thumbsucker

anchor books

new york

thumbsucker

a
novel

walter kirn

All rights reserved under International and Pan-American Copyright
Conventions Published in the United States by Anchor Books, a division
of Random House, Inc , New York, and simultaneously in Canada by
Random House of Canada Limited, Toronto Originally published in the
United States by Broadway Books in 1999

Anchor Books and colophon are registered trademarks of
Random House, Inc

Portions of *Thumbsucker* in slightly different form have appeared in *The
New Yorker, Esquire, GQ,* and *Allure*

Library of Congress Cataloging-in-Publication Data
Kirn, Walter, 1962–
Thumbsucker a novel / by Walter Kirn
p   cm   I   Title
ISBN 0-385-49709-1
PS3561 I746T48   1999
813' 54—dc21   99-13328
CIP

Designed by Terry Karydes

www anchorbooks com

Printed in the United States of America
10   9   8   7   6

For Maggie and Maisie,
in memory of
Rear Admiral Robert Knox

contents

Hundreds and hundreds were the truths and they were all beautiful. And then the people came along.

—SHERWOOD ANDERSON,
Winesburg, Ohio

thumbsucker

mouth to mouth

1

It was the one thing I'd always done. Even breathing did not go back to the womb. Being part of a circle of shoulder, arm, hand, mouth, connected me to myself. This circle is what they tried to break the summer I turned fourteen.

The appetite was neither thirst nor hunger but seemed to include them both. It could come at any time: while I was waiting in winter darkness for the school bus, fretting about Marcel, the French exchange student who sat behind me in social studies class and liked to rap his knuckles on my skull. Or I'd be walking past the downstairs bathroom, humming and pressing my hands against my ears to block out the sound of Mike, my father, singing high and tunelessly about the suppliers to his sporting goods store: "Oh, Orvis, you sons of bitches, get off my back," or "Give me a break, Smith & Wesson, just one small break." Or maybe I was downtown at Wayne's Cafe, watching my ravenous little brother, Joel, spread so much butter on an English muffin that his teeth left disgusting clifflike marks.

The effect when my thumb touched my lips was subtle and encompassing. Because I sometimes watched myself in a mirror, doubling my sense of self-communion, I knew how I looked at the moment of closure. Above my greedily flexing cheeks, my eyes would shine as though I'd just put drops in. My forehead would relax and lose its lines. From the rhythmic bullfrog swelling of my throat and the pulsing muscles along my jaw, it appeared I was actually taking nourishment. I believed I was.

~ ~ ~

When Mike began his campaign against my habit, the idea of it didn't seem to anger him. With his chewing gum and cigars and Red Man chewing tobacco, it's possible he even sympathized; he was a person who liked his mouth full, too. What riled him was that I'd developed an overbite and he was getting the orthodontist's bills. One night, when he was grouching about them, I said, "I thought your insurance paid for everything."

We were in the TV room watching Ronald Reagan, whom Mike had given money to and voted for. Mike still had a Reagan sticker on his Ford, nicked and shredded from my mother's attempts to scrape it off with a razor blade.

"You people must think insurance is free," Mike said. He spat brown tobacco juice into a beer can he was holding against his lower lip. "In point of fact, Justin, my entire store is paying for what you're doing to your teeth."

"I didn't know that," I said. "I'm dumb sometimes."

Mike gazed at Reagan's square, tanned face and sighed. "Insurance just *spreads* the costs, it doesn't erase them. Can't you people get that through your heads?"

That was what Mike called our family: you people. It made me feel like an intruder in his life.

Our dentist was a man named Perry Lyman. He worked in the northern suburbs of St. Paul and commuted from our little town of Shandstrom Falls. Before outsiders started moving there, in the early seventies, the town had been a sleepy trading center for hog and dairy farmers, but its large, inexpensive Victorian houses and proximity to the St. Croix River—a government-designated "wild river" that people said you could drink from, though I wouldn't—attracted a stream of outdoorsy young professionals. They brought with them new, exotic sports that hadn't yet spread across the Midwest: cross-country skiing, bike touring, kayak racing.

Rallies and meets were held every month or so, announced by flyers posted at Mike's store. Mike competed
in all these events. He held his own, but the first-place
trophies always seemed to go to Perry Lyman.

I could see why. Perry Lyman was steady, cool, and
able to pace himself, while Mike's approach of clenched
ferocity burned him out midrace. Perry Lyman seemed
to take pleasure in sports, while Mike's interest in them
was Spartan, almost survivalist, as though he were in
training for the day when modern civilization would collapse and men would have to paddle and ski great dis-
tances, gathering food and supplies. Mike's experience
playing college football (only a senior-year knee injury
had kept him from going pro) had taught him, in the
words of his old coach, that "winners treat every practice as a game." The saying decorated Mike's business
cards and hung in a gold frame inside his store.

Perry Lyman took a softer approach. He was a kind
of hippie, a social dropout, though with short, mossy
hair and normal clothes; he sometimes wore a bracelet of
tiny seashells but always removed them before touching
patients' mouths. He smoked pot—I saw a scorched
hemostat on his desk one day while he was adjusting my
retainer, and I knew what it was from the sheriff's
antidrug booth at the county fair. He was a hippie in
other ways, too. He preferred hypnosis to anesthetics
and liked to prescribe simple exercises for the correction
of minor malformations. The year before he gave me a
retainer, he'd actually had me using my fingers to push

my top teeth back. I pushed for an hour each night after supper and gave myself low-level headaches.

Though Perry Lyman knew the real reason, he pretended to blame my overbite on an odd nocturnal tongue motion supposedly common in boys my age. In explaining these spasms he introduced me to the term "subconscious pressure" and the idea of involuntary behavior. I instantly recognized the all-purpose excuse I'd been seeking all my life.

"So if people can't help things they do," I said, "why punish them?" I was thinking of John Hinckley, who'd shot Reagan.

"It has nothing to do with changing the offender," Perry Lyman said. "It's merely society working out its rage."

"I see."

"There's a group subconscious, too. It's complicated."

"It makes sense to me."

The day of my retainer fitting, I sat in Perry Lyman's padded chair and gazed around at rainbow-colored posters reminding me that "A Thing of Beauty Is a Joy Forever" and "If You Love Something, Let It Go." While I struggled to breathe through a stuffy nose, Perry Lyman packed my mouth with gray mint-flavored putty, then had me bite down to make an impression. Two weeks later he gave me my "appliance," a pink plastic, crab-shaped object ringed by wires and ridged on top to match my wrinkled palate.

I was supposed to wear the thing all night and as

much as possible during the day. I did this for two weeks, despite some problems. Its wires seemed too tight and made my gums sore. It caused me to speak with a lisp, which people made fun of. Also, the retainer smelled bad, collecting a fizzy yellow scum between its lifelike creases. It did have one important virtue, though: by heightening my awareness of my mouth, the retainer seemed to reduce the chance I'd forget myself in public.

This was a crippling, ever-present fear. Ned Lesser, a skin-and-bones foster child with digestive problems, had been hounded into switching schools when our eighth-grade class found out he wore a diaper underneath his jeans. I expected similar bullying if I lowered my guard. I'd learned that the trick was never to relax. Whether sitting alone in the lunchroom with a yogurt, trying to look noble in my unpopularity, or idling in right field during a softball game, wishing I shared my little brother's athletic skills, I had to maintain a vigilant alertness.

The person I had to be most careful around was Rebecca Crane, my first great crush. Far ahead of me mentally and physically, practically a woman at fourteen, Rebecca had long, brown, center-parted hair and a narrow, foot-shaped face. Like me, she rarely smiled, though it had nothing to do with her teeth, which happened to be perfect, straight and white. Rebecca was a dark and serious girl, devoted to endangered species. She wrote poems about the baby seal, using words such as "holocaust," and once got a warning from the principal for circulating petitions at school. Watching her fierce hazel eyes flash as she lectured me on the plights of porpoises and auks stirred my blood and absorbed my whole attention; I'm sure I would have forgotten myself in front of her without the retainer's irritating presence.

One day Rebecca and I went bird-watching along the Soo Line railroad tracks. Around us were hayfields mowed into stripes. My idea was to get her alone, outdoors, in nature, where our gaping social inequality wouldn't be so noticeable. With the retainer snug against my palate, I felt secure, protected against a slip, and I let myself relax completely—one of the first times I'd ever dared.

"It's hot. I'm taking my shirt off," I announced. It was a bold act for me. At fourteen, I had the physique of a sperm: an enormous oval head trailing a skinny, tapering body that, unless I started lifting weights as Mike was always badgering me to, would probably just drop off someday.

"Go ahead, take it off," Rebecca said, scanning a pasture with binoculars. "Look: a red-winged blackbird!"

"You take yours off, too," I said.

"My stomach will get a sunburn that my dad will see. He'll ask me what I've been up to."

"Your father looks at your naked stomach?"

"He checks my body for wood ticks. Doesn't yours?"

"With me it's Audrey, my mother," I admitted. "It's fine, though. She's a nurse."

Rebecca lowered her binoculars. "Why do you call your folks by their first names?"

"Mike says when I call him 'Dad' he feels old and I sound like a child. When he hears me call Audrey 'Mom,' then *she* seems old to him."

Finally, I got Rebecca to take her shirt off. Her bra straps made red nicks in her pale shoulders and I saw how the cups were cradling real weight. The sight thrilled me, but in bed that night, when I thought of Rebecca's father, a burly contractor, inspecting her body for ticks, I got anxious. When I opened my eyes in the morning my thumb was snugly seated in my cheek and the retainer was sitting on my pillow, staring back at me like an odd little sea creature. I never put it in my mouth again.

~ ~ ~

On the Fourth of July, as half the town looked on, Mike lost a kayak race to Perry Lyman. Mike finished a distant second, which might have been a close second if he hadn't flung away his paddle when he saw he wasn't going to win. That night, as he and Audrey and Joel and I sat on a blanket in the Lions Park and watched the volunteer firemen shoot fireworks, he suddenly clamped his hand on my right wrist and yanked out my thumb. It made a popping sound.

"You look like a baby," Mike said. "You're pathetic. When are you going to cut this out? My God."

On its own, it seemed, my thumb slipped right back in.

"You don't even *try* to stop," Mike said.

"I do, too, try," I mumbled with my thumb in.

"Well, I'm going to help you try a little harder."

Mike's first idea was Suk No Mor, a cayenne-pepper preparation whose label showed a throbbing thumbtip radiating jagged lines of pain. I sat at the kitchen table reading a *Modern Nursing* magazine as Audrey dabbed the liquid on my thumbnail using the plastic wand from the bottle. As always when she was treating my aches and pains—soothing poison ivy with pink lotion, removing earwax with a rubber bulb, extracting a splinter with an open safety pin—her face had a rich, focused beauty that made me blush. As stunning as any woman in a magazine, with eyes that were all bottomless black pupils and skin the color of a milk-dipped gingersnap, she seemed to come from another planet, my mother—one with a lighter atmosphere, less gravity. The men in our family were no match for her, not even Joel, whom all the girls called cute, and sometimes I wondered why she stayed with us.

"How much do you like this Rebecca?" she asked me, starting a line of questioning I found personal. "Have you tried to kiss her on the lips yet?"

"It says in here to inject adrenaline for severe reactions to insect stings."

"You can tell me, Justin. I won't be angry."

"Why would you be angry if I kissed someone?"

"I wouldn't be angry, I told you that. So *have* you?"

"I bet a shot of adrenaline feels good."

I spent the rest of that day by the river with Rebecca. Whenever she wasn't looking, I sneaked a quick lick of the Suk No Mor. She caught me once and I pretended I was biting my nail. The first hot, peppery shocks were followed by numbness, and by the time we turned to walk back home I'd licked the stuff clean off. I sensed Rebecca waiting for me to hug her or slide my hand up the front of her shirt, but I couldn't relax enough to risk the chance that once I had what I'd waited so long for, my thumb wouldn't drift to my lips from sheer relief. I had begun to be vigilant again.

~ ~ ~

"It's time we were honest and open," Perry Lyman said. We were sitting face-to-face: me in the dental chair, wearing a paper bib, and he at his little prescription-writing desk, his restless right foot playing with the pedal of his trash can. "The retainer won't work if you never wear it, and your father won't pay for braces," he said. "It's time to confront the underlying issue. I know what your problem is. I can help you stop."

I watched the trash-can lid flap up and down.

"It's an understandable habit," Perry Lyman said.

"In fact, what's strange is that people ever quit. It's nature's substitute for the female breast."

I knew this, but somehow it didn't help to hear it.

"How were you fed as a baby? From a bottle?"

"Might have been," I said. "I don't remember."

"Any tension at home? Anxiety?"

I nodded. "Plenty."

"Any bad memories?"

There were so many that it was hard to pick one. There was the time I quit the Peewee hockey team, complaining of bruised ribs after a check, and Mike reached over my shoulder on the drive home, stopped the car, opened my door, and pushed me out. Or the time when he picked up a shotgun in his store after a daylong argument with Audrey over her purchase of an antique mirror and warned me that he'd blow his head off someday if "you people don't come down to earth." Then there was the disaster of Camp Overcome, a summer program run by Woody Wolff, Mike's beloved football coach at the University of Michigan, that was designed to treat bed wetters, stutterers, and thumbsuckers like me. After two weeks of midnight mile runs, skimpy breakfasts of prune juice and cold oatmeal, and grueling four-hour lectures on self-mastery, my habit came back worse than ever. Intense. Unshakable.

I avoided my dentist's eyes. "No conscious ones."

"We never remember the big things anyway. The psyche is formed in the bassinet, the stroller. A cat drops a chewed mouse inside your crib and at seventeen you're a hand-washing fanatic. Some dimwit baby-sitter holds your mouth shut so she can watch her soap operas in peace and at forty you wonder why you can't stay married."

The conversation fascinated me. "What about the chromosomes? The genes?"

Perry Lyman glanced up at his wall clock. "Genetics, psychology, morality. The terminologies change, the problems don't. I'd like to try hypnosis, Justin."

"Hypnosis?"

"God knows it's better than essence of red pepper. Was that your father's idea?"

I said it was.

"I see he's entered the Labor Day bike race."

"He trains every day before work," I said. "Twenty-one miles."

"No kidding? What's his time?"

"He hasn't told me. Hypnosis, huh?"

Perry Lyman slowly let the lid down. "I think it can help you kick this thing. I do."

~ ~ ~

Because of a white-water rafting trip to Oregon, Perry Lyman couldn't perform the hypnosis right away. Each morning during my week of waiting, Mike used a pen with purple ink to print his initials, MFC—Michael Forrest Cobb—on the pad of my right thumb. He gripped my wrist to steady my hand, and my fingers went numb. At night he checked for fadedness and smearing. He promised me a portable TV if I managed to go a whole month, but I knew from experience he'd forget the deal if I succeeded in keeping up my end of it. He had a way of forgetting the bargains we struck.

"You *swear*?" I said the second night, after Mike inspected my thumb. "You swear it won't be like the Honda and the chin-ups?" Two years ago, Mike had promised me a dirt bike if I won the President's Physical Fitness certificate. I'd missed the award by two chin-ups and gotten nothing, a bitter reminder that a deal's a deal.

"What Honda? When?" Mike said.

I couldn't believe this. "I want you to buy that TV tomorrow morning and keep it in its box with the receipt."

One afternoon Rebecca startled me by asking what the writing on my thumb was. She had a chest cold and was at her house, wrapped in an electric blanket. She shared her codeine cough syrup with me. Her wet brown eyes looked drugged and trusting, and for a light-headed moment or two I considered telling her the truth. I felt the confession slowly rising inside me like a bubble in honey.

Then I panicked.

"MFC," I said. " 'Motherfucking cocksucker.' "

Tears came into Rebecca's staring eyes. Her line on me had always been that I was afraid of mature conversation, unwilling to share my fears and weaknesses. She assured me that doing this would bring us closer, but I noticed that she expected me to go first.

"Why do you have to act so tough?" she said. "Have I done something to hurt you? Don't you trust me? What's the point of spending time together if it doesn't lead to openness?"

"Motherfucking cocksucker," I said.

~ ~ ~

I shut my eyes and let my shoulders fall as music featuring harp, piano, and birdsong drifted from the tape player on Perry Lyman's desk. His voice was low and smooth. "Safety surrounds you. Peace pervades your being. Security such as you've never known descends." He circled me as he spoke, stirring currents in the Lysoled air. The sticky, peeling sound of his crepe-soled shoes made me wonder how often he mopped his floors.

"Imagine yourself on a path," he said after a few more minutes of warm-up. "You're deep in the forest. You glimpse a clearing. In its center, a shaft of yellow light shines down, illuminating a wild animal."

I wondered if I was "under" and concluded that if I could be wondering this then I wasn't. Perry Lyman's voice, annoyingly smooth and aware of its own resonance, kept on about the animal, calling it my "power animal" and urging me to see it in detail. Eventually, I managed to picture a deer. Seen straight on and eye-to-eye, it had the face of Ned Lesser, the diaper boy, but when it looked away it was a deer again.

"When you feel like sucking your thumb," said Perry Lyman, "call your power animal for help. It will comfort you and give you strength. Call it to you now."

"Come here," I whispered.

"Do it in your *mind*."

I did it in my mind.

When I got up from the chair, I was surprised at how limp and warm my legs felt. I remembered reading an article about a professional hockey team that had been hypnotized before a play-off game. I asked Perry Lyman if he used self-hypnosis to help himself win races.

"In fact, I do. I find it sharpens me."

"What's your power animal?" I said.

Perry Lyman glanced at the poster above his desk, a poster from the Sierra Club.

"That's personal."

"Come on."

"I'm sorry. It's just not the same, I'm afraid, if other people know."

The poster showed a pack of running wolves.

~ ~ ~

When people try to quit things, other things take their places. A woman stops smoking and starts inhaling pizza. A man cuts out doughnuts and heads off to Las Vegas. After Perry Lyman hypnotized me, my desire to suck just drained away, and so did all the pleasure. My thumb became a neutral object, like the end of a broomstick in my mouth.

"What's the despairing look?" Mike asked me one morning, sitting down to bran flakes after his bike ride. His face was red and sweaty and invigorated. "You wear a long face, it'll end up wearing you."

"Stop quoting Woody Wolff."

"That one was mine."

All I could think about was Rebecca. Suddenly, with leechlike intensity, I had to be around her all the time. As soon as her father's car drove off each morning, I hurried to her porch and rang the doorbell, loaded down with field guides and binoculars. When I sensed her interest in bird-watching decreasing, I started buying the movie magazines I'd seen her reading with her older sister. Day after day, I barraged Rebecca with Hollywood trivia questions and fun facts.

"What's Farrah Fawcett's beauty secret?"

"Do we?"

"She conditions her hair with egg whites."

"I said 'Do we?' "

"Do we what, Rebecca?"

"Do we *care*?"

I watched Rebecca grow to despise me. My shining moment with her—ordering her to remove her shirt and facing her down, bare-chested, until she did—seemed impossible to duplicate now that I cared so deeply about her opinion of me. My attentions took on a doomed and ingrown quality. I would insult myself in front of her, saying I was stupid, short, deformed, and then resent her for not defending me. When I saw how much she pitied wayward movie stars—drug addicts, wife beaters, hotel room wreckers—I began to regret not having confessed my weakness. That would have won her over, I felt sure, but now it was too late.

One day on her porch, with her father standing behind her, his broad, callused hands on her shoulders, Rebecca said, "Justin, we think you're bothering me. We think this isn't a healthy teenage friendship. We want you to stop coming over."

"Move it, son."

For the last time, I sought solace in my thumb. The deer with the face of the diaper boy appeared, but even after I chased the creature off, I felt nothing—no comfort, no relief. My thumb felt dead and so did my whole body.

I blamed them all, but especially Perry Lyman. He'd pretended to be my friend but had snatched my soul.

~ ~ ~

The course of the Labor Day bike race ran, for part of its last and twenty-fifth mile, through a highway tunnel. The cyclists emerging from darkness made for dramatic snapshots, so spectators liked to gather at one end. I stood with Joel in the barrow ditch on the other side, where no one could see what we were going to do.

Perry Lyman approached, head down, pedaling with

the steady, flowing strokes that usually guaranteed him victory. The hazy dot behind him was Mike. I signaled Joel to raise the poster I'd stapled to a stick, then broke into a trot along the road. I saw Perry Lyman glance over at Joel's sign and I noticed his front tire start to wobble. That's when I started howling. Joel howled, too. The howls came out of me like weird black scarves. They scared me. And they rattled Perry Lyman. He turned and flipped me the bird as he passed, a look of disintegration on his face. He couldn't have guessed what he'd done to deserve this—the Sierra Club wolf pack splattered with bloodred paint and my demented yapping. I knew at that moment that I'd broken his power, just as he had mine. In a photo Audrey took of him emerging from the tunnel, he had the face of a man who knew he'd lose.

He came in seventh. Mike was first.

That night at our backyard picnic table, when Joel and Audrey went in to get some knives, I said to Mike, "You owe me a TV set."

His hand grazed around in a bowl of salted nuts, pausing for the almonds. He was still lost in the haze of victory, and I knew I could get away with more than usual. In front of him was a foaming-over beer can and a can he hadn't opened yet. Mike had been having an extra drink with dinner ever since Reagan had been shot that spring.

"I knew you'd forget," I said, reaching for a beer. "I knew you wouldn't pay up."

"Pay up for what?"

Mike watched me open the beer and start to gulp it. I opened my throat and let the cold pour into me.

"Easy," he said. "Slow down. A sip or two."

I think we both knew that would be impossible.

2

Next I lost my desire for food, my appetite. It happened in late October and took four days. It was as though my mouth were turning against me, my one source of pleasure becoming a dry hole.

We'd been eating venison all month, trying to empty the chest freezer of game before Mike started filling it back up. We started with the chops, a cut I liked, and worked our way down to the sausages and roasts, which coated my mouth with waxy, rancid fat. I said I thought we should throw the meat away, the first time I'd ever spoken out like this, but Mike said a moral issue was at stake. With another bow-hunting season coming up, he just wouldn't feel right, he told the family, if last year's kill and this year's overlapped.

"Ah, the ethics of savagery," said Audrey. Smoke from the roast she'd been cooking all afternoon hung in thin gray layers above her head.

"Hunting's the basis of civilization," Mike said. "Read your anthropology."

"I have. While you were out vanquishing Óhio State, your sweetheart was actually attending classes. And the basis of civilization, my dear, is agriculture."

Mike bore down hard as he carved the roast and it slid around on its bed of wrinkled carrots. He'd managed to convince me over the years that venison tasted better than beef or pork, even though my own senses told me otherwise. This year, however, I wasn't buying it. I tasted what I tasted, and it disgusted me. I remembered reading an article once that said the muscles of hunted animals produce a fear hormone that cooking doesn't break down. I wondered how much of this substance was in me now.

Half the roast remained when we finished dinner. Audrey wrapped it in cling film and in foil and stashed it in the back of the refrigerator next to an open box of baking soda, which meant she didn't intend to touch it again. "Maybe your folks will take some venison home with them."

Mike's parents were set to arrive the following morning on one of their rare trips west to Minnesota, a state which they considered the frontier. Everybody was on edge about it.

"My mother thinks deer are precious creatures," Mike said. "She thinks they have feelings."

"So do I," said Audrey.

"Human feelings. Not just the primal drives."

"And what would those be?"

"Hunger. Thirst. Lust. Pain."

Audrey closed the refrigerator door. "It bothers me that you can tick them off like that."

Mike went into the yard after dinner to practice his archery in the fading daylight. His target was a paper bull's-eye pinned to a stack of straw bales. Joel, who'd never shown interest in the outdoors—unlike me, who'd faked it out of guilt—was allowed to go to a neighbor's house to play, but Mike demanded that I stay near and watch him. He notched an arrow, drew the string, let fly.

"I used to have to sneak out to hunt," he said. "My mother had some idea that it was cruel. What's cruel is not letting a boy grow into a man because you've had a bad experience."

"What happened?"

"Someone hit her once. A boyfriend. A smack me and Dad have been paying for all our lives. We snuck out to see a boxing match downtown once and when we got home she'd changed the locks on us."

"I'm surprised she let you play football."

"Dad drew the line."

Mike made a bull's-eye. Another. I pulled the arrows out.

"Your mother was wrong about civilization," he said. "Civilization is a perfect lung shot."

~ ~ ~

Mike's parents pulled in around lunchtime the next day in their new Winnebago motor home, the Horizoneer. Mike had asked them to visit at Thanksgiving, when it wouldn't interrupt his hunting, but Grandma had insisted on seeing Joel and me before the cold weather set in. She got her way. From what I'd witnessed of Mike's dealings with her, he'd never really been a match for her. At Christmas he sent her the presents that she asked for, luxury items like jewelry and crystal, then settled for souvenir coffee mugs in return. And though she called him home to Buffalo whenever she caught the flu or had a mole removed, she only came here when she was passing through anyway.

I felt anxious as my grandparents parked the camper. The last time I'd seen them was a couple of years ago at a family reunion out east, but all I could remember of the event was a sack race through a muddy field. Still, I told them I missed them when I hugged them. Grandma Cobb's body felt hard and armored, as if her underwear were lined with metal, while Grandpa's felt pulpy, like a bruised banana. Behind a pair of dandruff-speckled bifocals his hazel eyes were mild and remote and I immediately liked him more than her.

"Let me get your bags," Mike said. Already he sounded exhausted by the visit.

"We're staying in the Horizoneer," said Grandma. "All we need is a long extension cord."

"We made up the guest room," Mike said.

"We like our motor home."

Grandpa brought a brown case into the house and set it on the kitchen counter next to a package of thawing venison sausage that Audrey planned to make into spaghetti sauce. Inside the case, held by velvet straps that buttoned, were a silver cocktail shaker, a flask, four glasses, a jigger, and some swizzle sticks. "Long dry trip," he said, and smacked his lips, which were surprisingly juicy for his age. He mixed a double-shot Manhattan for Grandma and waited until she'd tasted it and nodded before making drinks for Audrey and himself. His hands, I noticed, were fat and padded, the fingers locked in a clawlike curl. They matched his thick, tufted eyebrows and pitted red nose.

Audrey browned sausage and diced tomatoes as Grandma brought Mike up-to-date about our relatives. My aunts' and uncles' names were unfamiliar to me, their life situations hard to picture, and hearing about them made me feel lonesome. When Mike left home for college, he'd told me once, he'd put his family behind him, where it belonged. He said he expected me to do the same someday.

"Wendy's back with the born-agains," said Grandma. "They practically hold her hostage in that church. She feels guilty about her miscarriages or some-thing, but that's no reason to sacrifice her youth."

"Mom," said Mike, "my God. The *kids*."

"And Rupert, your little nephew you've never seen, is still having tests. Poor baby's almost bald now. They're treating him at St. Joseph's, a Catholic place."

"Catholic hospitals bother you?" Mike said.

"You didn't grow up with an Irish mother," said Grandma.

"You're an Irish mother."

"Once removed."

"Removed by *what*?"

"Americanization."

Grandma turned from Mike and smiled at Joel, her makeup cracking and flaking around her mouth. Purple lipstick smeared her capped front teeth. "How nice to see you, dear. It's such a treat. I'd tell you you've grown, but I really wouldn't know."

Grandpa opened his flask and freshened his drink, making a show of measuring precisely but adding an extra splash at the end. A stillness came over the kitchen, a lull, as if a storm had cut the power off and left us sitting together in the gloom.

"Imagine," said Audrey, "a camper with a shower. Doesn't that sound cozy to you, Mike?"

Mike didn't respond; he was gazing out the window. Opening day was the day after tomorrow and the fore-cast was iffy, with a chance of snow. He had on his autumn face, calm and sorrowful.

"What's that smell?" said Grandma. "Something stinks."

"Tell Audrey about the Horizoneer," said Grandpa.

"I will in a minute. What's that awful *stench*?"

Mike rose from the table. "I've got a store to run. It's the busy season. Shotguns. Licenses. I can't afford to be away all day."

"It's deer meat," said Grandma. "You're making me eat *deer meat*."

Mike left the kitchen and Audrey said, "I'm sorry. I don't like venison, either."

"No one does." Grandma opened a silver cigarette case and drew out a Vantage. Grandpa flicked a lighter. He was her permanent bartender, her servant.

"So this is your life," said Grandma. "Does he make money?"

"He's building a business," said Audrey. "It takes time. I could microwave something for you. Some lasagna?"

"Not if it's been in the same refrigerator. Max, get our luggage from the motor home. I want to sleep in the house. I've changed my mind."

"Your bunk's all made up. Your sheets. Your special pillow."

"I want to be near my grandkids," Grandma said. "While you're out there, fetch me a potpie."

Grandpa drank up and went out to do his errand, leaving his minibar open on the counter. From the out-side it looked like a briefcase, inconspicuous, but the inner compartments were lined with crushed gold velvet. I wanted to curl up inside it and pull it shut.

~ ~ ~

Grandma got sick to her stomach the next day while showing slides to Joel and me. Mike was in the woods preparing his hunting blind, Audrey was at the county hospital working her emergency room shift, and Grandpa was under the Horizoneer draining and replacing the antifreeze.

"That's your cousin Brent," said Grandma. "He wins all his track meets. He'll do well. He's handsome."

"How old is he?" Joel said.

"Exactly Justin's age."

"He looks older," Joel said.

"It's his dress sense," Grandma said. "Here he is at the Park Club, on the cabin cruiser. That boy with him is the son of Homer Morse, the biggest wholesale grocer in Buffalo."

The slides annoyed me and I couldn't sit still. My cousins, two boys and two girls, looked spoiled and cruel, the sort of kids who can see into a future of Ivy League educations, good jobs, big houses. The boys had stylish, shaggy haircuts and movie-star suntans that showed off their slim builds. The girls wore pink polo shirts with the collars turned up and had professionally highlighted blond hair clipped into place with jeweled barrettes. They belonged to a world of country clubs and beach parties that might have been my world if Mike had stayed in Buffalo, where the Cobb family had a street named after it and Grandpa, an ad salesman for the morning newspaper, had been a vice-president of the Rotary.

Grandma clicked to an upside-down slide of Dr. March and Aunt Jean, Mike's older sister, racing a catamaran across Lake Erie toward a bank of glorious orange clouds. Grandma adjusted the slide but got it sideways. "Who cares," she said. "I don't know why I bother. You boys won't ever meet these people anyway." She coughed, and the cough sounded forced to me. An act.

"I'm gray," she said. "I'm gray and clammy. Feel me."

She took Joel's hand and pressed it to her forehead.

"Maybe you need something salty," Joel said. "Peanuts?"

"Nuts clog the small intestines," Grandma said. "What I need is ginger ale or Gatorade."

"We're not allowed to drink pop at home," Joel said.

"Gatorade has minerals. It's a health drink."

"All we have is water and milk," Joel said.

Grandma swayed forward, shuddered, spread her knees, and vomited into the slide-projector box. She ran a finger around inside her mouth to clean out the extra, then shook the finger dry. She sank back into the couch and shut her eyes, her hands closing on her lap like curling leaves.

"That venison smell's in the carpeting," she said.

"We don't notice," Joel said.

"It's inside you. You're immune."

Grandma bent forward as if to vomit again but nothing came out except a gassy burp. "I caught that one just in time," she said, patting and rubbing her chest. "I swallowed it. One of you boys go find Max. I need my bucket."

~ ~ ~

An hour later, the guest room was a sick room. Following Grandma's whispered directions, I set a Lysol-sprayed bucket beside the bed, plugged in a humidifier, and stocked the nightstand with Dixie cups and Gatorade, which Audrey had bought on her way home from the hospital. I also put out tissues, Tylenol, and a *True Detective* magazine retrieved from under the Horizoneer's front seat. Grandma sat up on a pillow, reading it. She'd let down her hair, a staticky gray horse's tail that shocked me with its length.

"I need a TV," she said. "My shows are starting. There's a portable in the motor home. Go get it."

"Grandpa drove to the pharmacy," I said.

"When he gets back."

"We have a radio."

"I hate the radio," Grandma said.

"St. Paul has an oldies station."

"I hate the oldies."

I was fetching a fresh box of Kleenex from downstairs when Mike came in wearing a camouflage jumpsuit and holding the new compound bow he'd been sent as a demo model for the store. He'd darkened his face with mud and grease, which made the whites of his eyes jump out. A hunting knife with a sawback blade hung from a leather strap on his right hip.

"Great day," he said. "She's out there."

"Who?" I said.

"The doe I've had my eye on since September. I like to have one picked out before the season starts. Makes it more meaningful. More one-on-one."

I told him about Grandma's vomiting.

"Where's Dad?"

"Out buying Aspercreme and magazines."

"Magazines about murder?"

"And detectives."

"Believe me, it's not the detectives she likes to read about. The woman has a fixation on random violence."

Mike clomped up the staircase and I followed him, picking up chunks of boot mud from the runner and slipping them into my pocket. Audrey emerged from the sick room with Grandma's bucket and Mike looked down at its contents.

"That's just spit. There's nothing but saliva in that pail."

"I realize that," Audrey said in a low voice. "Just talk to her. She wants her boy's attention."

I stood in the doorway next to the bucket as Mike stepped into the room and said, "It's me." Grandma lay on her side in bed, a heating pad folded underneath one cheek. She looked weaker than she had five minutes ago.

"Don't worry, honey," she said. "I'm feeling fine. Everyone's been so kind, so understanding . . ." Suddenly, she sat up and held her stomach.

"Mom, it's okay," Mike said. "You're safe. We love you. The only reason I wasn't home today was that I had to get ready for the season."

Grandma sat back. "It comes up, but then it stops." She blew her nose into a crumpled tissue, then carefully dabbed away the afterdrips. She opened the tissue and inspected it.

"You're letting yourself get all wound up," Mike said. "Those magazines, are they a good idea, Mom? Why not let Audrey find you a good book to read?"

Grandma lifted her glass and sipped some Gatorade, massaging her throat to help the liquid go down.

"I'll leave," she said. "I'm in your way. I'll go. I'm interrupting your blood sport."

"Suit yourself. I warned you what I'd be doing before you came."

"You can't even put it off until next weekend. Can't even wait a week."

"It doesn't work that way. The other hunters would get the jump on me."

"Fine, we'll stay in the camper. Just send the kids out. Have your fun and act like we're not here."

Grandma swung a pale leg out over the mattress and Mike stepped forward to help. She waved him back. She

planted one foot as if testing the floor for firmness, then
let out a long, sighing belch. I grabbed the bucket. By
the time I got into position, she'd splattered everything,
including Mike's boots. He looked down at them and
sighed.

~ ~ ~

Mike left the house at three in the morning. The smell of
the bottled buck scent he'd rubbed on drifted into my
bedroom, preventing me from falling back to sleep. I
turned on the radio beside my bed and listened to Ron
Ben Strong, a local evangelist, brief his flock about a
government satellite whose mission, he said, was to spy
on Christians' houses and track the titles of the books
they read. Like the rest of my family, I wasn't religious,
but I'd started to envy people who were. They seemed to
know just what and whom to be afraid of.

After a breakfast of eggs and venison sausage that I
only managed to eat two bites of, Joel and I went to the
motor home. I knocked. From visiting a nursing home
that Audrey worked in once, I'd learned the old people
needed their privacy because they were always fussing
with their bodies, dealing with ingrown nails and corns
and such. I was already feeling pangs of indigestion and I
didn't want to walk in on something sickening.

Grandpa showed us inside with a gesture that seemed
too sweeping for the tiny space. Grandma waved to us
from her fold-down bed in the sleeping compartment

behind the bathroom. A magazine lay open on her lap
and a cigarette in an ashtray on the sheet sent up a blue
plume.

"I just learned something important," she told Joel,
tapping a finger on her magazine page. "If you're being
assaulted in a lonely place and there's no one around to
hear you scream, scream anyway. It breaks the at-
tacker's momentum."

"Okay," Joel said.

"Assault is a crime of momentum," Grandma said.
"And it's not just the blacks you have to be afraid of
now. It's the Europeans, too."

"Hush, Alice," Grandpa said.

"He needs to know this."

"He doesn't need to know it now. Hush up."

We passed the morning playing along with game
shows on the motor home's portable TV. On the first
show, the object was to guess the prices of ordinary
household items. Grandpa's guesses were all dead-on, as
if he'd priced the items only yesterday, but Grandma's
guesses simply made no sense. She priced a gas barbecue
at a thousand dollars, a Mr. Coffee at three, a wok at
ninety. I wondered when she'd last been in a store. I
could only conclude that Grandpa did all their shopping.

As Grandpa prepared our lunch on the small stove, I
realized that the Horizoneer was growing on me. He
whipped up our macaroni and cheese in no time, maneuvering in the miniature kitchen like an airline pilot in a

cockpit. We ate at a table with an inlaid checkerboard, and without getting up from his revolving stool, Grandpa was able to open the refrigerator and get us bottles of Coke. Compared to the compact, convenient motor home, the house I'd grown up in seemed huge and wasteful—an echoey shell that I frequently felt lost in.

"Coffee, Justin?" Grandpa asked.

"No thanks. Don't drink it."

"It's good. It's time to start."

We drank the coffee out of plastic mugs whose bottoms were weighted so they wouldn't spill. The first sip burned my tongue. The second soothed it. By the third sip, I wanted another cup. It was that way with everything I liked.

"It's nice in here," I said. "I like this life."

"We'll take you boys on a trip sometime," said Grandpa.

"Fat chance," Grandma said. "Our son would never let them. They'd see we were fun, not the creeps he makes us out to be."

Grandpa refilled my cup. "Don't listen to this. She's not herself this week. There's a sedative that she's run out of and no one in Minnesota seems to carry it."

"They carry it," Grandma said, "but not in capsules. I only take capsules. My throat's too tender for pills."

She squeezed her neck and made a choking face. Then she reopened her murder magazine. "Everyone listen up: I have a quiz. Which are deadlier, pistols or blunt instruments? It's not what you'd think, so take a little time."

~ ~ ~

Mike seemed to be hiding something at dinner that night. He was too considerate, too gentle. His cheeks were rosy from scrubbing off the buck scent and he grinned between bites of greasy venison loaf. The film of smoke on the kitchen's picture window distorted the snowflakes that had started falling.

"Grandma gave us tips on crime," Joel said.

Mike spread fried onions over his slab of meat. "I'm glad you spent time visiting together. Mom and Dad have their quirks, but they're good people. I think that camper helps. Mom feels secure in it."

"Can we sleep out in the motor home?" Joel asked.

"Maybe that's not a bad idea," Mike said. "Give your parents some privacy tonight."

"That might be nice," said Audrey. "I think I'd like that."

Mike's smile broadened. "I got my doe tonight."

Audrey's mouth tensed.

"I aimed straight down at her. Easy shot. I bull's-eyed. Strong, clean chest shot."

"Where is it? Did you bring it home?" Joel said. My little brother loved dead animals. When Mike plucked ducks, Joel collected the chopped-off wings and ran down the driveway, flapping them and leaping.

"The deer's still out there. It bolted. Then the sun set. I'll find it tomorrow," Mike said. "She left a blood trail."

"You'll find it tonight," said Audrey. "Jesus Lord . . ." She stood up with her plate and scraped it into the garbage can.

"Fine," Mike said. "I'll get a sleeping bag and track the thing at first light."

"The *thing*," said Audrey.

"The animal, then."

"Just stop it."

"The precious Bambi."

My grandparents were right: life was nicer in the Horizoneer.

~ ~ ~

With Grandpa drinking bourbon sours and Grandma woozy from a sleeping pill, it was like a party in the motor home. To make up for dinner, which I hadn't touched, I shoveled down ice cream during our game of Scrabble. Grandma won by making nonsense words, including "plip"—a sound like *plop*, she claimed—and "clasque," which she said she'd forgotten the meaning of. Outside, the snow had turned to slush and sleet, and I thought of Mike in the forest, tracking the doe. The sleet would erase the trail and soak his sleeping bag, but facing difficulties in the woods was Mike's idea of fun.

After the game we popped popcorn in a popper whose

foil lid rose like a chef's hat during heating. Grandpa gave Joel and me pillows and wool blankets and we lay down in the aisle head-to-toe. Scattered popcorn hulls pricked my legs and back, and I was convinced I hadn't fallen asleep yet when suddenly I woke and noticed traffic lights in the small round window overhead.

The camper was moving, with Grandma at the wheel. Wearing only a flannel nightgown, a cigarette stuck in her mouth like a lit fuse, she stared at the fast-sweeping windshield wipers, eyes glazed. Grandpa was still on his stool at the table, his head down on the checkerboard, passed out.

I stumbled past him to the camper's passenger seat. Through the sleet-blurred glass I saw a town: rows of unfamiliar stores, all closed.

"Where are we? Where are we going?" I asked Grandma.

"Sometimes those pills have the opposite effect. They jazz me up," she said. "They make me restless."

The town petered out and we drove along through cornfields on a muddy, potholed country road. The gusting dashboard vents blew Grandma's hair back and pinked the tip of her nose. "We're lost," she said.

"This might be Wisconsin. Did you cross a bridge?"

"I might have. I wasn't looking down," she said.

She couldn't tell me how long she'd been driving or in what direction she'd set out. The fields grew flatter and went from corn to soybeans, indicating that we were headed west. We passed a few cars and another Horizoneer, which honked its horn in late-night solidarity.

Grandma eyed my reflection in the windshield. "We'll go to New York. You'll meet the other Cobbs. We're quite a clan out there—we have position. No one says boo to us; we protect our own. Your father thinks it's too dull, too sheltered there. Well, he can afford to—he's a great big man. Women and children can't risk that attitude."

I turned on the motor home's AM radio and listened for a clue to our location. Stations came in from everywhere: crop news from Omaha, polka from North Dakota, a Bible show all the way from Colorado. We were out on the plains, where all the signals cross.

"I think we need to turn around," I said. I rooted around in the glove compartment, looking for a map, but all I found were empty asthma inhalers and a crime magazine whose cover showed a woman bound and gagged with black electrical tape.

Grandma's head began to droop and sway; I braced myself to snatch the wheel from her. The only other vehicles on the road were pickups driven by hunters in orange caps. They steered with one finger, smoking and drinking coffee, and when the motor home drifted under forty, one of them honked at us and shook his fist.

All of a sudden, Grandma was fast asleep and I was pressed tight against her, steering us. I felt the Horizoneer's bulk, its sluggish tonnage, and I called out for Grandpa. Joel woke up instead. He cleared his throat, said, "Don't," and fell asleep again.

Keeping us straight required constant adjustments. There were crosswinds to fight and high spots in the highway. Our speed was a steady forty-three, governed by Grandma's wedged-in throttle foot. In time I got the hang of things. My pride rose. I managed to get settled on the seat and nudge Grandma's foot off the pedal with my own. I'd always suspected that I knew how to drive.

Moments later I heard Grandpa waking. I pumped the brakes and eased us toward the shoulder. He staggered forward, lost his footing, and ended up sideways in the passenger seat as I brought the vehicle to a stop. I waited for him to acknowledge my heroics but he was groggy and didn't have his glasses on.

I had to explain the situation for him. All my finest moments went unwitnessed.

"The woman gets confused sometimes," he said.

"She said she was driving to Buffalo."

"She's delicate."

"Mike says she's faking."

"He knows better than that. Your grandmother's nerves aren't her fault. She struggles with them. The people who should have loved her weren't always kind to her. Tough neighborhood. Tough family. Tough men. It wasn't a tea party, Irish Buffalo."

Grandpa took Grandma's hand and tugged her upright. Waking up, she muttered a string of curses—not the four-letter words that I was used to, but the ugly, peculiar ones you seldom hear.

"We know," said Grandpa, smoothing her tangled hair back.

"Cunt hole," said Grandma. "Prick."

"It's me. It's Max."

I excused myself, opened the door, and stepped outside. After so much venison and tension, the retching was a relief. It came in waves. And though I might have been able to swallow it back, I let it come up until it was all gone—not just the food but the desire for food, whatever that space was that the food had filled.

~ ~ ~

They were gone—to Florida, they told me, to join a convoy of other Horizoneers—when Mike returned with the gutted doe that morning. After I helped him unload it from the station wagon, he slit the tendons of the doe's back legs and threaded baling twine between the bones and hung it from a rafter in the garage.

I watched with gritty, tired eyes, my mouth still raw and sour from stomach acid. I knew better than to tell Mike where I'd been all night and turn him against his parents even more. My adventures had never interested him anyway. With Mike, there was no way to get around the feeling that everyone's in the middle of his own life and at the edge of everybody else's.

"She's a beauty, isn't she?" he said. "She ran for almost two miles, I don't know how. I only wish Mom and Dad were here to see this.'' He ran a hand along the doe's stiff flank, leaving a trail of fluffed-up, muddy fur. In the sticky cavity where the organs had been I saw a white spider walk across a rib.

"Those two have their ups and downs," Mike said. "I realize that. They sure do love you kids, though. That's what matters."

Blood dripped onto the orange plastic tarp spread out under the doe. It pooled and ran.

"They're sort of cute together in that camper. And Dad, what a saint. The man just gives and gives."

I looked at the ground. Mike was hard to listen to sometimes.

"Maybe you think hunting pleases me," he said. "It doesn't. Each season I think: 'That's it. Enough already.' I look at my deer and all I feel is sadness. Those big brown eyes, those elegant long legs. Let someone else be the bad guy for a change."

The spider crawled up the doe's neck onto its tongue and started down its throat.

"But then, the next fall, another thought comes over me. I can't control it. It pops into my skull. The next thing I know I'm out there with my bow again."

"What thought?" I said.

"It's stupid. It doesn't make sense."

"Tell me," I said. "I want to understand."

Mike touched the doe's forehead.

"Another year of meat."

Mike let the deer age for a couple of days, then butchered it himself. He tossed the slabs of flesh into a bucket while I stood by with his knives. I couldn't watch him. In my shirt pocket was a postcard from Grandma describing her trip and ending with a P.S.: "Don't let him make you eat anything you don't want to. That's how allergies develop, swallowing things you hate." My chance to heed her advice came right away. When Mike finished hacking and scraping he held a steak out and asked if I'd like to taste it raw. I didn't. He bit off a chunk and grimaced as he chewed, as if he were forcing down a dose of medicine. To *each his own*, I thought. Everyone in our family had his medicine, and the bug it was meant to drive off was one another.

3

Knox gelatin drink for stronger, healthier nails held an essay contest that winter on the subject of "My Most Attractive Feature." Audrey decided to enter—as a joke, she said. First prize was a "Miami dream date" with the actor Don Johnson, "America's swingingest vice cop." The package included round-trip airfare, deluxe accommodations, a Palm Beach shopping spree, and dinner and drinks at a South Beach nightclub. Audrey said Mike would go crazy if she won.

The whole idea spooked me. I wanted her to lose.

One afternoon while Mike was at work demonstrating a new wide-bodied tennis racket that he'd won the exclusive regional rights to, Audrey sat at the kitchen table with a legal pad and a violet Flair pen. Instead of starting her essay, she doodled circles and swirls and diamond shapes and gazed at Johnson's picture on the Knox box. He had dimples. His hair was a sweaty, devilish mess. He reminded me of photos I'd seen of Mike during his playing days at Michigan, except that Johnson's eyes were narrower. The man looked untrustworthy, dangerous. A threat.

When Audrey's coffee cooled, she poured a fresh cup, and then let that cup cool. Her doodles grew hard and spiky, angry-looking.

"Help your stupid mother," she said. "You've always had a knack for things like this."

I stood over the sink and poured myself another ruby spoonful of codeine cough syrup. I was home from school with a case of made-up flu, but the hacking cough I'd been faking since waking up had given me a genuine sore throat. The air around me boiled with filmy clouds, an effect of the syrup. My arms felt long and apelike.

"I'm sick," I said. "I can't think."

"Oh, be a sport."

Audrey was right: I was good at things like this. Once, the *St. Paul Pioneer Press* had published a letter I'd written to the editor arguing that habitual drug offenders ought to be put to work in mental hospitals. The idea was Mike's, from a comment I'd heard him make after his store was robbed by an employee high on angel dust; I thought he'd be pleased to see his views in print. When the letter was published, though, Mike was in Sioux City at a fishing tackle trade show, and I was too shy to show it to him later. My gym teacher read it, however, and seemed impressed, so I began to write letters on other issues, from welfare mothers to nuclear disarmament. Having no opinions of my own, I took random positions, pro and con.

Audrey flipped to a fresh sheet of paper. "I have to find something distinctive about myself. And not some cliché like my eyes or sense of humor."

I pictured Johnson in his trademark shades helping Audrey out of a black limo. Red neon splashed his face and her bare shoulders. Around them milled a crowd of nightclub-goers in tippy high heels and loose Italian jackets.

"Your smile," I said.

"That's worse than sense of humor. This contest's nationwide—we need a gimmick. Something to set me apart from all the other gals."

It struck me that Audrey knew what she was doing and might end up meeting Don Johnson, after all.

"It's five," I said. "Mike could come home at any minute."

"Shush. I'm thinking." Audrey started writing. Her letters were steeply slanted, almost flat, and she held her

chin just inches above the page. The cane in her chair
seat creaked as she bore down, but once she'd filled half
a page she lost momentum.

"Aren't you making dinner tonight?" I said.

Audrey scratched a sentence out. "I'm having Mike
grab a pizza at Giorgio's. I told him I'm weak from
giving blood. Don't snitch."

I broke into a codeine-muffled panic. Only once had
Mike let us eat pizza for dinner—a brittle, tasteless
store-bought pie bought because Audrey was groggy after having her wisdom teeth removed. A rich, sticky
restaurant pizza might spoil us and upset the budget
Mike was trying to keep us on. Joel, who seemed to be
eating for both of us now that I could barely manage a
bite, would probably want one every night, and Audrey
might lose interest in her kitchen duties. Even her language, *grabbing a pizza*, had taken on an alarming
breeziness.

"Listen," said Audrey, "and tell me what you
think." She flattened out the page so she could read it.
"A woman's beauty isn't just external. Faces and figures
fade. What counts is *inside*."

"It's good. It's on the mark." I felt relieved. Such
corniness, I was convinced, would never win.

"Nevertheless," Audrey continued, "the outside often
reflects the inside, lending a shape to invisible qualities.
The body is a mirror of the spirit. So it is with my scars.
It's true: my scars. I consider my scars my most attractive feature, for each one tells a tale about my life."

My neck prickled and my earlobes heated up. This scar idea was ingenious. A winner, maybe.

"My plan," Audrey said, "is to tell where each scar came from. For example, the time when Joel fell through the ice and I cut my legs up wading in to rescue him. Or the scar from when I was changing an IV and the patient woke up delirious and bit me."

"I don't know," I said. "It's pretty strange. Maybe you should just write about your hair."

"What do you mean? My hair is limp. It's ordinary."

"Do you have to send photos?"

"No photos."

"So exaggerate."

Audrey pushed out her lower lip and made a grumpy, dimpled chin. The ease with which I'd discouraged her surprised me. She set down her Flair on the pad and gazed again at Johnson's lethal grin. "I know this seems stupid to you, but it's important. I want to see the expression on Mike's face. Maybe if you're still sick tomorrow," she said, "you could help me take another stab at it? We could drive to St. Paul, have lunch, go shopping. Brainstorm."

I glanced at the level inside the codeine bottle: there wasn't enough to last another sick day. Still, I felt I couldn't run the risk of letting Audrey write the essay herself.

"If I go, can we stop at the pharmacy?" I said.

~ ~ ~

Sometimes, after a late-night ambulance call, if the call had been especially sad or bloody or if someone young had been involved, Audrey would come to my room when she got home and sit on the edge of my bed with a drink and talk about her life, her memories. It was always worth staying awake for, what she said, and if I felt my eyes closing I'd pinch myself; there was no other way to learn about her past. She hadn't kept pictures, both her parents were dead, and her only sibling, a sister, lived in Florida and didn't keep in touch. Her father, who'd been the team physician for the Michigan football pro- gram, hadn't been kind to his daughters, I'd gathered, and going their separate ways when they grew up was their way of forgetting their time with him. As for their mother, they'd never really known her; she'd died of breast cancer when they were small.

The story Audrey told most often was the story of how she'd met my father. They'd come together at a Rose Bowl party when Michigan beat USC in Pasadena. Mike was a linebacker nicknamed "the Hatchet" for his low and devastating tackles. Audrey was a nursing stu- dent. Her father had brought her along to see the game, wangling her a seat on the team plane, where Mike first caught her eye. Sitting next to Woody Wolff himself and obviously a leader and a star, he wore a buzzcut, a loud Hawaiian shirt, and was actually exercising in his seat; curling a pair of dumbbells with his eyes shut. She'd never seen such concentration, she told me, or such a lean and tightly made male body. "He interested me as a specimen," she said. "I know that sounds cold, but I was cold back then." She asked her father about him before the party and learned that Mike had the slowest pulse and largest lung capacity he'd ever come across.

The victory party was held outside, under the first real palm trees Audrey had ever seen. She never forgot to mention the trees. Mike couldn't dance, so she had him to herself, and as they drank and talked he let a secret slip: he'd heard something tear in his knee during the game and was finding it hard to stand up. "That did it," she told me. "The thought of such a perfect man in pain sent me around the bend somehow. I swooned. Here I'd been muddling along through nursing school as a way to please my dad, and suddenly up pops this god who needs my help." In fact, Audrey told me, she sensed immediately what Mike would only decide after his surgery—his football career was finished—and it thrilled her. A man who might have cast her off if his future had played out as planned had ended up dependent on her care. They married before Mike's senior year was out, while he was still on crutches.

I found it hard to look Audrey in the eye during these late-night chats in my bedroom. I couldn't stand her beauty. It made me fidget. To have such a good-looking woman for a mother didn't seem fair to me; it raised expectations for my future love life that I feared would never be fulfilled. When Audrey was my age, I felt, she wouldn't have noticed me; the only way someone like me could hold the gaze of someone like her was to be her child. Her son.

"You'll always be my baby," she sometimes said, rising from my bed after our talks, and nothing made me madder. I felt cheated. Unlike Mike and the other young men she'd known, who'd had the chance to make winning first impressions, I'd met her when I was helpless, speechless, tiny.

Wrecking her essay was my chance to get even— with her, with idols like Johnson, with the Hatchet. I wasn't proud of myself, but there it was.

~ ~ ~

At breakfast the next morning I played sick again. I coughed into a tissue and pretended I couldn't eat my bowl of Oat Rings, a cheap bulk cereal Mike made Audrey buy instead of Cheerios. As a retailer himself, Mike knew the cost of building national brand names, and he refused to pay the premium. He forbade us to wear Levi's or brush with Crest or relieve our headaches with Excedrin.

Mike sipped coffee and scanned the front page as Audrey checked my glands. I couldn't help comparing his looks to Johnson's. Mike had the same cleft chin, a straighter nose, and his cheekbones were, if anything, more prominent, but unfortunately he hadn't learned the trick of skipping shaving to let his stubble grow out. Touches like that were what made Johnson a star.

"They're inflamed," Audrey lied. "No school for you today."

Joel shot me a jealous look and sulked. He hated school as much as I did and only attended because of sports, it seemed. He played them all, with an ease and natural grace that pointed to great achievements down the line, maybe even greater than Mike's had been.

"I think what Justin needs is *air,*" Mike said. "He's been indoors for two days running now."

Audrey gave Mike a cutting look; this was an old argument between them. According to Mike, fresh air cured everything, while Audrey maintained that rest was the best medicine. All of my parents' other disagreements, from where to go on vacation to whom to vote for, seemed to me to be versions of this one. Reagan, because he rode horses, had been the outside candidate; Carter, a scientist, the indoor man.

The debate about how to make me better continued as Mike got up from the table and put his coat on. I opened the bottle of codeine, held it high, and poured, but all that came out was a paltry thread of syrup.

"By the way," Audrey said, "I'll be busy all day today, so maybe you could get a bucket of chicken."

Mike bent down to tie his shoes. "I see a pattern here. Have you stopped cooking?"

"Twice is not a pattern," Audrey said. "Fried chicken or pizza again, it's up to you."

Mike snapped on his rubbers and straightened up.

"There's another divorce on the way. The Andersons. Anna's run off to Chicago with some gigolo."

"The man is an accomplished sculptor, Mike. What does that have to do with anything?"

"Staying together takes sacrifice. It's work. Certain people seem to be forgetting that."

~ ~ ~

On the drive to St. Paul we discussed the Johnson essay.

"I want to work in the word 'gamine,' " said Audrey. It was snowing and we were driving behind a sand truck whose amber warning light strobed her face and hair and made her look like an actress in a suspense film.

"I prefer 'petite.' "

"Petite's a commonplace."

"Miniature?"

"Too technical. Too awkward."

"Wee?" I said. "Pint-size? Trim?"

"You're just confusing me."

Confusing her was the essence of my plan. Last night, I'd let myself picture Audrey's dream date in greater detail than before, and I was terrified. I could see the blue tropical cocktails on the bar as Johnson led Audrey across the nightclub's dance floor through a crowd of partying celebrities: Burt Reynolds kissing a teenage fashion model, Joey Heatherton hugging an NFL receiver.

"We're taking the wrong approach," she said. "Instead of getting hung up on language, Justin, imagine you've never seen me. We've never met. You round a corner and there I am, in front of you. And what strikes you first is . . . ?"

The exercise was difficult. I tilted my head to change my perspective and tried to see Audrey anew, as a stranger. Her skin, I noticed, was darker than I realized, as though she had a trace of Indian blood, as well as surprisingly moist and shiny. Pores loomed. Freckles. Blackheads. Oily spots. In school I'd been taught that the skin is an organ—a kind of stretched-out liver or kidney—but only now did this idea make sense to me.

"Talk," Audrey said. "Describe. Immortalize."

I was thinking of fancy words for Audrey's skin tone when I noticed the tendons in her hands, fanned like the wire ribs of an umbrella. Her fingers were beautiful, too. Like the idealized fingers on the Knox box, they curved and tapered perfectly, ending in bladelike crimson nails that I could see my reflection in.

I knew it then: the winning essay would focus on hands and fingers. It was obvious.

"You've got it," Audrey said. "You've solved the puzzle."

"It's just a thought. It's stupid."

"Go ahead."

"When are we going to find a pharmacy?"

"As soon as you stop stalling me. Let's hear it."

Grit from the sand truck rained against the wind-

shield. I pictured Audrey sitting on a hotel bed as Johnson splashed on cologne in his beach house, preparing for
their evening out. A towel was tied loosely around his
narrow waist and even the tops of his feet were darkly
tanned.

"Fine. No cough syrup," Audrey said.

I stiffened. Everything inside me reversed itself.

"I think you ought to write about your hands."

"What about them?" Her voice was low, excited.

"You have to promise me that if you win you won't
forget who helped you."

"Promise," she said.

A minute later, I'd told her everything, betraying myself for a mild narcotic. Idiot.

~ ~ ~

We wrote the essay at lunch in a department store. The
cheese in my French onion soup disintegrated as Audrey
took my dictation. I was flying. I'd snuck some cough
syrup into my Pepsi and suddenly I felt lyrical, fearless,
my brain a lubricated spool of words. I described Audrey's hands folding laundry, forming piecrusts, stroking
hospital patients. They turned pages in hymnals and
helped deliver newborns.

"Let's change hymnals to novels," Audrey said. "We
don't go to church."

"Write 'hymnals.' Take my word for it. A little religion makes a person sound modest."

The waitress whisked away my untouched soup and set down two Reuben sandwich platters. Audrey laid her pen aside and drew out the frilly toothpick from a sandwich half. Our table was on a balcony overlooking the perfume floor, and I could smell lilies, cinnamon, and vanilla mixed with the salty odor of corned beef.

"It doesn't sound like me," said Audrey. "That's the whole point, the whole dream: that he'd like *me.*"

"Johnson's not judging the contest. Knox is."

"Good point. I forget that. I'll owe you one for this."

"No problem," I said.

"I mean it. This must feel strange, helping your mother refine her image."

"It does."

Audrey picked up a sandwich half and nibbled at the overhanging sauerkraut. According to my changed idea of things, helping her with her entry was in my interest, regardless of the outcome. If she lost, as was likely, she'd know I'd stood behind her. And in the event she won, which seemed impossible, she'd know that the credit belonged to me, her son, and not to herself for being smart or special. She'd feel humbled, grateful, in my debt.

"The point," I said, "is to show your hands in action and not just describe their appearance. That's our gimmick."

"I still like my scar idea. This seems conventional."

"Trust me on this. I've really thought about it."

Audrey wedged a nail between her teeth and picked out a bit of sauerkraut and nodded. She pushed away her plate and got the pen.

~ ~ ~

After Audrey submitted her essay, I started seeing Don Johnson everywhere: profiled in magazines, posing on billboards, pitching aftershave on TV commercials. I'd always assumed, without giving it much thought, that somewhere in America there was a border between famous people like him and people like us, but I wasn't sure how far away it lay or how easy it was to cross. If Audrey made it to the other side, there was no telling when she'd come back, if ever. The only person I knew who'd made the trip was a gorgeous blonde high school senior named Jeanna Meade who'd left for Los Angeles three years ago, appeared in a soap opera for a couple of months, and never been heard from since. Her parents had closed their motel and gone to find her and they had vanished, too.

One night Mike and Audrey attended a seminar on marketing upscale vitamins and supplements and Joel and I stayed up late and watched a talk show. Johnson was a guest. Women shrieked as he strode onstage, his collar open, his trousers loose and flowing, and when he sat down beside the other guest—a female singer with a double chin and long false eyelashes that looked like bat wings—she hiked up her skirt and fiddled with her blouse buttons.

"Do you always have this effect?" the host asked Johnson.

Johnson shrugged. The actress clutched her heart. She rolled her eyes and pretended to be fainting.

"Medic!" the host yelled. "We need a medic here!"

As the waiting period went on, Audrey developed a certain swagger, as if merely mailing the essay had transformed her. She made pizza night a weekly ritual. Tasks that I knew she'd been putting off, she suddenly dove into, such as talking to Joel about sex. Instead of teaching him as she'd taught me—with the help of college nursing texts that made the sexual organs look like plants—she used the new *Penthouse*. I wondered where she'd bought it.

I grew bluer and moodier by the day. Though I'd come to believe that Audrey would lose the contest, one scene that I'd imagined from her dream date seemed bound to haunt me always: Johnson filling glasses of champagne while Audrey applied mascara in a compact mirror. Whether this moment ever came to pass didn't matter now that I knew the truth: Audrey's life with us was a compromise, a sham.

To ease her dissatisfaction, I pampered her. At night, when we watched TV, I rubbed her shoulders, digging into the muscles with my thumbs. I watered her plants and washed and waxed her car and plumped up the sofa cushions before she sat on them.

One day she said, "You're all over me. Get off."

"Your neck looks tight. I thought I'd rub it down."

"I can rub down my own neck. Get away."

I went to the kitchen, where Mike was cleaning wall-eyes. He'd been ice fishing on Elkhorn Lake. His thermal undershirt glittered with bloody scales as he poked a fillet knife into one fish's throat, then pulled straight back. Dark guts came tumbling out.

"You're spilling blood on Audrey's clean tile," I said.

Mike dropped a paper towel on the floor and wiped it around with his foot.

"You're making it worse."

Mike rinsed his bloody hands in the sink and dried them on a white dishcloth.

"You're going to lose her."

Mike hung the cloth on its hook and stared at me. "What's going on?"

"You've given up," I said. "You talk about all these couples getting divorces and then you treat your own wife like she's a cleaning lady."

I said nothing more, but Mike seemed to get my message. A few days later, for no special reason, he came home with flowers and a box of candy and took Audrey out to the Hund, a German restaurant with a strolling accordion player. They returned after midnight, which thrilled me. I'd waited up. I listened to their voices in the hallway.

"Well, I think he's cute."

"He's a homo."

"Women love him."

"My mother loves Liberace, for God's sake. If any-thing, that's *proof* the guy's a fruit."

I heard my parents' bedroom door close and then, a few minutes later, it opened again. Mike appeared in my bedroom, shirtless, shaking. He stood at my footboard and glared, his hands in fists.

"Get up," he said. "I know what you've been up to."

"She asked for my help. I had no choice. You're drunk."

"You bet I'm drunk. I have a right to be."

I shrunk back against the headboard as Mike sat down and slapped the edge of my mattress with one hand.

"You're right, I don't deserve her. Never did." He unraveled a thread from my blanket's satin border and wound it around one finger like a tourniquet. "I played on her sympathy. She felt sorry for me. A linebacker with a limp. She ate it up. Then the limp went away and I had nothing to offer her."

"It's not just you," I said. "It's Joel and me. We have to make more of an effort."

"She dreams," Mike said. He tightened the thread. His fingertip turned white. "Still, you'd have thought she'd have better taste. *Don Johnson?*"

"He dresses well."

"It's my fault. I'll do better. Maybe she was right to play this game with me. Maybe I've let things slip fur-ther than I realized."

Mike opened his arms and leaned his weight against me. The hug was hot and soggy. I didn't like it. I pushed him back but he only held me tighter, squeezing the air from my lungs. Such force, such mass. I wondered sometimes how my mother stood it.

~ ~ ~

The manila envelope looked official. In its cellophane window I read the words: "Audrey Cobb, You're a Winner! Claim Your Prize!"

I stashed it unopened in a dresser drawer and tried to continue normally with my day, but every time I looked at Audrey my mind said good-bye. I watched her do the laundry, measuring out detergent and setting dials. She matched up my socks and tucked them into balls and tossed them free-throw style into a basket. I happened to know from reading certain magazines that women were tired of performing such chores for men and that the day was coming when they'd quit doing them.

When I finally handed over the contest envelope, resigned to yet another defeat from a world that seemed determine to strip me bare, I saw Audrey's eyes go dewy. She ripped it open.

"I don't believe this!" She slid the letter out. She flattened it on the table and started reading.

Her face fell. She turned the letter printside down.

"What?" I said.

Audrey crossed her arms and hugged herself.

"You didn't win?"

"Of course I didn't. Don't tease."

Later, I read the letter for myself and learned that Audrey had, in fact, placed third, along with five hundred other Johnson fans. The prize was a year's supply of gelatin drink, but when the carton arrived she didn't open it. She stashed it high on a kitchen shelf, behind a box of generic instant rice.

A few days later, I noticed her nails were breaking. She trimmed them back and started chewing them. She gave up polishing them and using emery boards.

One night I found the courage to tell her how bad I felt.

"I'm sorry," I said. "I shouldn't have interfered. I should have let you write the essay yourself. That scar idea was a winner."

Audrey looked up.

"I blew your big chance," I said. "You could have met him. You could have seen Palm Beach. You could have stayed up all night in Miami, partying with stars and fashion designers."

Audrey held up one hand and spread her fingers. She looked at them close up, then farther away.

"Just so you know that," she said. "Just so you know."

4

Because I'd been drinking cough syrup all winter and generally letting my health and hygiene go, forgetting to dress warm, skipping meals, and rinsing with mouth-wash instead of brushing my teeth, I wasn't in any shape that spring to go out for baseball, as Mike had hoped I would. I joined Mr. Geary's new speech squad instead.

He recruited me as I was walking home from school one day. He stopped his road-salt-corroded Mercedes die-sel, turned down the classical music on the tape player, and motioned to me with the very gesture—a crooked index finger—that I'd been taught as a child to beware of.

"I'll give you a lift. We need to talk," he said. "Here, let me clear this seat off."

"That's okay."

"If cleanliness is next to godliness, I'm a fallen angel, I'm afraid." I sat on a heap of flattened Penguin Classics and button-down white shirts with yellow armpits. Empty cola cans rolled around in back, and on the dashboard were hairbrushes and combs snarled with colorless hair. The key chain hanging from the steering column was one of those plastic Buddhas whose tubby stomach supposedly gives you luck if you rub it.

"I've noticed you're quite a communicator," Mr. Geary said. "I think you have an oral gift."

I frowned.

"That's not a diagnosis, it's a compliment. Me, I'd do anything to have your talent."

"What makes you think I have talent?"

"Little clues. Of all pupils I've had in ninth-grade English, you were the first who knew what 'simile' meant. Also, you have a certain lively eloquence that can't be taught. It's organic."

"I hate that word. It reminds me of mold or something. Bacteria."

"See how sensitive you are to language? Nurture that, Justin. Never let it go. I assume you're a reader."

"Not books. I've never finished one. Now and then I skim a Hardy Boys."

"Nothing wrong with the Hardy Boys. Cute duo. I always preferred the dark one. Joe?"

"It's Frank."

"So, are you on my team?"

"I'll think about it. My father might not be happy."

"I'll talk to him. I have a bit of a golden tongue myself."

It worked. I stopped in at Mike's store that afternoon to help him unpack a shipment of Louisville Sluggers. Joel stood behind the counter taking practice swings. "Going, going, *gone*," he said. Mike grinned. Last year, Joel had tied a grade school home run record and he was looking to top himself this spring. His arms were like little fence posts from lifting weights.

"You just missed your teacher," Mike said when he saw me. "Quite a fan you've got there."

Joel swung his bat. "Am I choking up too much?"

Mike shook his head. "So," he said to me, "speech. It could be worse. He told me it's pretty competitive, in fact."

"He thinks I'll be good."

"As long as it's competitive. As long as it's not just a lark. Some feel-good thing."

"It's out of the park!" Joel cried. "It's in the street!"

"If you let me, I'll give it my best. I swear," I said.

"We all deserve to win at something. Fine."

~ ~ ~

The speech team's first meet, a divisional match, was held ninety miles away, in Chippewa City. My teammates, five girls, were already on the bus, huddled in the back around a beauty magazine, when I boarded with Mr. Geary. He'd had a crisis. Five minutes before, I'd found him in the boys' room standing in front of the mirror with a scissors, attacking his bangs with jerky, hectic snips. Hair clogged the sink.

"I wish that I was *bald.*"

"I think your hair looks good," I said.

"Don't patronize me."

"I'm sorry."

"You're making it worse now."

Mr. Geary wet his hands and patted his hair down. I felt sorry for him. He was our school's youngest teacher and a bachelor, so plain in his looks that when he took his glasses off he seemed to have no face. His skin was the neutral hue of turkey meat and his thinning, straight hair required constant perms. In the days immediately following his stylings he'd wisecrack, laugh, and jiggle as he taught, but as his curls went flat, he went flat, too.

When the bus pulled into Chippewa City, Mr. Geary stood up in the aisle and addressed the squad. He urged the girls to emphasize their eyes by freshening their mascara before they spoke, and he stressed the importance of posture and breath control. "It's spring," he said, "and I've noticed some stuffy noses; I brought along some

decongestant pills. They'll clear your heads and maybe
pep you up."

None of the girls expressed interest in the pills, but I
took four, which was twice the normal dosage.

"That should give you a tingle," Mr. Geary said.

The speech event he'd signed me up for, Small-Group
Discussion, had been created that year. The goal, according to a pamphlet I read, was not to vanquish the other
side as in straight debate, but to "fruitfully interact
with peers concerning issues of national and global interest." The match was held around an oval table in the
high school's counseling office. I arrived to find my
group already seated: two boys and three girls, all well
dressed and smiling, wearing paper name tags on their
chests and chatting about a documentary broadcast on
public TV the night before.

I disliked my opponents instantly. Beside one boy's
chair was a patent-leather briefcase with a built-in com-
bination lock, while three of the girls had equipped
themselves with card files marked with colored tabs. To
make myself look as serious as they did, I went to a rack
of pamphlets against the wall—"So, You Want to Be an
Electrician?," "Pregnant at Sixteen"—and grabbed a
stack of them to set in front of me.

That season's general topic was the media. The sub-
topic, chosen that day by the judges, was TV violence.
"Begin," one judge said. A stretch of silence followed. A
girl named Elise spoke up first. "It's sick," she said.
"TV violence just *kills* morality, particularly among

teens. The studies prove it. Day after day kids watch these shows with gunfights and suddenly it's like, Hey, let's rob a store. The next thing you know someone's dead. It's really a shame."

"I concur," said Mark, the briefcase boy. "But let's go further. TV decays the family. And once the family goes, everything goes with it. Down go our institutions. Up goes drug abuse. Ditto gambling and pornography."

I sensed the group recoiling against Mark's vehemence. Interrupting him might win me allies.

"Images aren't reality," I said. "Violence in art goes back to . . . Egypt? What's important is teaching people to be skeptical—to draw a line between images and life."

I knew that I'd taken the lead with this remark. The judges, three older women with tall, sprayed hairdos, scribbled on the clipboards on their laps. Pushing for extra interaction points, I turned to the shy girl cowering next to Mark, her lower lip sucked back into her mouth.

"What's your view, Lisa? The group needs more perspective."

"You're right," she said. "TV's not real. It's pictures." She flashed me a bashful grin. "It's nice you asked."

"Hold on," Mark said. "Reality's not the point here. Social decline is."

"Kate?" I said. "Reaction?"

"Go ahead."

"Mark," I said in a measured, gentle voice, "I understand the spirit of your objection, but reality and society are inextricable." I held up my hands and laced my fingers together.

I was bound to win, I knew it then. Small-Group Discussion was all about maneuvering—harassing the proud, encouraging the meek, and making oneself a trusted central figure. Knowledge of the topic was irrelevant. My victory seemed even more assured when the decongestants took effect. They made the room expand and brighten and keyed me in to the play of group emotion. I found myself finishing the other kids' sentences and recombining their conflicting positions into satisfying compromises.

Mr. Geary was pacing in the hall when the discussion concluded. He clutched my elbow. I saw that he'd cut more hair off near his temples, giving him a funny, monkish look.

"How'd it go?"

"You were right. I have a flair."

"Told you."

"It's the first thing I've ever been good at."

Mr. Geary stepped aside as the judges lined up to shake my hand. After they'd gone, he said, "You're on you way. Winning suits you, Justin."

I agreed.

~ ~ ~

The regionals, held in Duluth on a Saturday, required a
Friday night stay in a motel. We drove for hours along an
interstate whose median was planted with tiny pine
trees. The smell of sunbaked soil filled the bus and the
driver turned on a Bemidji radio station whose fast-talk-
ing D.J. was counting down the hits. I had a feeling of
being bound for glory.

When we registered at the motel Mr. Geary asked
the clerk to place the squad's three remaining girls in one
room and me and him together in another.

"I think we should do this by age," I said.

"Against school policy. No males with females."

"I'll say I sneaked in. I'll take the blame," I said.

"Justin, what precisely is this about? You don't feel
comfortable being alone with me?"

"I like to be with people my age, is all."

The girls unpacked their gym bags on the beds and I
sat on the floor and watched the news. Now that I had a
forum for my opinions, current events and social issues
gripped me. What's more, I suspected there might be
money in them. TV was filled with analysts and experts
who sat around tables politely arguing just as I did in
Small-Group Discussion. For the first time since coming
back shattered from Camp Overcome, I glimpsed a future for myself. A goal.

I analyzed the news reports as my teammates showered. They emerged from the bathroom in baggy football
jerseys, their shampooed hair tied back in fragrant
ponytails.

"Who besides me needs a drink?" said Heather Hall. "I brought some licorice schnapps. I just need ice."

Janna Lindgren produced a rolled-up Baggie. "I've got weed, but I need a beer to smoke it with."

"I could use a beer, too," said Dora Muntz.

The girls looked at me to solve the problem. I was the man, the favorite, the leader. I dialed the number for Mr. Geary's room and got an answer before I heard a ring.

"The girls want a twelve-pack of Michelob," I said. The trick, as in Small-Group Discussion, was confidence.

"You're asking me to buy alcohol for minors?"

"People do it all the time."

"Not teachers."

"We think of you more as a peer," I said. "A friend."

A half hour later a knock came at the door and Heather opened it just wide enough to snatch the beer and put money in the hand.

We drew the blinds and cranked up the air conditioner and sat in a campfire circle on the bed talking about Mr. Geary and passing a joint. The girls felt he needed a wife. I disagreed. At one point I touched Heather's leg by accident, causing a pop of static that made her jump. This led to an experiment. After rubbing against the blankets to raise their charges, Dora and Janna lifted their jerseys and pushed their chests together bra-to-bra. Green sparks flew. When it was my turn I pulled my shirt off and Heather pulled off hers, then reached behind herself to unhook her bra—a white bra with a pink heart between the cups and frilly stitching along the underside.

The phone kept ringing and we kept ignoring it. The next thing we knew Mr. Geary was in the doorway. The desk clerk must have given him a key. He had on blue flannel pajamas with white stripes and reading glasses that enlarged his eyes.

The girls draped sheets and blankets over their bodies.

"Out in the hall, Justin. Now," said Mr. Geary.

"I can't. I'm not dressed." I held a pillow against myself.

"The honor system is wasted on you people. This is outrageous. I smell dope in here."

"Stop being such an old woman," Heather said. "All we're doing is having a normal slumber party."

"How did you just refer to me, young woman?"

Heather looked at her friends as if for backup, then faced Mr. Geary square-on. "I think that what I said was: disappear, queer."

Mr. Geary's face went white and taut and his soul seemed to shrink away behind his eyes. He backed up into the hall with three quick steps and closed the door so hard it rattled the latch. I dialed his room repeatedly for an hour, then called again when I woke at one A.M., and each time I sensed the presence of his hand hovering near the receiver.

Finally, I went down the hall and knocked. Blue TV light filtered under the door.

"It's Justin. Open up."

"Fuck off. Get out of here."

The bad language startled me. "Are you all right?"

"I took some pills. I'm trying to fall asleep."

"How many pills?"

"Not enough. Just let me be."

In the morning, when everyone gathered at the bus, Mr. Geary had shaved his hair clean off.

~ ~ ~

In the days leading up to the statewide finals, I became impossible at home. Filled up by my first-place showing at regionals, I demanded new privileges, shirked my chores, and argued with Mike about stories in the newspaper. Recognition and the decongestant pills had given my voice an authoritative ring I couldn't get enough of.

"Don't let the liberals dupe you," Mike said one morning as we debated the headlines. "Organized labor's a form of legal blackmail."

"Blackmail. Black male. Have you ever noticed that?"

"Meaning what?"

I wasn't really sure. In the swell and surge of my nonstop jabbering, I'd started seeing patterns in the language that struck me as significant and ominous but didn't seem to interest other people. Therapist. The rapist. Coincidence? And why was "live" spelled backward "evil"? My oral gift had turned on me somehow.

At school my arm ached from raising my hand so often. The hinges of my jaw hurt. I couldn't shut up. In social studies one morning, during a lesson on life in the ghetto, I sprang from my desk to state my views and sent my chair crashing backward into the wall.

At lunch hour a man's voice on the P.A. ordered me to visit the school nurse. She tested my blood pressure twice and took my pulse, then picked up her phone and summoned the principal.

"Whatever drug you're on," he said, "you'd better not be bringing it to school. I've ordered a locker search."

"Go ahead. Use dogs."

"Empty your pockets."

I turned them inside out. Nothing but lint and change, which I let spill.

"Pick that junk up."

"I want my coach," I said.

Mr. Geary explained my condition to the principal as a case of prestate-tournament jitters and offered to drive me home so I could rest. In the Mercedes I thanked him for his help. Sunlight bounced and flickered off his scalp, which he'd begun to wax. He wouldn't look at me.

"What's wrong?" I said.

"You're a monster."

"You used to love me."

"Don't be grandiose."

"Then what was all that business about my 'gift'?"

"Flattery. Ego building."

"But I keep winning. There must have been something to it."

"I made a monster."

With the meet just two days away, I couldn't sleep that night. At school the next morning the nurse rechecked my blood pressure and warned me that if it didn't come down soon she'd check me into Children's Hospital.

"The weight loss, the agitation. You're taking something."

I glanced involuntarily at my sock, where I'd stashed the decongestant pills. It wasn't them, though. It was me; my mind. Maybe I really had become a monster. Maybe winning didn't suit me, after all.

I decided to confess. "I can't stop blabbering. It's like I've turned on a switch I can't turn off. I'm out of control."

The nurse softened. "Close your eyes. Imagine a peaceful lake."

Hypnosis again.

"I'm doing it," I lied. "It's helping."

"Still, blue, fresh water. A sunset. Gliding gulls."

Why were they always trying to put me under?

~ ~ ~

The finals were held on a Saturday morning at the Minneapolis Sheraton. We checked in the night before: one room, two beds. The girls had been eliminated by then.

In the soaring glass lobby coaches, judges, and students signed registration forms, consulted schedules, and filled out sticky name tags with Magic Markers. The only student I recognized was Mark, my opponent from divisionals. He had on black loafers, gray flannels, and a blue blazer whose sleeves fell short of his wrists.

"God, how pretentious," I said to Mr. Geary.

"The boy has pizzazz. It takes courage. Good for him."

A dinner buffet was held in the Red Room. I got in line in an effort to seem sociable. Men in chef's hats wielding metal tongs heaped our plates with roast beef and mashed potatoes. Mr. Geary passed by my table, ignoring me, and sat down next to Mark. I overheard him call himself "a fan of yours" and I watched the two of them instantly grow close, tilting their heads together, laughing and smirking. Mr. Geary poured Mark a glass of wine from a bottle reserved for the adults.

I left my plate and headed to the room to wash up for the dance that night. I rubbed on cologne, thought twice, and scrubbed it off. I sat at the desk to wait for Mr. Geary. I didn't want him to find me on the bed, but when a half hour had passed I changed my mind and propped myself on one elbow on the mattress. I turned the TV on, mussed up my damp hair, and tried to think only cool and careless thoughts. It was time for revenge. He deserved it. He'd betrayed me.

An hour passed and Mr. Geary didn't show. I opened the box of chocolates on his pillow, took a small bite from each one, and put them back.

Downstairs at the dance I spotted my coach with Mark again, huddled in a corner near the stage. From the lively arching of their eyebrows, I guessed they were being sarcastic about the band. I asked a middle-aged female coach to dance and guided her back and forth past Mr. Geary, my hands pressed into her hips. He turned his back to us.

"I've heard of you," said the woman. "You're quite the prodigy."

I watched Mr. Geary light a cigarette and pass it to Mark, who cupped it in one hand, stole a few drags, and exhaled down and sideways.

"Thanks," I said. I twirled the woman, dipped her.

"Is that your coach with the fat boy? We've been commenting. Not exactly the time or place."

"Ignore them."

"It doesn't offend you?"

"The kid's just playing with him. Trying to psyche me out before the match."

"They look to me like a pair," the woman said.

I returned to the room after midnight. Mr. Geary's bed was empty. I opened the bathroom door and snooped around. A cigarette butt turned slowly in the toilet bowl and I smelled two colognes in the air that didn't blend well. The two red rings on the sink were wine. I sniffed them.

I ordered a pot of coffee from room service and sat up in bed until two, watching issues shows. When I heard a key in the lock I pulled the blankets up and pretended to be asleep. I listened to Mr. Geary unbuckle his belt and fluff his pillow with two or three firm slaps.

"Where were you?" I said as if I'd just awakened.

"Wasting my precious time. As usual."

"I could have told you he wasn't a nice guy."

"Go back to sleep." Mr. Geary took his shirt off.

"I want you to take back that monster thing you said. I know you didn't mean it and it hurt me. I like being liked by people."

"Don't we all."

Mr. Geary folded a pillow around his head and I sat up and poured myself more coffee. I watched the windows lighten behind the curtains. At seven-thirty, still awake, I swallowed my last two decongestant pills. The match wasn't for another two hours, but I needed the boost. Mr. Geary woke at eight, stumbled into the bathroom, locked the door, showered for a solid hour, then shaved his scalp with his electric razor. I gave up on cleaning up and put my clothes on and went downstairs to the gift shop to find more pills.

~ ~ ~

The topic that morning was "TV News: Too Negative?" A blond girl with a daisy in her hair spoke of the need for upbeat reporting. Mark disagreed. Another boy took the girl's side. The judges, who all looked hung over, yawned and fidgeted. It occurred to me that we were losers, every one of us, the tournament just an excuse to feel important before returning to towns that didn't notice us.

Mr. Geary sat in a chair behind the judges' station, a

half-eaten jelly doughnut on his lap. Whatever had happened with Mark had worn him out, while Mark seemed energized, his voice a bell.

"The human condition, as presently evolved, is not a pretty sight," he said. "Face facts, Kim. It's not the news that's to blame, it's us, the populace. Welcome to the Fall of Rome, part two."

"I totally reject that, Mark," said Kim. "Pessimism's a *product*. It sells papers. The media needs to look inside itself."

I felt the words rise up. I made my move.

"I think we're confusing tone and content here. Content isn't negative or positive. Content just *is*."

"You're missing the point," said Mark.

I looked at my coach. He was dozing, eyes half shut, powdered sugar sprinkled on his chin.

"*Tone* can be negative, though, and that was Kim's point. Maybe the answer is: lighten up the tone but let the content stand," I said.

"Report on rapes and murders with a smile. That's absurd," Mark said.

He was right; it was. I'd cornered myself. My brain spun like a tire in mud as Mark leaned over the table and slashed away at me, his lips forming vicious shapes. I glanced at Mr. Geary for a prompt, but he was napping, his doughnut on the floor. With time running short, I tried to push Mark back and mount a defense of the nonsense I'd slipped into, but when I opened my mouth no words came out. My throat closed tight like a fist around a coin.

When the judges called time and Mr. Geary woke up, I sneered at him and hurried toward the door.

Mark blocked my exit with his outstretched hand. "Nice discussion," he said.

"You, too."

"You're good."

"Shut the hell up."

"*That's* gracious."

"Kiss my ass."

I packed my bag, turned my key in at the desk, and stood outside beneath a dripping awning, smoking a menthol bummed from a bellhop. Gray shreds of cloud were falling with the rain.

Mr. Geary found me. "Back inside. The ceremony's starting. Show some class."

I grunted. No clever comeback, just a noise. Forming whole words seemed pointless suddenly.

"None of us win all the time. Get used to it."

Another grunt.

"You disappoint me, Justin."

After the prizes were handed out Mr. Geary drove me home. I rested my head against the passenger window as he reviewed my performance for the season. My strengths, he concluded, were drive, intensity, and an understanding of group dynamics. My weak points were glibness, resentment, sloth, and arrogance. Mr. Geary became so absorbed in the critique that he let go of the steering wheel now and then, nearly driving us into a ditch while waving his hands and fluttering his fingers to illustrate my lack of discipline.

For almost an hour I sat there, taking it. To lose a gift I might never have known I had felt worse than not being gifted in the first place.

"I'm sorry if I sound cruel or blunt, but somebody's going to tell you these things someday. You can't just bob and weave your way through life. Fakes get found out. At bottom, the world is *fair*. A knack for ad-libs is a bonus. It's no foundation. If it's true that someday you'd like to be a commentator, what you need to develop are reasoned opinions, not clever tactics for winning brownie points."

By this time we were parked in front of my house and the car had been idling for a while. I could have left at any time, but I was letting Mr. Geary finish. I'd decided to grant him his dramatic wrap-up speech, if only because I knew how good it felt. To know what you're saying and know you're saying it well, to speak with momentum and confidence and spirit, is no small pleasure, he'd taught me. It changes everything.

When Mr. Geary was done condemning me, he shook my hand and let me out of the car. We waved to each other and he rolled down his window.

"I forgot. I got your third-place medal for you." He held it out for me. "To show your father. And don't let my little critique just now discourage you. There's always next year."

The medal went into my pocket. When Mike asked me how I'd done, I didn't show it to him. Placing third was nothing to be ashamed of, and I was pretty sure that he'd be proud of me, but it would require a bit of explanation, and I was tired of hearing my own voice by then. Instead, I just told him I'd lost and saved my breath.

5

The speech team had been an experiment in concentrating on what came out of my mouth instead of what went into it. When the experiment failed I had a hole to fill, a hole I sometimes feared was larger than I was. I tried eating again, but the nausea from the venison years came back with a vengeance, so I turned to smoking. I liked it, but I hated the company. The smokers my age were a depressing gang. They came from broken families, dressed in black, and were always swearing idiotic pacts to kill a certain teacher, kill themselves, worship the

devil, bomb the school, or run away to St. Paul and form
a rock band. Eventually, out of boredom and contempt, I
drifted away from them.

I made a play to join the drinking crowd—anything
for a habit I could share—but it wouldn't have me because I didn't play sports. This was just as well. Our
town was dry, no bars or liquor stores, and the jocks'
drink of choice was 3.2 beer, a weak concoction that
smelled like soapy water and tasted like the glue on enve-
lopes. I had to drink a whole six-pack to catch a buzz,
and even then I felt maddeningly alert.

My need for a painkiller was made more urgent by
the fact that Mike and Audrey were fighting. One issue
was who worked harder for less acknowledgment. Mike
had paid Woody Wolff a thousand dollars to visit his
store at the start of summer vacation and autograph
shoes and balls. Over a hundred people showed up, but
few of them purchased anything, having Wolff sign
pieces of paper instead, and Mike accused Audrey of
failing to sympathize with this great betrayal. Audrey,
for her part, charged Mike with underestimating the
thanklessness of the nursing profession.

The other issue between my parents was Joel, who'd
fallen in with the rich kids on the hill. He'd demanded
tennis and riding lessons, which Audrey had gone ahead
and paid for out of her own earnings. Mike went ape.
The night he found out he stayed awake till dawn piling
up items in the living room—lamps and books and
clothes and kitchen gadgets—which he sold at a garage

sale the following weekend. One by one, Audrey replaced the lost items with more expensive equivalents, and each time she brought one home Mike kicked a door or pounded a table. It was hell at home.

I decided that the answer was hard liquor. I approached the town drunk to find out what his source was. A hairy-nostriled old man named Willy Lindt, he lived on a houseboat whose windows were soaped over like the windows of the dirty bookstores I'd seen on Hennepin Avenue in Minneapolis. He fished for crappies and smallmouth from the deck and took his low-life role seriously. He milked it. Three summers ago a movie production company had come to town—a costume drama about the pioneers—and Willy was cast as a drifter by the director. The only local to land a speaking part, he still wore his costume of canvas dungarees and spoke with the Swedish accent he'd been coached in.

Willy seemed pleased to have a visitor. I sat on a velveteen couch whose caved-in cushions made me feel inadequate and short as he scurried around with a broom and tidied up. He dumped his trash through a portal in the floor, where the river floated it away.

"I want to know how to get liquor," I said.

"Steal it from your folks."

"I can't. They'd catch me. I'd get sent somewhere."

Willy smiled. "There's nothing wrong with that. I got sent to Pine Island Juvenile. I learned to play chess there. Mastered archery. Far and away the best year of my life."

"What if I gave you money for vodka?"

"Don't drink clear spirits. Don't go down that road. They say they're purer. They're not. Drink rock and rye. The fruit in the bottle adds important nutrients."

I fished in my jeans for the crumpled fives I'd stolen from Mike's basement workshop. One reason for his despair about money might have been his inability to keep physical track of it; he rarely got through an entire checkbook before losing it down the seat crack of the car, and he littered the house with change and crumpled bills. When he came home from the store at night, he'd fling what was in his pockets on shelves and tables as if he were ridding himself of built-up poisons, not seeming to notice when his property vanished. What disturbed him was spending money, buying things; misplacing money was just a part of life.

"You sure you want to go this route?" said Willy, counting the fives. I felt patronized, insulted. He'd done quite well as a drunk—he'd won a movie role.

"Buy me some booze or I'll get it from Fred Hurley." Fred was our other town drunk, Willy's rival, younger and less picturesque by half, but possibly more authentic. Not an actor.

"You'll get it from me," said Willy. "I'm your guy. How much do you want?"

"Enough to knock me out."

"This isn't a suicide thing, I hope."

"Just buy it."

I came back three days later, as directed, and found

my connection unconscious on the couch. His head hung down over the edge and grazed the floor and the blood pooled in his face had turned it purple, swelling his lips into froggy blobs. I rifled cupboards and yanked out drawers, freeing clouds of midges and flying ants. I couldn't find my vodka.

"Out. Get away!" I heard Willy shout behind me.

I turned, harassed by the insects in my face.

"It's you," Willy said. "I'm sorry."

"Where's my liquor?"

"Never give an alcoholic money, kid."

I made him sit up, then searched his dungarees. He held his arms in the air and didn't protest. But besides some empty food stamp booklets, all I found was his actor's union card, laminated in plastic. What a fake.

~ ~ ~

I soon discovered that marijuana was easier to get. I followed a smell to the woods behind the Lions Park and found a group of older girls in tube tops passing a stone pipe and gossiping. They were comparing the size and shape of the school's top athletes' penises. When I joined the girls the next day the topic was "assne"—who had pimples on their butts. In return for a couple of hits off the pipe, I sold out half the boys' locker room. It was something that I'd been waiting to do, I realized.

The girl I grew closest to was Donna Prine, a redhead with freckles the color of new pennies. She lived alone with her famous father, the only Shandstrom Falls celebrity other than Willy Lindt. His twice-weekly column for the St. Paul paper was syndicated throughout the northern plains and took as its theme the decline of basic values. I wasn't a fan of his politics, but I admired his wordplay. He called Hollywood actors "movie scars," abortions "vacwombs," politicians "kleptocrats," and people on welfare "food tramps." Due to his highly sensitive skin—the result, Donna said, of attending H-bomb tests during his 1950s army days—he seldom left the house. The one time I'd glimpsed him working in his yard, he'd worn a hooded sweatshirt and his face was smeared with white zinc oxide.

One night I went with Donna in her Skylark to buy an ounce of pot. She blindfolded me before we left, wrapping my eyes in a sheer black nylon stocking fragrant with sweat and soap and baby oil. I inhaled deeply as we drove along. "Are you getting off on that?" said Donna. She took my left hand and sucked the middle finger, then guided it knuckle by knuckle through her zipper. "Just touch, don't look," she said. "That's my rule, okay?"

"Why can't I look?"

"I'm saving myself."

"For who?"

"The area's changing. New guys are moving in. Richer, more experienced. More eligible."

When Donna untied my blindfold we were parked in front of a lopsided white farmhouse whose windows were covered with sheets of plastic. The place was a

dump like many local farms, surrounded by weedy fields
and rusting implements. Government programs paid
farmers not to plant, so they'd taken to selling things
instead: Amway detergent, gizmos that boosted gas mileage, knickknacks made of weathered wood. And drugs.

"Be cool," Donna said as she knocked on the screen
door. "And don't make a fuss if he pulls the baby stunt."

The dealer, whom Donna called "Munch," was tall
and in his twenties, with moles on his eyelids the size of
pencil erasers. He led us to a makeshift table fashioned
from a door raised up on cinder blocks. He cleaned the
pot with a putty knife. A Nazareth album, turned down
low, warbled from the stereo and I noticed that the floor
was out of true. Getting my money out, I dropped a
quarter, and it rolled forever, out of sight.

"Hey, Grit!" Munch yelled. "Get down here! Customers!"

"Grit's Munch's girlfriend," said Donna. "They have
a son." She seemed to be preparing me for something.

A young woman appeared at the foot of the stairs.
Her breasts hung out of the sides of a black halter top
and her jeans rode high and tight against her crotch. In
her arms was a baby whose head lolled, unsupported. Its
face was grim and pinched and vaguely mummified, like
something that had been buried and dug up.

"Duncan's a weed freak, too," said Munch. "Kid
Cannabis."

"What do you mean?" I said.

"Likes to feed his head."

The girl laid the baby down beside the pot and went into the kitchen. Munch tickled the infant's bare stomach. It didn't react. He scratched under its chin. It didn't twitch. The baby's stoniness seemed to be the point.

The girl returned with a large cardboard carton and opened the lid and set the baby inside it. She closed the lid and sat down next to Donna as Munch flicked a Zippo and lit a joint he'd rolled. The joint sparked and sizzled as Munch inhaled, choking back a heroic load of smoke. He leaned across the table over the box and blew out his hit through a hole punched in the cardboard.

Smoke leaked out through the lid. I heard dull thumping sounds. The box moved a couple of inches across the table.

"Imagine what he must think in there," Munch said. "It's Disneyland in a box. It's Disney *World*."

I looked at Donna, stunned, wondering how many times she'd seen this horror and how she'd managed to harden herself to it. She dropped her eyes and folded her hands and sighed. I wanted to go, but I also wanted the pot. Maybe smoking enough of it would help me forget buying it.

"Babies are naturally high," the girlfriend said. She steadied the box as it rattled toward the table edge. "It's because they don't have language yet. They're pure. They think in pictures."

"Of what?" Munch said.

"Of animals."

"That's a guess."

"It's what I like to think. It makes me feel good."

Munch blew more smoke in the box and it stood still.
The girl untucked the lid. She lifted out the baby by its
armpits and held it so we could look. Its skin was gray,
its toes and fingers curled up tight like paws. Oddly, the
kid didn't seem to have a belly button, only a sort of
bumpy reddish smudge.

"Watch now, here's the amazing part," said Munch.
The girlfriend sat the baby in an armchair and started
untangling a power cord running to a pair of headphones. She seated the headphones on the baby's skull
and crossed to the stereo and turned a knob. Instantly,
the baby started kicking. An eerie bugling sound escaped
its throat, followed by a clamor of grunts and squawks in
which I heard crowing roosters, rooting pigs, a whole
excited barnyard.

"We're programming him young," said Munch.
"He'll be a star someday. Bigger than Jethro Tull. Than
Jimmy Page."

An hour later, parked above the dam, Donna and I
divided up the pot. "Munch is sick," she said. We were
good and stoned by then. "Sometimes I'd like to steal
that baby from him. Leave it in a church."

"Probably not a bad idea," I said.

"A child should be a beacon. A light of hope."

"I agree."

"They're scrambling its little brains."

An ember jumped onto the thigh of Donna's Levi's; I brushed it onto the floor mat. I touched her shoulder. She didn't shrink or flinch. My hand slid down her slick acrylic sweater onto her breasts. "My rule," she said. "Eyes closed." My hand felt her ribs, her speedy little heart.

"I'm taking that kid. Will you help me?" Donna said. I would have promised her anything just then.

~ ~ ~

The marijuana lasted us two weeks. We smoked most of it in Donna's bedroom in the basement beneath her father's study. It spooked me to hear his castered desk chair scrape across the ceiling. He dictated his columns in headlong bursts, adopting a screechy, politician's tone.

"Vacwombs outnumbered live births this year—a milestone. The old and infirm are next. The march is on, folks. Next stop the crematorium. All aboard!"

I feared Mr. Prine might detect our marijuana fumes, but Donna said not to worry. "He's very tolerant. The column is all an act. It's showbiz, really. As a matter of fact, that book was his idea. He gave it to me on my sixteenth birthday."

The book was a deluxe-size paperback: *The Sensual Gourmet.* We'd been working our way through it chapter by chapter. We rubbed ourselves down with olive oil and perfume and wriggled like fish in each other's greasy arms. We positioned ourselves on chairs and stacked-up pillows and tested the limits of human flexibility, sometimes crossing the line into real pain. Playing Donna's puppet, I wore the blindfold as she twisted us into taut, ecstatic knots. I realized passivity suited me. No pressure.

Unfortunately, we were running low on pot and I was nervous about buying more. Our noble talk of snatching little Duncan, a subject Donna inevitably brought up after we'd closed the book and caught our breath, had grown into a plot I didn't like.

"Fine," Donna said one day. "I'll go alone. By the way, we're finished here. My teenage experimental phase is over."

"America, wake up! Ignore the movie scars! Look to your friends and families and clergy."

"I told you I'd help," I said. "I won't go back on that. I love you, Donna."

"That's not what we've been doing here."

"I know. It just happened."

"Well, nip it in the bud. When Daddy and I decided I needed experience, we thought I should get it at home. In a safe setting. We also decided that picking a kid, like you, would keep down the chance of someone getting attached."

"You're kidding me."

"We love each other, okay? We tell each other everything. Get used to it."

"Fine, but I think it's strange. You're father and daughter."

"I think *your* family's strange. Go home," said Donna.

Upstairs, I heard her father start to type.

~ ~ ~

I had trouble leaving the house that night. Mike was throwing a fit in the kitchen over our family's failure to come to grips with the rising cost of groceries. He flung open drawers and cabinets, removing cans of soup and vegetables and quoting their prices in a high, scared whine. "Cut green beans for thirty-seven cents. A dollar for brownie mix. A dollar fifty for raisins." Next, he'd drop the items on the counter, where they'd burst open or roll onto the floor. "We have to stop eating," he said. "We're going under."

I got up from the table as Joel slipped out of the room. I heard him turn on the TV to Wimbledon.

Mike kicked a jar of spices at my chair. "Where are you going?"

"A movie."

"What kind of movie?"

"Whatever's showing. I can't digest my food here."

At the end of the driveway Donna's red Skylark idled. Her dilated pupils reflected the glowing gauges. She'd combed her bangs straight down and put on lipstick and donned a pair of tight black driving gloves.

"After we make the buy," she said, "we'll hide out-side until they put the baby down. Then you can climb through a window and hand him out to me."

"I'm scared. I can't do it. It's wrong."

"What's wrong is leaving him there."

"We could call in a tip to the cops," I said.

"Like Munch isn't already paying them off. Get real." Donna held out a pill bottle, uncapped it. "It's Daddy's phenobarb. Sometimes his skin's so itchy he can't sleep."

"Give me two."

"You'll pass out."

"I wish," I said.

The lights were out at the farmhouse and the cars were gone. In a crate on the porch a litter of runty kittens nursed on a sweat sock, their mother nowhere in sight. I peered through the screen door and saw the lit-up stereo but heard no music.

"Lucky break," said Donna. "They're at the bar. They leave the baby home."

We went on in. My bravery surprised me. To my small but growing list of talents I could add nighttime burglary.

The baby was on its back in the armchair, the head-phones hugging its ears. Its eyes were open. It appeared to have grown some since we'd seen it last. The legs sticking out of the diaper were longer, trimmer, and a ridge in its forehead suggested a heightened intel-lect.

Donna removed the headphones. A bass guitar blared. Suddenly, the baby spoke: "Ma pa ma pa."

"Jesus!" I said.

"Just hold him, shitbrain. Here."

I cradled the baby as Donna opened a closet and climbed on a chair to hunt for Munch's stash. Something seemed wrong with the baby's nervous system. I moved a forefinger across its vision, but the pupils failed to track the progress.

"You're safe," I whispered. "We'll take good care of you." I didn't believe myself.

Donna stood down off the chair holding a plastic trash bag wrapped in duct tape.

"Take it all," I said. "Just take it all."

"They'll notice. They'll freak"

"They'll notice their kid's gone, too."

I made a nest from a cheerleading costume and bedded the baby down in Donna's backseat. She drove an inconspicuous forty, taking right turns on unmarked gravel roads. Once we'd lost track of where we were, Donna killed the engine and lit her pipe.

"Not in the car," I said. "The baby."

"Sorry."

We stood in the ditch and got higher than we should have. The pot Munch kept for himself was stronger than the stuff he sold. An owl glided past just feet above our heads and Donna yelled and ducked.

"I think we should drive to the Lutheran church," I said. Each word was a labor, like hoisting a stone slab.

"Ixnay," said Donna. "Lutherans are too strict."

"The Catholic church? The Methodists? The Baptists?"

"I want to take him home to show to Daddy. He's lonely, Justin. A baby might lift his spirits."

I didn't answer. I couldn't lift the words.

Donna smoked as she drove, braking for animals only she could see. She parked in front of her house and cut the lights. The baby chirped and whinnied and made clicking sounds. In the glove compartment I found a Tootsie Pop, which I put in the baby's mouth. It spit it out.

"I'm sorry. I need my daddy now," said Donna. "We shouldn't have done this. I blew it. Don't be mad at me."

I snugged the baby against my chest. I felt possessive suddenly. No church that I knew of deserved him. No one did.

Donna opened her door and swung her legs out. "Try the Episcopalians," she said.

~ ~ ~

Where I went next—I felt I had no choice—was Willy Lindt's houseboat. The baby didn't faze him. I chalked up its presence to "a screwed-up dope thing" and Willy said he understood and knew how to fix things.

"Sit, I need the company. I'm drying out and it's rough as hell tonight."

Willy opened two cans of 3.2 beer and brought out a bag of pretzels. For the baby, he dipped a finger in some milk but it jerked its head away. Its tongue was pale.

"I'll drop him at the sheriff's in the morning. I'll say I woke up from a binge and there he was. They expect this kind of thing from me."

"Why are you trying to quit drinking?" I said.

"I've got a line on a role. In Minneapolis. I play a corpse in a trunk. A crime-spree movie."

The baby's condition worsened as we talked. A film formed on its eyes. New sounds erupted. They rose from deep in the baby's heaving chest—the scrambled upshot, I supposed, of so much heavy metal over headphones. Willy paced with the baby, rocking it, but the sounds kept coming. The baby flailed its arms.

"Maybe it's allergic," Willy said, "and it's having some kind of reaction. Or epileptic."

"The parents kept it high on pot," I said.

"That's what it wants, then. Roll a joint."

"That's sick."

"We need what we're used to. Take an old bum's word."

I argued but eventually Willy prevailed. Once the joint was rolled and lit, we knelt on the floor. Willy stroked the baby's head. I gazed into its face and saw no soul, nothing but a blurry, rubber mask. This changed with my first exhaled puff. The baby cooed. Its mouth opened wide for more. I sucked more smoke in. Shame burned my face and split me into two: the kid who knew better and hated what he was doing and the kid who didn't know a thing and let other people who claimed to know control him. I positioned my mouth above the baby's thin dry lips and blew until I was crying and had to stop.

"The thing to remember," Willy said afterward, "was that we didn't start this mess, now did we?"

I was bawling. "We didn't stop it, either."

"We got here in the middle. It's not our fault. Look at him—like it or not, he looks much better now."

Willy was right. The baby looked revived. So why did I feel dead?

The middle of things was a lousy place to be.

~ ~ ~

I saw them together again a few weeks later—Munch, his girlfriend, the baby, and Donna, too. She'd broken things off with me after the baby caper and taken up with a handsome college sophomore who was home for the summer from Marquette, where he supposedly edited the newspaper. I'd seen them at the movies a couple of times, smooching away at the foot of the screen while Donna's father sat a few rows back, sucking a Coke and pretending not to watch them. I got the feeling the joke was on the college kid and that he was being spied on without knowing it. For all Donna's talk about catching a rich man someday, I strongly suspected that she'd never leave home.

Munch, his girlfriend, and Donna looked thoroughly stoned as I pedaled past them on my ten-speed. They were standing around a fire pit in the Lions Park, cooking hot dogs on sticks. They jabbed them at each other and horsed around and their hot dogs flopped off the sticks into the fire, causing hissing flare-ups of burning fat. The baby lay on its back on a picnic table, wedged between a tape deck and a six-pack.

They saw me and I was trapped. I had to stop. I steered my bike across the grass and leaned it against the table and got off.

"In the mood for a tube steak?" Munch said.

"No thanks."

"Finest ground-up entrails money can buy."

Donna grinned like an idiot. She was one. The baby, asleep with its arms stretched over its head, looked markedly healthier than when I'd seen it last. Its eyes were moving under their flimsy lids and when I tickled its chin it jerked and kicked, showing normal reflexes for once. I liked to think that its night away from home had startled its parents into taking care of it. I noticed it had on blue socks against the chill.

"Don't wake him up," the girlfriend said. "He's fried. Just got back from his infant play-group hour."

"Good for you. Looking after him," I said.

"Munch is like the perfect dad now," Donna said. I could smell her beer breath from yards away. "He bought like a dozen books on modern parenting and made an appointment with a pediatrician."

"Glad to hear it."

"Smoke a J?"

"Not now."

I swung my leg over my bike seat and pushed off.

Even the worst were trying to do their best today. Tomorrow or the next day they'd probably lapse, but the
hope was that they'd recover and try a new thing. Nothing solved everything. Some things didn't solve anything.
You just had to treat every practice as the game.

hyper

1

Other people's weaknesses and failures settled in their hearts, their minds, their consciences; mine, however, collected in my teeth. I didn't know when the destruction started, the microscopic melting of enamel, or which of my bad habits was most to blame for it, but there was no doubt about when it crossed the line. It happened that fall at a mock United Nations when I drank from a cold carton of two percent while making a speech on behalf of Argentina. With the first chilly sip a bolt of pain forked up from my jaw behind my ears.

Everything light in the room went dark and dark objects pulsed white.

"Are you okay?" said the girl beside me, who represented Spain.

"Headache. Bad headache."

"Want a Midol?"

"Yes."

The pain struck again at dinner with a hot food, a grilled breast of pheasant riddled with shotgun pellets. I ran to the sink and gulped water from the tap as a kind of black executioner's hood fell over me. I woke on the floor with Audrey kneeling close and Mike standing over me, looking miffed. He'd just returned from a trip to Michigan, where Woody Wolff had been hospitalized for liver failure and placed on a long list for a new organ. Mike couldn't believe they were making the great man wait and had already been on the phone to Woody's congressman.

"Where does it hurt worst?" said Audrey.

"All through my head, but starting in my cheeks."

She opened my mouth with her fingers. "I smell it now. Wow, do I smell it." She fanned the air between us. "Completely abscessed. You must be miserable."

"The kid couldn't bother to floss, and now his teeth hurt. Excuse me if I save my tears," Mike said.

I was taken to see Perry Lyman in the morning. His office had changed since my retainer days. As his dental technician prepared a tray of instruments I surveyed the new posters on the walls. The messages of peace and love had given way to patriotic scenes: the Stars and Stripes being planted on the moon, a row of crosses in Arlington National Cemetery, the Blue Angels flying team streaking past Mount Rushmore.

"He'll be another minute," the technician said. "Sit back and unwind. I'll start you on the gas."

"He gives patients gas now?" The technician was new. "He used to use hypnosis."

"Out of vogue. Dentistry's a living, changing science."

I held the mask snug. The gas was cool and sweet. The technician told me to inhale normally but the moment she left the room I sucked and gulped. I slipped back deeper and deeper into my mind until I seemed to be sighting down a telescope with a foggy lens. When Perry Lyman walked into the room—a man I'd teased and tortured and provoked, and who had every right to hate me for it—I felt a wave of compassion and forgiveness. "Good morning. I'm glad you could see me on such short notice."

"It wasn't short notice," Perry Lyman said. "Two years without a checkup or a cleaning usually tells me the patient will be back."

He picked up my chart from his desk, which was cleaner and tidier than before. He was wearing a silver flag pin on his lab coat and seemed to have put on muscle in his shoulders.

"I owe you an apology," I said. "My stunt at the bike race."

"Depressing time for both of us. You'd lost your security blanket, I'd lost my marbles. Credit the Guard for turning me around. From pothead pacifist to citizen soldier." He tilted the chair back. "Feeling any lighter?"

"Starting to. You joined the National Guard?"

"I suffered from an organic disorder, Justin. First I dealt with it medically, through drugs. Next, I realized I needed a shot of discipline."

Perry Lyman turned a dial on the nitrous tank, then switched on the spotlight angled at my face. "Let's see what's doing inside the old black hole."

The nitrous oxide acted on me like truth serum. As Perry Lyman scraped and picked, I chattered away about things I rarely spoke of: my plan to become a TV issues-analyst and stir the nation with controversial insights. My notion, inspired by a recent dream, that the original Bigfoot was a hoaxer who'd found that roaming the woods in pelts and skins was the life he'd wanted all along. I even let slip my shameful wish that Woody Wolff would never get a liver.

As I rambled, a lot was happening in my mouth. I coughed out blood clots the texture of cottage cheese and watched the water whirl them down the spit sink. I swallowed gritty bits of tooth enamel.

"We have a job ahead of us," Perry Lyman said, cutting the gas off and raising the dental chair. "First, your

gums: they're receding and infected. The abscessed mo-
lar needs a crown and root canal and your bottom wisdom teeth are terminal."

The gas wore off as he spoke and left me wondering if
I'd made a mistake in coming back here. Perry Lyman
had already taken my thumb—what would he take next?

"That's just the dental dimension," he said. "Your
heavy bleeding during the exam suggests malnourish-
ment."

"I had a bad meat experience last fall."

"School?"

"They hate me. Impulsive and disruptive. Doesn't
work up to potential. Self-absorbed."

"Homelife?"

"You want the whole checklist?"

"A to Z. I like to see my patients in the round."

I ticked off the facts in the tone of a reporter. "Joel
gained fifteen pounds this summer, lost ten at a tennis
camp, then gained back twenty. My grandparents came
for another visit last month but Mike accused Grandma
of faking an asthma attack, so they left after only being
there two hours. Then Mike got his crossbow and shot
up the garage. He's having business troubles. He's building a health club but no one's signing up and there's a
petition going around town to prevent him from selling
guns, his biggest moneymaker."

"Your mother?"

"The same."

"What's the same?"

"I wish I knew."

Perry Lyman let a silence go by, then slipped a me-chanical pencil from his lab coat, clicked up the lead, and faced his calendar, which was illustrated with paintings of aircraft carriers. He drew X's through a number of squares, rubbed his chin, erased a couple, then added a few more.

"I'm blocking out a month for the whole process. But I need your commitment you'll press on to the end; oth-erwise I'm wasting both our time."

"What whole process?" I said. "To fix my teeth?"

Perry Lyman retracted the pencil lead. "If I threw the whole thing in your lap at once, you'd panic. You'd think I was overreacting. But I'm not. I'm going to do what I should have done the first time."

I looked into his eyes for clarification.

"Treat the disease," he told me, "not the symptoms."

~ ~ ~

Mike dropped me off for stage one, the root canal, on his way to the airport. He was headed back to Ann Arbor to visit Wolff and help sell his house to cover medical bills. I braced myself for the usual lecture about the cost of my sloppy oral hygiene but instead Mike apologized for his recent tantrums, explaining that his old coach's collapse had shaken his faith in human goodness.

"How is he?" I said.

"Still waiting. Something stinks. Plane crashes every

evening on the news but a man who won four Rose Bowls can't get a liver."

Mike pulled into the clinic's parking lot. "About Perry Lyman—he's been to hell and back. Listen to him. Show him some respect."

"What happened?"

"He lost his father to Lou Gehrig's. Then his wife left. Killer alimony. He went to a clinic in California somewhere and came back squared away. A solid citizen. He's behind that new tax-cut petition that's going around."

Thanks to novocaine and extra gas, the root canal was loud but painless. The drilling and digging prevented me from speaking, but Perry Lyman kept me busy listening.

"I'll spare you the sob story introduction—you've probably already heard it through the grapevine—but a couple of years ago I hit a wall. Sensitive there?"

"A little."

"Bottom line: I reexamined everything. Values. Attitudes. Relationships. Most crucially, I went on medication. Result: I've become the man I always wanted to be. I fly and maintain my own small helicopter. I tutor illiterates. I go to church. The stoned neurotic on the water bed is dead and gone."

I held up my hand to keep my mask from slipping. I wanted all the gas that I could get.

"Which brings me to a question, Justin."

I waited.

"Have you ever suspected you're different from other

teenagers? Not as patient. Can't finish what you start? Terrified of being left alone but angry when you feel crowded?''

He'd nailed me. "All of it."

"It isn't your fault," Perry Lyman said. "It's mine. I saw the syndrome when you came two years ago. And what did I do? I let you go on suffering. Classic hyperactive teen, textbook attention deficit disorder, and Dr. Counterculture here tried the subconscious suggestion.''

"It worked. I stopped."

"You switched," said Perry Lyman. He changed his drill bit. "I want to start you on Ritalin."

"You're a dentist, though."

He stepped on a pedal and revved the drill. "I like to think of myself as more than that."

~ ~ ~

The pill was the driest thing I'd ever swallowed and seemed to absorb all the moisture in my throat during its scratchy, slow descent. I drank from the glass of juice Audrey gave me and thought about Garrett Blount from fifth grade, who'd also been diagnosed as hyperactive. Garrett had pierced his own ears with a pencil, Krazy-glued his hands to walls and blackboards, and regularly wet himself in class. I still remembered the puddles under his desk, so hot they gave off visible wisps of steam.

"They're wrong," I said to Audrey. "I'm normal. I'm fine."

She answered me with a story. When I was six years

old, she said, I'd trimmed our living room carpet with pinking shears because I'd thought it was growing.

I didn't remember this.

"Or think of when you were ten. The milk phase. You had to pour milk on everything you ate."

I dropped my head. There was no denying the milk phase.

I was walking to school when I felt the Ritalin hit. The air seemed to thicken and mold itself against me. The sky expanded and revealed its curved shape as my peripheral vision spread and sharpened until I could almost see over my shoulders. Moments later, I noticed my stride had changed. My footsteps felt involuntary, guided, as if governed by magnets buried in the ground. To walk I just had to let myself be pulled.

My first class that morning was English. We were supposed to be reading *Moby Dick*. As Mrs. Rand chalked theme words on the blackboard—Whiteness, Sea vs. Land, Revenge & Pride—I opened my paperback copy for the first time.

"Who'd like to talk on Whiteness?" Mrs. Rand asked.

I opened my mouth and out flowed several ideas I wasn't even conscious of having thought about. Whiteness stood for eternity, I said. It represented both innocence and extinction.

"I see you read the preface," Mrs. Rand said.

This wasn't true. I hadn't read a line.

It happened again in biology. I pronounced "mitochondria" correctly, despite never having heard it spoken before.

After school, I swept into the house to share my news. I found Joel in front of the TV watching a tape of his serves at tennis camp. The counselors had told him he showed promise but that it was buried under all the weight.

"You're out of breath," he said. "What's wrong?"

"I've changed. I'm better. It works. It really works."

"Why are your eyes like that?"

"Like what?"

"So huge."

The conversation depressed me. I felt inside my pants and found the pill I was meant to have taken at noon. An hour later, feeling better, I settled onto the couch with *Moby Dick*. When Audrey called me to dinner I said, "One minute," but I kept on reading until eleven o'clock. I woke up at five and took another pill and by the time Mike and Audrey came down to breakfast, I'd finished all but two chapters of *Moby Dick*. No skimming or skipping, either. Every word.

~ ~ ~

I didn't take nitrous oxide for my crown fitting; I preferred the new clarity of Ritalin. Perry Lyman held up a mirror afterward and showed me the jewel that was bonded to my jaw. He'd urged me to get a porcelain crown out of consideration for Mike's budget, but I'd chosen gold. The new me deserved the best.

"How's the medication?" Perry Lyman said.

"Great. I read my first whole novel last week. Also, I mowed the lawn the other day and managed to make a perfect crisscross pattern."

"Mood swings?"

"No swings. Just up and up. Straight up."

"Any other breakthroughs besides the mowing job?"

"Only little ones," I said. "It used to feel like a hassle to put on underwear, but now I wear it every day. Also, the Pledge of Allegiance. It gives me chills now. I never really listened to the words before."

"Don't pull my leg."

"I'm not. I'm being honest."

Perry Lyman slid open the drawer in his desk where he kept his giveaway toothbrushes and dental flosses. He took out a fat red book and looked a page up. "You're describing a common side effect: euphoria."

I'd heard this word but was fuzzy about its meaning.

"Let's keep an eye on that," Perry Lyman said. "You don't want to get to feeling so high and mighty you do something stupid like try to leap tall buildings."

A shadow of the old distrust fell over me. What could be wrong with feeling good?

My wariness lingered during my next visit. After fil-ing and readjusting my crown, Perry Lyman gave me a psychological test. He assured me that there were no wrong answers, but I knew better. There were always wrong answers.

"Now and then, when things don't go my way," he

said, reading from a clipboard, "I feel that life is blank. Fill in the blank."

I couldn't decide what kind of answer to give. One that made me sound confused and jumpy, confirming the original diagnosis, or one that made me sound calm and healthy? Cured. The stakes were high: if I didn't respond correctly, I could lose my prescription.

I tried a nonsense answer first. Depending on how Perry Lyman reacted, I might get a clue as to how to play the other questions.

"A miracle," I said.

Perry Lyman remained expressionless. "When I'm away from home, I miss my blank."

I hesitated. "Family. I miss my family." This was the cured approach.

"My teachers are blank?"

"Mature adults," I said.

"You're faking this. Don't play games with me, Justin. This is serious."

"I thought there were no wrong answers?"

"Don't get cute."

I switched my tactics after that and answered like a hyperactive person.

"When I see other people suffer, I feel . . ."

"Nervous?"

"My friends don't know how blank I am."

"Impatient."

"Baby animals make me feel . . ."

"All jittery."

Perry Lyman set the clipboard on his desk. "I'm giving the medication another week. I'm worried this isn't organic, after all."

Betrayal loomed. I thought back to my thumb.

My dentist was not going to break me twice. No way.

~ ~ ~

What Perry Lyman didn't know as he arranged the IV drip was that I'd ignored his order to skip my pill that morning. What he'd told me he didn't want to happen—a clash between drugs that would lighten my sedation—was precisely what I wanted. Given Perry Lyman's proven ability to enter my brain and rearrange my thoughts, I was prepared to suffer increased pain in exchange for greater alertness.

As the fluid moved down the plastic tube the overhead lights broke into silver stars. The textured ceiling tiles became mountainous. Perry Lyman's eyes and cheeks wrinkled and warped and dripped like melting cheese.

It wasn't the urge to blab I felt this time, though sentence fragments careened inside my head (". . . words, the opposite of food . . . ," ". . . forward divided by backward equals sideways . . ."), but a deeper, fiercer impulse. I wanted to eat my dentist, to consume him. Next, I'd chew my way through the whole building, the cars in the parking lot, the landscaped grounds. I saw myself as a mammoth caterpillar lengthening and swelling with each bite until there was nothing left but air and everything that had been outside, in my way, was finally inside, a source of strength and energy.

"Suction. More suction," Perry Lyman said. The technician swooped in with her tools. The office roared.

As the hammering, cracking, and drilling went on, the sedatives seemed to get the best of me. Soon, it was not just dead tissue being removed, but diseased impressions, infected memories. The rank taste of deer meat was whisked out of my skull by a pair of sparkling diamond pliers. Next, I felt my need for Audrey gripped by steel pincers that sparked like jumper cables. It wouldn't come loose, though, and slipped back down my throat, lodging in my stomach, where it burned.

"Flatten your tongue," Perry Lyman said. "Stop talking."

"How could I be talking? I'm not talking."

My dentist howled. A peaceful blackout followed. When I came to he was bandaging his forefinger with a cotton ball and white cloth tape.

"You bit me," he said.

I fell asleep again. When I woke up, it appeared that time had passed. Perry Lyman had changed from his lab coat into a sports jacket and seemed to be about to leave the office.

"I'm sorry I bit you."

"I understand," he said. "It's not surprising, considering our history."

"Is my father here to pick me up?"

"His friend got a liver. Your father's been called away. Your mother's at an all-day paramedic class." Perry Lyman buttoned up his jacket. "You can hang out at my house. See my helicopter."

"Are they out?"

"They're out. Completely out."

~ ~ ~

My cheeks were packed with bloody gauze as Perry Lyman walked me to the helicopter parked on a concrete pad behind his farmhouse. The craft had no doors, just a see-through plastic bubble shielding an instrument panel and two small seats. Using gestures to spare my swollen jaws, I asked Perry Lyman to take me for a ride.

"Maybe someday," he said. "Now, about your medication . . ."

I crossed my arms, prepared to stand my ground.

"Personally, I don't see much improvement. In fact, I see warning signs. But I'm not you. I used to try to be everyone, of course, but that got tiring. Awfully lonely, too. Conclusion: you do what you want. It's your own chemistry."

I took the gauze out. "Thank you."

"Hush, you'll bleed."

"The pills make me feel like me. I never did before."

"Then how would you know what it feels like? Shush. Don't answer."

Perry Lyman changed his mind about going up in the helicopter. We strapped on seat belts and put on cush-

ioned headsets with microphones that extended in front
of our chins. We left the ground with the cockpit tilted
down, as if we were going to crash into the trees, but a
few seconds later we leveled off.

"To answer me, tap on your mike," said Perry
Lyman. "One for yes and two for no."

I tapped.

I didn't recognize the local landmarks; Perry Lyman
had to point them out. The school was a black rectangle
of roofing tar strewn with silver puddles. The golf
course being constructed west of town was a collection
of dirt piles and shallow trenches where the clubhouse
and condos were going in. I managed to spot my house
and yard because of the dozens of yellow tennis balls left
over from Joel's practice sessions against the wall of the
garage.

"Like it up here?" said Perry Lyman.

Tap.

"Ready to set her down yet?"

Two taps. No.

"You're like me: I go up, I like to stay up. Just fly in
circles and see what I can see until there's no more fuel.
I hate the ground. The only reason it's there is to take
off from."

Tap.

"Sometimes I worry myself."

Tap, tap.

We flew for another half hour, buzzing the river,
hovering over the bluffs. I envied the new life that Perry

Lyman had found and sensed it would be more lasting than my new pill. He'd told me once that Ritalin was just a bridge, that someday I'd have to come off it, but onto what? I watched him consult his gauges, move his stick. I didn't have a stick. I was flying blind.

2

My learning to fly-fish that summer was Mike's idea. I'd told him I wanted a hobby, not a sport. Me, I'd been pushing to attend a drama camp sponsored by the U of M, but something Mike said to me changed my mind. He told me how, after his knee operation, fly-fishing for trout had kept him sane by giving him something to focus on and care about besides the fact that he'd never play pro ball.

I wanted this: a pastime I could care about. Something to fall back on besides the pills.

To get me into the mood to learn, Mike gave me some magazines to read. What grabbed me were the pictures of the fishermen. In their caps and sunglasses and hip boots, their vests adorned with elaborate metal gadgets, they had the intelligent ruggedness of airline pilots, a look that was part engineer, part athlete. Fly fishermen, according to the magazines, were patient, meticulous, thoughtful. A cut above. They were forever making one last cast after getting skunked all day and suddenly hooking the trout of a lifetime, only to release it for conservation reasons.

First I had to learn to cast. I practiced in the yard. Mike stood next to me gripping my elbow as I stripped a few feet of line off the reel and raised my rod to forty-five degrees. Once I got the line into the air, the trick was to let it straighten out behind me and reach its full extension on the backcast.

I kept flubbing it. My fly, its barb removed for safety's sake, bounced off my head as my fly line lost momentum and fell in sloppy coils around my shoes.

"Don't pause," Mike said. "Keep it moving, nice and even." He guided my arm, too firmly for my liking. "Ten o'clock. Back to two o'clock. Repeat."

"Let go of me," I said.

"Don't force it."

"I'm not!"

Eventually, my casting improved and Mike let me choose a fishing vest from the Orvis display at his store. I filled the pouches with leaders, hooks, weights, clippers, and various bottles of dressing meant to help the fly to float or sink. The finishing touch was a slim aluminum box containing flies Mike had tied over the winter: Pale Morning Duns, Royal Coachmen, Goofus Bugs.

"What makes these special," he said, "are the materials. The ones you buy at the store use synthetics, but I tied these from natural materials."

I already knew the secret of Mike's flies. Now and then, while driving in the country, he'd see something in the road, pull over, get out, and toss a dead grouse or pheasant in the trunk. He stored his finds in the basement freezer and didn't always bother to wrap them up, forcing me to confront their carcasses whenever I went for ice cream or a Popsicle. Once, when I threw out a woodcock he'd been saving, Mike went ape and made me dig through garbage bags until I found the bird.

I shut the fly box and tucked it in my vest. "Thank you."

"You're going to love this sport," Mike said. "It isn't like Joel's tennis. You never master it. Every river is a whole new ball game."

~ ~ ~

On summer Saturdays, rain or shine, we woke up at six and drove a hundred miles to the Winnikick River in southern Wisconsin. The river flowed through an Indian reservation and Mike had to buy a license from the tribe permitting us to fish. The tribe was poor. Hitchhikers in surplus combat jackets trudged along the shoulders of the road, raising their thumbs when they saw our car approach and lowering them when they saw that we weren't Indians. Instead of advertising cars and clothes, the billboards along the reservation's main highway promoted suicide hot lines and nutrition classes.

Before we hit the river for the day, Mike always made a point of stopping in at the reservation trading post, which sold tax-free tobacco as well as sporting goods. I liked the store's smell—old leather, pipe smoke, bait— but one day Mike ruined the place for me by buying chewing tobacco.

"I'll take a pouch of Red Man," he told the clerk.

Outside I said, "I can't believe you did that."

"If they didn't want people to buy it, they wouldn't stock it."

"I saw the clerk's face."

"White sportsmen support that outfit."

The Winnikick was a tricky river to reach. After parking our car at the end of a dirt road, we had to walk a mile through brushy swamps, aiming our rod tips between the trees and brambles to keep from snagging them. Mike lived in fear that I'd break the rod he'd bought me, an Orvis eight-footer so slim and delicate that wrecking it seemed to be just a matter of time. My bulky rubber waders weighed me down, and I was worn out by the time I reached the river, my hair snarled stiff with burrs, my hands scratched raw. Mike, who walked faster than me and hated waiting, was usually in the river by this time, aiming elegant casts at the green banks.

I waded in well downstream from him that morning. The sudden squeeze of water around my calves felt like when the doctor took my blood pressure. I chose my fly—a fluffy deer-hair caddis made from a buck Mike had shot—and tried to tie it to my hair-thin leader.

My clinch knot unraveled. My neck muscles cramped solid. The same way certain people can't learn to dance no matter how many lessons they receive, I couldn't learn to tie fishing knots. They baffled me.

"Need any help back there?" Mike shouted. He knew from our previous outings that I did and that I'd say I didn't.

Five minutes of frustration became fifteen. Behind me I heard a splash: a feeding trout. I twisted and looped the nylon line at random, hoping to tie a knot by accident.

"Got one!" I heard Mike shout around the bend. "Beautiful rainbow. Gorgeous. Come on up here."

I slogged upstream, bent forward against the current. The rocks underfoot were slick with moss and seaweed. By the time I reached Mike he'd already landed the trout and released it back into the river.

"Any luck back there?" he said.

"I couldn't tie my fly on."

"You need more tippet." From his vest Mike took a coil of line, measured out a section along his forearm, and snipped it off with a pair of nail clippers attached to a retractable key chain.

"For joining two sections of line we use the blood knot. Remember the blood knot?"

"I think so. Show it to me."

We'd tried this the week before. We tried again. Mike flipped up his clip-on Polaroids and guided my smooth white fingers with his rough brown ones as I overlapped the lengths of line. I felt a frustrated tension in his thumbs as I braided the sections together, threaded a loop, pulled the ends tight, and watched the knot undo itself.

Nearby I heard a trout jump. Then another.

"Go on and fish," I said. "I've almost got it."

"Like hell you do. Gimme." Mike took the line from me. He joined the two pieces of leader, spit on them, and cinched the blood knot tight.

"What fly were you thinking of using?"

"A Royal Coachman?"

"I'll put one on for you. Try to pay attention."

By noon Mike had caught and released four trout and I'd caught none, though I'd had a couple strikes. The second strike snapped my leader and took my fly. I tried to tie on a new fly, failed, and chose to go on pretending to fish rather than pester Mike for help. I put on quite a performance for myself, casting, reeling in, and stripping line as though I actually stood a chance of hooking something with an empty line.

We ate our lunch in the shade of an oak tree. Acorns

plopped onto the ground, knocked loose by squirrels, and daddy longlegs high-stepped over leaves. Mike sliced a hard salami with his fillet knife and I squeezed cheese from a tube onto Ritz crackers. Mike ate the salami slices off the knife blade, which made me nervous.

"What's wrong?" he said. "Tough morning?"

"Be careful, you'll cut your tongue."

"You're mad at me. You wish you were studying drama with the rich kids."

"I can't tie knots."

"You bear down too hard. Ease up some."

Mike peeled his waders off after lunch and stretched out under the tree for a nap. I walked down to the stream to drink a beer I'd stashed in my fishing vest.

"Any luck?" a voice said.

I looked up. On the bank across from me two Indian men were fishing in a way I'd never seen before. Their poles were short and stout, like sawed-off pool cues, and were propped in the crotches of Y-shaped sticks.

"My father caught four," I said. "He threw them back, though."

"A purist," one of the men said. "That's too bad. A person should eat what he catches. It shows respect."

"How about you two?" I said.

The second man reached his arm out to the side and hoisted a black plastic garbage bag off the ground. The bag looked heavy, about to split and spill, and the man only managed to lift it for a moment. What Mike had told me once was true, it seemed: the Indians fished for food, not sport, and would empty the whole river if they could.

"What were you using?" I asked.

"Just crawlers. Want some?"

"My father says we have to fish with flies."

"I think I know your old man," the first man said.

I drank the rest of the beer. "How's that?"

"I work at a store he comes into." The Indian looked at his friend. "Mr. Red Man."

The two of them laughed. I waved good-bye and left.

On the drive home Mike found a dead raccoon.

~ ~ ~

Mike tied his flies at a workbench in the basement. One end of the bench was strewn with spools of thread, boxes of hooks, and cards of colored yarn. The other side held stacks of pheasant wings, bundles of squirrel tails, and sections of furry deer hide. Sitting in front of his tying vise, listening to a Twins game on the radio, Mike would poke through his collection of remains, looking for the feather or tuft of fur that matched the photographs in his book of flies.

"You want to stand here and learn?" he said.

"I'm busy."

"Fly-tying teaches attention to detail. Woody always said I had a problem there. Thank God I had someone to point out my deficiencies."

"It never made you angry?"

"Sometimes, sure. But that's where I got the energy

to improve myself. Men who don't get angry, in my experience, tend to end up carrying other men's luggage for them."

While Mike wrapped thread around a tiny hook I sat on the floor with a fishing magazine containing an article on tying knots. It recommended practicing with rope. I went upstairs and found a coil of laundry line, cut off two equal pieces with a steak knife, and returned to the basement.

"Admirable persistence," Mike said. "At some point you have to say 'Hey, I'm on my own. It's me versus myself. That's all there is.' "

As I switched my gaze between diagrams and rope, trying to align them in my mind, it dawned on me that knots were not my problem but only a symptom of some deeper chaos. Basic issues of left and right had always been cloudy for me. When asked to recite the Pledge of Allegiance, I never knew which hand to cover my heart with.

After tying a few more knots that wouldn't hold I dropped the rope and closed the magazine.

"Grasshopper season's coming up," Mike said. He opened the jaws of his tying vise and a deer-hair hopper dropped into his palm. "Even the beginners can catch trout then."

"I don't care if I ever catch a trout."

"You will once you've caught one."

I stared at the limp rope. "I want to fish with worms."

"The easy way."

"What's wrong with things being easy?"

"I think you know." Mike reached for a pheasant neck, plucked a feather off, and clamped another hook inside his vise.

"I *don't* know," I told him.

"Then I feel sorry for you." He drew a length of red yarn from a spool and bit it off with his teeth.

~ ~ ~

That week we went fishing with Jerry, Mike's attorney. Mike's age, but without a wife or kids, Jerry was known for having young blond girlfriends and taking vacations in places like Aruba. We picked him up at his house in White Bear Lake, idling in his circular brick driveway while Jerry brought out his equipment load by load. His rod, his vest, and his waders were all brand-new, and when he'd finally arranged them in the car and settled in next to Mike in the front seat, he revealed that he'd never fished before by saying: "First one to catch a ten-pound trout buys drinks tonight."

Mike told Jerry that ten-pound trout were rare, particularly in small midwestern rivers.

"Two five-pounders, then," said Jerry. "The total's what counts."

I was glad to have another novice along. "You and me," Jerry kept saying. "You and me, kid."

Mike grinned at Jerry's jokes and funny lines, but I got the sense that he looked down on him as someone who didn't take the outdoors seriously. When the talk turned to fishing, Mike was stern with Jerry, insisting that he release his trout and not tire them out by playing them too long.

"Your father's the Führer of fly-fishing," said Jerry. He gave a one-arm salute.

"Enough," Mike said.

We stopped at the reservation store so Jerry could buy a carton of tax-free cigarettes. I hung back by the beer refrigerator, praying that Mike wouldn't ask the clerk for Red Man. The clerk recognized me and waved. I nodded back.

"A carton of Raleighs," said Jerry. "Make that two." He turned to Mike beside him. "Anything?"

"No thanks. I'm fine."

The day was starting well.

Once on the river, Mike left Jerry with me and headed downstream to fish his special hole. I watched Jerry struggle to tie his fly on, glad I'd already tied mine on at home. Jerry's damp pink fingers jerked and shook.

"Not an easy night," he said. "Lost a battle with a Wild Turkey."

We fished side by side. The day was bright, poor fishing weather, and steam poured out of my waders into my face. Jerry lit one Raleigh after another and spat out his butts in the river. We chatted, told stories. Jerry asked what career I had in mind and warned me not to pursue the law.

"It's brutal. For guys like Mike, who frighten people

naturally, it might make sense," he said. "But not for our type."

I asked him what he thought that our type was.

"The guys who'd rather take the elevator. The guys who buy their buns already sliced."

From his fishing vest Jerry produced a silver flask and tilted it smartly back. "The pause that refreshes," he said, and wiped his mouth. "Don't tell Hemingway, but fishing bores me. I bought all this gear because *Esquire* says it's in this year."

Jerry lounged on the bank while I kept casting. A hatch had started—hundreds of tiny green mayflies. I felt a strike and pulled back to set the hook. The trout wriggled off but a cast or two later another one hit. Jerry whistled. I played the fish. It was small but it liked to jump. "My first!" I shouted.

I was lifting the trout from the water when Mike walked up. He stood over Jerry and held out an open palm.

"What are all these?" he said.

Jerry rolled his eyes. I held up my fish but Mike didn't look over.

"They floated down to me," Mike said. "This river is not an ashtray, Jerry. Reel your line up, Justin. Fishing's over."

"But I got one," I said.

"You'll get another. Let's go."

Jerry sat in back on the ride home, blowing Raleigh smoke through his rolled-down window and nursing his flask. No one spoke. The car was stifling. As we were about to leave the reservation Mike touched the brake and pulled over on the shoulder. "Are you going to make me walk home?" Jerry said. Mike got out of the car and looked both ways, then quickstepped across the highway and bent down.

"Tell me he's not going to eat that," Jerry said.

Mike walked to the back of the car with a dead mallard, holding it by its neck. He opened the trunk. There was a thud and then the trunk lid slammed.

"Someone should tell your old man the news," said Jerry. "It's the nineteen eighties. The West's been won."

"We've tried," I said. "He disagrees." I didn't know if this made me proud or sad.

~ ~ ~

A couple of Saturdays later I was browsing in the reservation store, waiting for Mike to fill the car with gas, when a kid with a push broom asked if he could help me. The kid had bad acne, like cinders under his skin, and a smile I had to look closely at to see.

"Thanks. I'm set," I said.

"You need some fishing flies?"

"My dad ties his own."

"That's your dad there?"

I looked down.

"You're the one," said the kid. "My uncle met you. He watched you fish the other day."

"Your uncle the clerk?"

"He said you can't tie knots."

The kid held a finger up, signaling me to wait, and disappeared through a canvas-curtained doorway marked "Employees Only." He came back holding one hand out.

"Six bucks," he said. "Everybody says they do the trick."

The knot-tying gadgets were made of stainless steel. One was U-shaped. The other resembled a pen. I bought them both. It didn't have to be me versus myself now.

Outside, Mike was pointing to something on our windshield: a grasshopper with its wings caught in the wiper blade. I noticed another one clinging to the aerial.

"Look at your shoes, they're everywhere," Mike said. "This is the day. Today's the day. You ready?"

I sat on a log and practiced using the knot tools. The weather was hot and humid and overcast and sweat rolled off my nose onto my leader as I managed to tie my first unassisted clinch knot and then, a few minutes later, my first blood knot. Though the tools did most of the work, I felt proud anyway.

All around me hungry trout were feeding, some bursting right out of the water to snatch the grasshoppers struggling in the surface film. The larger, heavier fish left visible wakes as they missiled toward their targets, struck, then dove, resting for a moment near the bottom, where I could see their shadows on the gravel. The sight made me sick with excitement, a deep-down fishing greed I hadn't known was in me.

I had a sport.

My first cast was perfect, depositing my hopper at the head of a deep green pool. I watched it float. It swerved past a jutting rock, accelerated, sliced through a wrinkle of foam, and vanished. A strike. I lifted the willowy rod and felt a pull followed by a sturdy, pan-icked jerking that meant I had something of size on.

My knots were holding.

When I lifted the big rainbow from the water, its belly was tense and stretched from gorging on hoppers. I shouted for Mike to come look but got no answer.

I knew what I was expected to do next according to the honor code of fly-fishing: let the trout go. I couldn't, though. I wanted it. Not as a trophy or a souvenir, but as something wild to give me strength. I opened the mesh pouch inside my vest and slipped the trout inside and snapped the flap.

There. It was mine. And the next one would be, too.

They were all mine that day, all seven of them, which was two fish over the legal limit. The first three came to me in quick succession, as if to pay a debt that I was owed. Then my leader broke. I tried to fix it. My fin-gers, gloved in fish slime, didn't grip, and I felt the old confusion creeping back. Then Mike walked by on the bank and said, "Still fussing?" and suddenly I felt sharp again, from spite.

I worked hard for the last few fish. I earned them. One was too small to keep. I kept it anyway. The fish pouch hung down bulkily behind me as I trudged through the swamp to the car. Mike wasn't back yet. I stashed the trout on the floor in the backseat and covered them with my waders and vest. I planned to eat them in secret, I wasn't sure how.

On the drive back I was quiet, full of thoughts. The moon was full but strangely dim and the dashboard lights glowed yellow on my hands.

"Admit it," Mike said. "Today made everything worth it. I understand I'm hard on you sometimes, but that's because I take the long view."

"Huh."

"Drama classes will be around forever. Clean wild trout streams won't. It's now or never. How many you catch today?"

"A few." I could smell my fish in the backseat and it made me anxious to leave the reservation.

Mike recapped his day's big moments as we drove. We passed a hitchhiker with a khaki knapsack, a billboard offering aid to unwed mothers. When the trading post's neon arrowhead appeared, Mike shifted his hands on top of the wheel.

"I need something."

"What?" I said. I knew what. "Don't."

"I've had a perfect day. I want my chew."

We pulled up in front of the store and Mike got out. A tribal police car was parked beside the gas pumps. I could see the cop inside the building, talking to the clerk.

Mike strolled inside. While he was making his purchase, the cop came out and looked at our car. I slid lower in my seat. I prepared myself to be punished for my fish lust.

The cop rapped on my window. I rolled it down.

"I see your permit?"

"They're in my father's wallet."

"Out of the car, please."

"I do something?"

"Get out."

The cop walked around the car with his flashlight, playing its beam across the seats and even aiming it up into the wheel wells. I stood with my hands in my pockets. Mike walked up. One of his cheeks bulged with chew.

"I'd like you to pop your trunk lid, sir," the cop said. "I've had some reports."

"Of what? I don't believe this. We shop your store, we support your businesses."

"We're grateful. I want to look inside your trunk."

Mike opened the lid with his key and stalked away. The flashlight beam glinted off glassy eyes, bright feathers, a shard of white bone in a broken pheasant wing. There was a flattened weasel with matted fur, a gray squirrel without a tail. The mallard from the day we'd fished with Jerry lay bent-necked and stiff on top of the spare tire.

The cop looked at Mike and shook his head. Fleas hopped off the bodies and caught the light.

"Interfering with tribal wildlife. The law applies to remains."

Mike mumbled something.

"Whatever that is in your mouth, sir, spit it out. I can't understand you," the cop said.

Mike spat. A little.

"Do you know where you are, sir?" the cop said. "*All* of it."

~ ~ ~

That was it for trout fishing that summer. We surrendered our fishing permits on the spot, and in place of a bond, which Mike refused to post, the cop confiscated our sporting goods. I piled the rods, vests, and tackle in the parking lot while Mike, wearing rubber gloves the cop had given him, put the roadkill into plastic sacks. When I removed my waders from the car, the cop saw the fish I'd stashed in the backseat and asked me to count them for him.

"There's seven," I said. "I finally learned to tie knots, and I got greedy. I could barely catch a fish before."

"I don't understand you fly fishermen," the cop said. "You take something simple and make it complicated. It's like you can't have fun unless you're struggling."

We didn't discuss the incident afterward, but I could tell Mike was feeling bad about it when he offered to enroll me in the drama camp, which had added an extra session. I turned him down. After a summer on the Winnikick, the idea of learning to cry on cue and simulate knife and sword fights bored me stiff. I missed the strangeness of the reservation. I missed forgetting myself in the cold water. I missed that moment when you cast your fly, tied with a knot you can't be sure will hold, and something hidden grabs it, and you're caught.

3

North of town, on the shores of Heron Lake, where I sometimes went to be alone to worry about my family and my future and whether or not I would ever settle down inside and find a path that would lead me out of the middle of things, there was a famous rehabilitation clinic for drug addicts and alcoholics. Maple Glen treated celebrities and millionaires. Elvis Presley was rumored to have stayed there, as well as a Norwegian prince and the wife of a former president, but it was hard to know the truth. The clinic's employees were sworn to secrecy and the windows of its long green shuttle vans were tinted with a dark reflective film that grew more opaque the harder you stared at it.

Still, I had a couple of close calls, and they were enough to fill me with resentment toward those whom the world seemed to favor for no good reason. One day I walked into the Shell station downtown just after one of the vans had left the pumps.

"Guess who just used a rest room?" the attendant said. "Elizabeth Taylor."

"Right."

"I shit you not."

"What did she look like?"

"A woman with a cold. She bought some Fritos out of the machine."

This brush with fame so close to home unnerved me. I felt strangely diminished, pushed aside. Elizabeth Taylor's type, it seemed to me, belonged on television and in magazines, where ordinary people could look at them but they could not look back at us. The thought that she might have glimpsed me from the van and formed some opinion of my clothes or hair made me queasy with self-consciousness.

My next close call with a Maple Glen celebrity was less direct but even more discouraging. I was manning a booth at the Muscular Dystrophy Fun Fair held every fall in the high school parking lot. My job was to sell tickets for a guessing game involving a fish tank filled with jelly beans.

A girl, a senior debater I had a crush on, plopped down a dollar, guessed sixteen hundred and twenty, and asked me if I'd heard the news.

"Truman Capote was here. He got his fortune told."

"Who's Truman Capote?"

"He walked right past your booth. You really don't know who he is?"

"Not really."

"Pathetic."

"A politician?"

"Pathetic. Get a clue."

The pain of this conversation took days to heal. I changed the route I took to school each morning, avoiding the streets where I'd seen the shuttle vans. And if one of my friends even mentioned Maple Glen, I changed the subject. I didn't want to hear it.

Then one night at dinner disaster struck.

"Audrey got a new nursing job," Mike said.

"It's only part-time. It's nights," she said. "It's nothing."

"Where?" I said.

"Maple Glen."

"She's stunned," Mike said. "Guess who she saw in the lobby before her interview?"

"Stop it," said Audrey. "I can't go leaking names. I signed an agreement about it."

"That writer," I said.

Audrey gave me a hard look. "Eat your venison."

I put down my fork and asked to be excused.

~ ~ ~

The long morning baths were the first sign she was changing. When Audrey would get home from work at breakfast time, she'd put on a robe and slippers, tie her hair back, and run the water in the claw-foot tub. The downstairs bathroom adjoined the kitchen, and the smells of the salts Audrey sprinkled in her bath—lavender, hyacinth, vanilla, cinnamon—penetrated the refrigerator and tainted the milk I poured over my cereal. When her tub was full, Audrey would shut the door and stay in there, soaking, until I left for school.

One morning I couldn't find my Ritalin. I rapped on the bathroom door.

"I left my prescription in the medicine cabinet."

"I'm meditating. Go away."

"Just check."

"It wouldn't kill you to skip a day."

"You're *meditating*?"

When Audrey finally opened the door a crack and handed me my pills, I glimpsed something next to the tub: a flickering candle. To burn a candle so early in the day seemed wasteful to me, a troubling self-indulgence. When I smelled the candle again the next morning. I said something about it through the door.

"It's sunny out."

"So?"

"You lit a candle."

"So? Let your mother do something for herself for once. She can't just take of others all day long."

This was the last time I tried to speak to Audrey during one of her baths. I listened instead. Sometimes, over the slip and slop of bathwater, I could hear her reading from a book written by one of the doctors at Maple Glen: *One Year in Recovery: A Spirit Log*. I'd sneaked a look at the book one day and I hadn't liked what I'd seen. The pages were divided down the middle, with a little prayer on one side and a brief quotation on the other: "I will stop comparing my insides to others' outsides." "Don't just do something, sit there." "Easy does it."

One morning school was called off because of snow and I was still home when Audrey left the bathroom. She'd been soaking by candlelight for ninety minutes.

"How was work?" I said.

"Quiet. Very quiet." She set a kettle on the stove and opened the cupboard where she kept her tea. Instead of the Lipton she normally drank, she took down two color-ful boxes of herbal tea I hadn't seen before: Chamomile Cloud and Licorice Life Force.

"Any interesting patients?" I said.

Audrey hung a bag of Licorice Life Force on the rim of a mug from Maple Glen. A motto encircled the mug in silver lettering: "Growth is Change is Growth is Change is Growth."

"Give me a hint," I said.

"You know the policy."

We'd been through this routine before. Audrey
seemed to take great pride in shielding her patients'
identities, as if it allowed her to share their fame somehow. In fact, since going to work at Maple Glen she'd
started to act like she was better than other people. Just
yesterday, for example, while watching the evening news
with Joel and me, she'd dismissed the entire United
States Senate as a "bunch of senile white male narcis-
sists." Even Joel did a double take at her new haughti-
ness.

"It must get awfully depressing," I said, softening my
interrogation tactics, "seeing people who have everything throw it all away."

"Addiction doesn't play favorites," Audrey said, pour-
ing hot water over her herbal tea. "I'm learning something, Justin: the higher their status and level of achievements, the needier human beings tend to be."

I sensed her relaxing, lowering her guard. If I could
make her spill just one big name, I thought, we would be
equals again. Just one big name.

"Truth be told," Audrey said, "I pity these characters. Back where they come from—Los Angeles, New
York—they're surrounded by flatterers, by hangers-on.
No one ever tells it to them straight. They smash up a
sports car or run a traffic light and the cops let them off
for an autograph. It's sad. They have to come all the way
out to Minnesota just to hear the truth about themselves."

"You tell them the truth," I said.

"It's pretty obvious: they worship their own egos. They're sick with selfishness. No higher power."

"Like who, exactly?"

"Stop it. There but for the grace of God go you."

That was as far as I got that day, but it was further than I'd gotten before. The trick, I'd found, was to play on Audrey's pride. The excitement of rubbing elbows with celebrities, and maybe even believing that she was saving them, was bound to get the best of her eventually.

A few days later I renewed the pressure. It was Audrey's night off and I found her on the sofa watching a late-night talk show with the sound turned low.

I sat in the recliner. "Can't sleep," I said. "How come you're up still?"

"I'm staying on my schedule. The secret to working nights is turning nocturnal."

Audrey sipped a mug of herbal tea as the talk show host welcomed a bald comedian with pink runny eyes that wobbled in their sockets as if they didn't fit snugly in his skull. I saw her attention home in and grew suspicious. The comedian, whose name I'd missed, jogged out onto the stage and snatched the mike and cracked a series of jokes about Las Vegas. Audrey, who'd never been to Nevada so far as I knew, laughed like an insider.

"You know that guy?"

"Go back to bed," she said.

I was onto something. When the comedian wound up

his bit, he crossed the stage and flopped down beside the host, who congratulated him on his comeback.

"So what's he like?" I said, adding up the clues. "Is he funny in person, too?"

"I wouldn't know."

"Who are you afraid I'm going to tell? Don't you trust your own son? Come on, it's *me*."

Audrey wrapped her hands around her mug. "Why is this so important to you suddenly? You're acting obsessed. Have you been skipping your pills?"

I watched the comedian pat his forehead with a damp white hanky. He looked unwell.

"What was he in for? Booze or drugs?" I said.

"Are you afraid I'll fall in love with one? Is that it?" said Audrey.

I leveled a stare at her.

"They're sick, sick people. They're lost. They're dead inside. I don't care how many millions of dollars they make or how many Broadway shows they've starred in, they're not my type. I don't go in for junkies."

I kept up my stare. Audrey fidgeted, looked down.

Her promises meant nothing, and she knew it.

~ ~ ~

The van was so new it had dealer plates and its windows hadn't been blacked-out yet. I spotted it on Highway 9 while practicing for my driver's license road test. My driver-ed instructor, Mr. Graf, whose favorite teaching aids were bloody film strips with titles such as *Death*

Drives Ninety, had turned me into a timid, defensive driver—and yet when I saw the van I lost my caution and executed a U-turn so I could follow it.

Through the van's rear window I could see a man sitting all alone in the backseat. His hairstyle was one I'd only seen in magazines: long in the back and spiky on the sides, but perfectly proportioned to his head. He flicked a cigarette butt out the window which bounced on the pavement and showered orange sparks.

I tailed the van for another mile or two, working up the courage to accelerate and drive alongside it for a better view. Up ahead was a diner with a gas pump. When the van turned into its driveway, I turned, too.

The driver, a woman in nurse's shoes, opened the van's sliding door. A man got out. He was so tall he had to duck his head and the driver reached out one hand to help him down. The man looked familiar but I couldn't place him. His short-sleeved sport shirt showed muscular tanned arms; his face was lean and prematurely rugged, with scars on his nose and cheek that looked like beauty marks. Certain people led such charmed lives, apparently, that even their wounds worked out to their advantage.

While the driver filled the van with gas, the man took off his dark glasses and rubbed his eyes. I recognized him then. He looked thinner than on TV, but it was him: Matt Schramm, the private eye, a character in a show called *Malibu Nights*. A maverick who didn't carry a gun because of his mastery of martial arts,

Schramm solved his cases by "thinking with his gut," and his trademark line—"I'm onto you like glue"—had caught on at school a couple of years ago. I'd used it a few times myself.

I put the car in reverse but didn't back up. Schramm was leaning against the van, tilting his face to the sun, arms crossed. I found myself picturing Audrey drawing blood from him—rolling his sleeve up and sliding in a needle. I imagined her weighing him, writing down his height, quizzing him about his allergies.

I backed up slowly and started to turn the wheel. Schramm looked over at me and raised one arm.

"Hang on there," he said.

He approached my car. I stopped. He leaned in my open window, held up a cigarette, and flicked an invisible lighter with his thumb.

"Can't use the one in the van. I'll blow it up," he said. "Too many gas fumes."

I pushed in my lighter and waited for it to pop. I could smell Schramm's cologne in the car. The lighter ejected. I held it red end out and Schramm bent closer and cupped my hand and inhaled. His skin was icy.

"Gracias, kid."

"You're welcome."

"You from this town?"

"Over the hill there."

"Great area. So *real*. I'm a midwesterner, too, originally."

"What part?" I said.

Schramm ignored me and moved off.

"Thanks for the light, kid. Take it sleazy," he said.

As Schramm climbed back into the shuttle van, I noticed that a small crowd had gathered on the diner's front step. He gave them a wave and they waved back at him, not stopping when he slammed the sliding door. Then a woman pushed forward, fluttering a napkin. "I love you!" she yelled. "I *love* you! I *adore* you!" The van pulled away from the pumps, the woman ran after it. She pounded on a window. I saw Schramm duck.

That night when Audrey went to work I said a prayer for her. For both of us.

~ ~ ~

I couldn't help it: I became suspicious. When Audrey came home from work in the mornings, I scrutinized her face and posture, alert to any change in how she greeted me. I tracked the TV shows she watched. I rifled her purse. In the glove compartment of her car I found a roll of sugar-free breath mints that I checked on daily for a week. The roll decreased steadily, one thin mint per night, but I didn't know how to interpret this evidence.

There was one clue I couldn't ignore, though: the sudden change in Audrey's beauty regimen. I'd never known her to suffer from dry skin, but suddenly she was moisturizing constantly. She dabbed cream on her elbows after her morning baths. She slicked on cocoa butter while watching TV. And she couldn't seem to settle on just one product; she switched from bottle to bottle, jar to jar, as if she were searching for something. Perfection, it seemed. What's more, she began spritzing perfume on her uniform and wearing earrings to work.

At dinner one night I brought up *Malibu Nights*. There were risks in being so direct, but I had to see how Audrey would react.

"I watched it last week," I said, trying to sound casual. "It was part one of a special two-part episode about a mysterious string of call-girl murders."

Audrey went on eating. Drinking, actually. Her schedule had thrown off her appetite, she said, and instead of having pot roast with the rest of us, she'd made herself a yogurt drink with brewer's yeast. She said she preferred to eat dinner later at night, but I knew the truth: she was dieting. For him.

"Why don't you watch it with me? Part one was great," I said.

"Sure," Audrey said. "Sounds dumb. I love dumb shows."

At eight we sat on the sofa and turned the set on. Audrey squirted a wavy line of lotion onto one arm and rubbed it in in circles. I ate a handful of popcorn I'd just popped, and offered her the bowl.

"No thanks. Too much butter." She patted her stomach.

"You're skinny."

"I'm just not big on butter lately. Thanks."

Matt Schramm was not at the center of that week's

episode, which made it hard to analyze Audrey's responses. His partner, Ronald, dominated the plot. Hired by the wife of a movie producer to check out her husband's connection with the dead women, Ronald went undercover as a rich john while Schramm, in a secondary assignment, interviewed men who'd used the call-girl service. According to the show's familiar formula, this meant Schramm would find himself in danger sometime in the last part of the show and Ronald, this week's star, would rescue him.

For the first half hour nothing happened. Audrey seemed bored during Schramm's infrequent scenes and only once did I see her pay attention: when one of the call girls kissed him on the cheek and asked him if he was free that night. "For what?" he said. "For love," the girl said. "I don't need love," Schramm said. "I need the truth."

I went to the bathroom during a commercial and stood in front of the mirror, gripped with shame. I had my own bad habits and weaknesses; someday, like Schramm, I might need help with them.

Malibu Nights had resumed when I returned, but something had changed, on the show and in my mother. Schramm had been kidnapped, just as I'd expected— locked naked in a sauna by the murderer. Jets of steam were boiling him alive and Audrey seemed spellbound, rubbing yet more lotion into a hand she'd already moisturized. Her feet were jiggling, though she seemed unaware of it. When Schramm passed out while pounding on the door, the jiggling stopped for a moment, then sped up.

Something in me came loose. I lost control.

"Admit it," I said.

"Admit what? Stop acting crazy."

"He's there. He's your patient."

Audrey shook her head. "Someday you're going to realize. You're going to have to."

"What?"

"I'm a *mine*, not a *yours*. I have an *inside*. And that inside has boundaries. You can't just barge right in."

These were all lines from *One Year in Recovery* and I was too worked up to figure them out. I left the sofa, charged through the back door, and locked myself in the garage in Audrey's car. I turned on the radio and squeezed the steering wheel. I stabbed the button on the glove compartment, causing it to fall open. I looked inside. Audrey's roll of breath mints, new that week, was already down to two.

And I found something else, something worse: a rolled-up photograph. I spread it flat on the seat and turned the dome light on. The photo showed Schramm bare-chested on a beach, and there was writing on it: "Audrey Cobb, I'm onto you like glue. Hugs, David Baird."

My eyes stung. I went rigid. She not only knew him, the bastard had a name.

~ ~ ~

"I'm calling for a patient there," I said.

"It's one in the morning. Our patients are asleep."

"This one's awake." I gave the woman Baird's name.

"I'm sorry, sir, but it's our policy not to disclose the identities of residents."

I hung up the phone and sat in the dark kitchen. They were there together, this minute. I was sure of it.

I asked for the nurses' station when I called back.

"Did you just phone here?" the operator said.

"This is a family emergency. Put me through."

The phone at Audrey's station rang and rang. Each ring seemed longer than the ring before and struck my ear with the empty, hollow tone that means there is no one on the other end——or else that they've consciously chosen to ignore you.

Either way, it was time to act. I got Mike's car keys.

A red-striped gate blocked the driveway to the clinic. I drove a quarter mile past it, turned off on a side road, pulled over on the shoulder, cut my lights, and started through the woods, my hands in front of my face to push the branches back. Though I'd never been to Maple Glen before and didn't know the layout of the grounds, I knew I was headed in the right direction because my anger grew with every step.

Several cars were parked around the entrance, including Audrey's. I didn't see any people. I crossed the lawn, then dropped into a crouch and followed a flower bed along a wall, peeking in every window that had lights on. In one of the rooms I saw a naked fat man lying facedown on a mattress with its sheets torn off, his back tattooed from shoulder blade to shoulder blade with a coiled snake. In the next room a woman sat yoga style on the floor, watching TV with her nose right up to the screen. Neither of the two patients looked rich or famous, which didn't mean they weren't. After all, Truman Capote had walked right past me.

The last of the windows was larger and better lit. I peered in sideways, my back against the wall, and saw a horseshoe-shaped desk and filing cabinets. Audrey's coat was hanging over a chair, and on the desk, held open by a stapler, was her copy of *One Year in Recovery*. Over the desk was a poster of a chimp perched on a toilet eating a banana. The caption read ''Thank God for Simple Pleasures.''

As I waited for Audrey to come back, I found myself hoping she wouldn't be alone. Only solid, final proof of her betrayal could harden my fears into facts that I could act on. Indeed, I'd already sketched out my plan of action. Blackmailing Audrey with what I'd seen, I'd demand to be sent away to school, preferably to an eastern prep school with a good debate team. I'd never come home or send a single letter. I'd go on to college, graduate with honors, then move to New York and become a TV journalist. I'd drink away the nights. I'd snort cocaine. I'd blow my paychecks betting at the track. Finally, after a major nervous breakdown, I'd fly back home and check in to Maple Glen. Audrey and I would lock eyes. She'd weep. Embrace me. "What did you expect?" I'd ask her. "What did you expect?"

I was still lost in this fantasy when a man in a hospital smock and jeans stepped out of the shadows and sidled up to me. He didn't seem to recognize my face but I knew his. I couldn't get away from it.

"I guess I've found the smokers' lounge," Baird said, holding out a pack of cigarettes.

I took one. Baird clicked his lighter. A flame leaped up.

"A guy can only kick one thing at a time. You in the juvenile wing?" he said.

I nodded.

"What's your poison?"

My mind raced. "Dope."

"What flavor?"

"I don't know. Everything, I guess."

"Join the fucking club," Baird said. "Never met a drug I didn't like. Except maybe acid. Too profound for me. I guess if I have a favorite, though, it's tranquilizers."

Baird smoked no-handed, exhaling through his nose, and hugged his chest for warmth. He took a deep, rasping drag, then tipped his head back and blew a forked gray plume across the moon.

"How old are you anyway? Sixteen?" Baird said. "Me, I was still a choirboy at your age. Didn't even take aspirin. A Christian Scientist. Then I broke my leg. A compound fracture. My mom and dad prayed for me. No pills, just prayers. But then I met a guy who had some morphine tablets. Believe me, they helped. I saw visions. Jesus Lord. A grizzly bear ate my entire head one night and shit out a Barbie doll. Mention *that* in group!''

I smoked and said nothing. I was in over my head. The best thing to do was to listen, to be still.

"Move over," Baird said. "She'll see us."

I turned and looked. Audrey was back at her station, in her chair, eating dinner off a plastic tray. Judging by the heap of mashed potatoes and the slice of chocolate cake, she wasn't on a diet, after all.

"You know that nurse?" Baird said. "She saved my neck."

"Her?" I said.

"She's a tough one, but she's good. In fact, I consider her my guardian angel. I wouldn't be sober without her."

"You're friends?" I said.

"It's deeper than that. You want the whole sad story? That's what this place is all about: confession."

"I have to get back. They'll start searching."

"I'll condense it for you." Baird bent his neck to one side until it cracked, pushed back his hair, and cleared his throat. An actor. "Three weeks ago I fly here from Los Angeles. I work in TV. My studio commits me. Maybe you've seen my show."

I shook my head. Baird didn't hide his look of disappointment.

"Well, anyway, I get sent here. Against my will. So naturally I smuggle in a stash. Tucked up my rear; some pills in a balloon. And the first thing I do after check-in, I hit the boys' room, but son of a bitch, the stash is too high up. I try to extract it in bed that night. No dice. Now I'm panicking. Thing could break and kill me. I ask Dr. Frost for an Ex-Lax, but he refuses. No drugs, he says, and laxatives are drugs. Next day I eat raisin bran breakfast, lunch, and dinner, but still no action. That Valium is *up there*."

I looked over Baird's shoulder at the window. Audrey had fallen asleep in her chair. Her plate was clean, not a crumb of cake remained, and on her desk I spotted a framed certificate: my award from the last state speech tournament.

I'd wronged her.

"So anyhow, it's night three by now," Baird said, "and I'll try anything. I'm still backed up. I steal a dessert spoon at dinner—I'll *scoop* it out. But something goes wrong and I cut myself internally. I'm bleeding like crazy on the bathroom floor. I know I need help right away or I'm a goner, but who do I call? It's the middle of the night. Plus, if the studio hears what's happened, I'm toast. No more Ferrari. Good-bye Sunset Strip."

Baird paused, lit two more cigarettes, and passed me one. I sucked the filter, hard. I needed a lift.

"So I realize it's life or death now," he continued. "My fate is in my hands. I crawl to the phone and dial the nurses' station. My legs are soaked in blood. I'm losing consciousness. Nurse Cobb picks up and says she'll be right down, so I climb up onto the bed somehow and wait. She gets there, she sees the blood. I'm swimming in it. She asks me what happened. As usual, I lie: I was wiping my ass and I nicked it with my fingernail. Luckily, she sees right through my bullshit. She turns me onto my stomach, kneels behind me, and in goes her hand, her bare hand, no rubber glove. And no Vaseline to grease it; just my blood. And that's when I woke up, kid. Then. That moment. That's when I finally got real about myself.''

Baird gazed at the back of one hand and flexed the fingers. "I'm David and I'm an addict," he announced. He looked back up. "That's my story, what's yours?"

~ ~ ~

I should have known that as soon I stopped hounding her, Audrey would start confiding in me. It happened suddenly. We were watching *Eyewitness News* one night and the anchorman stumbled pronouncing the governor's name.

"Speed freak," Audrey said, nodding at the screen. "Beats his girlfriend with a tennis racket."

A few days later at the supermarket, I picked up a magazine and skimmed an interview with a British actress I had a thing for. Audrey leaned over my shoulder. "You think she's cute?"

"Sort of," I said. "She's okay."

"Her nose is plastic. A surgeon had to rebuild it. Too much coke."

At first I assumed that Audrey was trying to scare me, to warn me about the dangers of fast living, but as she continued exposing people's secrets it became clear to me that she was bitter. Despite everything she did for them, she told me, most of Maple Glen's well-known patients relapsed, sometimes within hours of being discharged.

"Drama. They're all hooked on drama," she said. "Look at me. Love me. That's the *real* addiction. We're all in pain, but they make a big show of it. And we eat it up. The so-called little people. Which is what keeps us little, I suppose."

The morning of my driving exam I turned on the *Today* show in the kitchen and sat down to study my book of traffic laws. Audrey came in from work and put coffee on. She'd quit drinking herbal tea some time ago. She'd quit a lot of things, in fact: the candlelit baths, the lotions, the recovery books. It was over, her whole experiment.

The host of the *Today* show announced a guest. When I heard his voice my head jerked up.

"It's him," I said.

Audrey put down her coffee cup. Baird, unshaven and dressed in a black muscle shirt, couldn't seem to get comfortable in his chair. The interviewer asked if he was "back" and Baird crossed his legs and ran an index finger along the stitching of one cowboy boot. "Frankly, it's been a struggle,'' he said. He paused. "I've learned some tough lessons.'' Pause: "About myself. But I like to think I'm a better person for it. More sane, I guess. A little bit more real.''

"Baloney,'' said Audrey. "He's high right now. He's loaded.''

"You mean he's lying?''

"You're watching a professional. This joker stayed stoned his whole time at Maple Glen. Total con man. Total sociopath. Handed out autographed photos to all the nurses and swore to each of us no one else had gotten one. Lost his mind when we took away his drug stash and started drinking Lysol from the cleaning closet.''

I looked down at my book, at the silhouettes of road signs. I'd doubted her, I'd spied, and I'd been punished for it. But maybe my anguish had been unnecessary. If Baird was such a notorious liar, maybe he'd lied to me, too.

I had to know. "Who found his drugs?''

Audrey turned off the *Today* show. "I think I'm going to have to quit that place.''

I repeated my question.

"I did,'' Audrey said.

To stop halfway would be pointless. I'd gone too far. "Where were they hidden?''

She avoided my eyes. "I honestly don't remember.''

Such love, such concern for my feelings—I didn't deserve it.

As usual, I took it anyway.

4

The deal was I could buy a car if I got a summer job, and because I'd always liked the smell of gasoline, as natural to me as the smell of grass or wood, I put in an application at the Standard station out on Highway 9. Within a few days the owner called me back and invited me to his house to chat. Thinking that hard, honest work and pride of ownership might be the things that would finally set me straight and end my dependence on the Ritalin, I wet-combed my hair and ironed a white dress shirt and rubbed a deodorant stick around my armpits.

My body odor had never bothered me, but Mike said it had bothered other people who'd been too polite to let me know.

"Now remember," Mike said, "you have to sell yourself. No one knows what you can do but you." This was a reference to Joel, the sudden boy wonder, who'd come in third in a St. Paul junior tennis tournament that no one had thought he'd had any business entering.

"All this guy needs is someone to pump gas," I said.

"You never know. He might need more than that."

The station was owned by a man named Scott Dekalb, who'd moved to Minnesota just six months ago. According to the gossip I'd heard in town, he'd owned a Burger King franchise in Colorado which had been destroyed in a tornado. He lived with his wife in a glass-faced model home on the edge of the new golf course, Pheasant Bluff. The locals had said the place would never take off, but the lots had doubled in value in a year. A Minnesota Viking had even bought one.

Scott was waiting in the arched front door when I turned into his driveway on my bike. He had on a polo shirt with a turned-up collar, khaki shorts, and a fat gold chronograph whose luminous dial lit his forearm green. Instead of shaking my hand he squeezed my shoulder.

"Great. Come in. Terrific. Justin Cobb. He needs a summer job, we hear. Fantastic."

The floor of the house was beneath ground level; I had to walk down a short staircase when I entered.

Spindly trees in brightly painted pots ringed the room. I smelled fertilizer, peat moss. From somewhere I could hear a woman's voice counting slowly to ten and back to zero in what I supposed was a yoga exercise.

"Eva, my wife, made some great fruit tea," Scott said, directing me to a U-shaped leather sofa on which a couple of fat books lay open. "You can add sugar, but it doesn't need it. It's naturally sweet. You should try it without sugar."

"I will," I said.

"Sugar's a killer. It shrinks the glands. They've autopsied people who've eaten lots of sweets, and where their adrenals are supposed to be, there's nothing. The American way of death."

While Scott poured our drinks I leafed through one of the books. The pages were heavily underlined in yellow marker, their margins covered in stars and exclamation marks. I glanced at the title: *The Abundant Mind*. The cover showed a unicorn with wings soaring over a rainbow toward a mountaintop. On the unicorn's head was a radiant gold crown.

The tea was sour, thick with grit and pulp, but I took long swallows to be agreeable. The interview went well, I felt. Scott did most of the talking, using strangely lofty language to describe his business. His name for the gas station was "the enterprise." Gas and motor oil were "the product," customers were "extended family," and employees were "service channelers." He also talked about money, which he called "inflow." Most people, he said, had mixed feelings about inflow and thought that earning it required struggle, but nothing could be further from the truth. Inflow was like oxygen, Scott said.

"I want you to take two breaths for me," he said. "First, I want you to actually *suck* the air in."

I did this.

"Let yourself exhale. Good. Okay. Now this time, instead of making a strenuous effort, I want you to gradually expand your lungs. Forget the air. Just open up your lungs."

I inhaled the second way.

"Tell me now," Scott said. "Which breath felt fuller, more satisfying?"

"That one?"

"*Voilà,*" Scott said, "the principle of inflow. You see, the universe *wants* us to be wealthy. It *wants* to fill us up. We choke it off, though. We choke it off because we worship *scarcity,* this man-made idea that the world is basically *hostile.*"

"My father thinks that way."

"Don't fall for it. So what are your goals for the summer?"

"Nothing special. Mostly I'm trying to save up for a car."

Scott set down his tea, which I noticed he'd barely touched. "Personally, I prefer the German makes. Benz, BMW, Porsche."

"Expensive. Nice."

"It's all a matter of what you think you're worth. When can you start? This Saturday?"

"No problem."

Scott picked up *The Abundant Mind*. "I've hired a manager, Chris, my wife's kid brother. He doesn't start until next week, however, so in the meantime I have some homework for you. It's kind of our personal bible around here."

He passed me the book and I tucked it under my arm. Scott put his hands on his knees. We stood.

"Now, that was easy, wasn't it?" he said. "Success is like sailing: sit back and catch the wind."

~ ~ ~

I couldn't have wished for a better job. I loved leaning over windshields with the squeegee and drawing it squeakily across the glass. I loved unscrewing the plugs from oil pans and watching the glossy fluid drip through my fingers. Most of all, though, I loved my uniform: light blue shirt, red cap, and navy pants. My name was sewn into the pocket of the shirt, and the cap had a torch-shaped patch, the Standard Oil emblem.

By my third or fourth day I had the job down cold, so when Scott stopped by to check on me one morning, I suggested that he could keep expenses down by delaying hiring his brother-in-law until I went back to school in the fall. I'd tested the idea on Mike and he'd said it showed initiative and guts.

Scott frowned. "That's the scarcity rut that I was talking about. Do more with less. Conserve. Scrape by. Scale back. Didn't you read that book I lent you?"

"I started it." In fact, I'd misplaced it and couldn't find it now.

"Study the chapter on potential energy. Within every molecule, every human being, there's a vast reserve of latent power." Scott picked up a pencil lying on the cash drawer. "If a person knows how to tap it, there's enough energy in this stick of graphite to heat every home in St. Paul for a whole winter."

"Really?" I said. "A whole winter?"

"You're skeptical. That's because you've been programmed. We've all been programmed." Scott held up the pencil near my nose. "Unfocus your eyes. The pencil splits in two. See how it splits into two?"

"I do."

Scott nodded. "And what does that tell you? About reality?"

I pretended to think for a moment, then said, "A lot."

Scott smiled, then presented me with the pencil as if it had some mysterious new value. I took off my cap and put the pencil behind my ear.

~ ~ ~

Chris showed up two hours late his first day on the job. He pulled up next to the premium pump in a custom Chevy van whose sides were painted with desertscapes and stars. He walked around to the pump, unhooked the nozzle, and started filling his tank—all while holding a lighted cigarette. I shot him a look of warning. He shrugged and then stamped out the butt with a sharp-toed roping boot.

"I've worked with petroleum products all my life," he said. "Unless you drop a lit match in them, you're fine."

Chris parked his van while I rang up his fuel. When I handed him his receipt he tore it up. His uniform shirt was unbuttoned and untucked and he had on one of those T-shirts underneath that show the anatomy of the human body: all the muscles, bones, and organs in their actual colors. The shirt repulsed me.

"Void that. My gas is on Scott and Eva," he said.

"You pumped almost twenty gallons."

"Gas is water. There's more of it than Standard Oil lets on. They jack up the price by holding back supply."

"As long as they gave you permission."

"I don't need it. Nickels and dimes don't interest them, believe me. Those two have bigger fish to fry. They're players."

"What do you mean?"

"You don't want to know," Chris said.

I voided the purchase but kept the register tape in case there were questions later on. Chris spent the morning poking around the station and pointing out its flaws. "Check it out: this oil additive's phony. It doesn't increase your mileage, it *lowers* it." Later, he raised the shop's hydraulic hoist. "Hear that wheezing sound, that noise it makes? Just watch: this baby'll fail and drop a car on me. Hell of a workmen's comp claim—that's the bright side."

At noon, Chris unlocked the station's pop machine and helped himself to a can of RC cola.

"It's funny: these products that companies get rich on are basically just water. Colored liquid. It's like we have this *need* to waste our money."

"So business is all a big joke to you?" I said.

"I'm twenty-six. I've gained a certain perspective." He held out a can of RC for me.

"I'm fine."

"You look thirsty," Chris said.

"I like to pay for things."

That afternoon Chris serviced a station wagon crammed with Little Leaguers in caps and jerseys. I watched him work as I filled a VW Bug. When he went to the car's rolled-down window to be paid, the driver, a woman, pointed to a sign: "Declaration of Total Satisfaction." It said that unless the attendant checked the tires, washed the windows, and offered to check the oil, the customer was not obliged to pay.

"You forgot my tires," the woman said.

"I checked them visually. Your pressure's fine."

"We'll compromise," the woman said. "We'll split it." She dug in her purse as the bratty Little Leaguers pressed their sluglike tongues against the windows. Chris flipped them the bird and the kids began to holler.

The woman twisted around to shut them up and Chris grabbed her purse through the window, ripped some money out, tossed the purse back in the car, and walked away.

Chris handed me a five. "For standing backup."

I gave him back the money.

"I like your honesty. Leaves twice as much for me," he said.

Later, after five or six more cars, Chris stole another RC and lit a cigarette. He gazed out at a field across the highway where a Farmall tractor was mowing hay. The acne scars in his cheeks resembled fossils and his bony Adam's apple looked like a skull.

"My sister and brother-in-law are sharks," he said. "I'll take all the five-finger discounts I can get. Truth is, all I'm doing here is marking time while the game plays out on higher levels."

"What game is that?"

"High finance. Tax shenanigans. You really think people get rich by selling gasoline?"

"Rockefeller did. He founded Standard."

"Rockefeller was a crook," Chris said. "His father was a small-time flimflam man."

The driveway bell rang twice. Chris flicked his smoke away.

"I'll take the Mustang," he said. "You grab the motor home."

~ ~ ~

I was showering after work with Lava soap when Mike came in and sat down on the toilet. He bowed his head and spat tobacco juice into the bowl between his open knees.

"How's work?" he said.

"Okay."

"You sound unsure."

I scoured my armpits with the gritty soap. "It's not like I expected."

"Never is."

"I have this manager, Scott's brother-in-law. He's stealing company property."

Mike spat. "A cost of doing business, I'm afraid. Half the price of milk these days goes to make up for shoplifting, they say."

"People shoplift milk?"

"They shoplift everything. Milk is where they recapture the lost profits."

I held out my arms in the spray. Gray water rolled off. The grease wasn't on my skin but underneath it—a spreading, shapeless black tattoo.

"How much oil is there?" I asked Mike. "Chris says that Standard has wells in Lake Superior that if they ever started pumping them, gas would go down to a dime a gallon."

Mike flushed the toilet; my shower water ran scalding. "I wouldn't be surprised. I've heard these stories."

I scrubbed at the grease; I felt let down, betrayed. The company uniform had made me proud.

~ ~ ~

By my third week of working under Chris, I was drinking my fill of RC cola and eating free lunches from the snack machine. Chris was partial to pretzel twigs and corn nuts, but I was too modest to steal such popular items. I held myself to the peanut-butter crackers.

Scott stopped in every few days to check the books. He smelled of VapoRub and cough drops and always seemed to be searching for a shop towel to wipe his dripping nose on. Chris said Scott had a problem with cocaine and hosted all-night parties at his house, whose guests included stockbrokers and bankers.

"Basically, they're the power elite," Chris said. "You and me are just chits. We're human currency."

"I'm saving for a car. That's all I care about."

"Big Oil's got you exactly where they want you, then. Another young American bites the dust."

Slowly, under the pressure of Chris's teasing, I began to cut corners in my work. I ignored people's tires. I left windshields bug-streaked. For three days running I put off cleaning the rest rooms, leading to a catastrophic spiral of plugged-up toilets, overflowing trash cans, vandalized towel dispensers, and flooded floors. The men's room graffiti grew filthier and bolder, climaxing in a life-size drawing of revving chain saws attacking a woman's crotch. I tried to erase the drawing with steel wool but only succeeded in scuffing up the wall, which made the image look more obscene somehow.

One morning, during a cola and pretzels break, Chris informed me that he was dropping acid.

"Leave me out of it," I said.

"Tough. I already slipped some in your pop."

A station wagon pulled in with three flat tires caused by driving over a construction site. While Chris put the car on the lift, the passengers—a mother, a father, and two cute little girls—leafed through old *Road & Track*s in the office. We brushed the tire treads with soapy water to locate the punctures, then removed the rims. I sanded down the rubber around the bad spots, glued on patches, and remounted the tires. When I finally double-checked for leaks, soap bubbles formed where air was still escaping.

"Something's wrong," I said.

Chris scratched his scalp, raising a flurry of dandruff. "We're reptiles, man. We shed our skins. You see this?"

"Why are these tires still leaking?"

"We're goddamn *lizards*."

The father stepped into the service bay. "You finished, fellows?"

"Our work is complete," Chris said oddly. "You're on your way."

When the station wagon drove off, Chris waved at it but no one waved back, which seemed to hurt him.

"Those were nice people," he said. "I didn't charge them."

"Their tires weren't patched right."

"No."

"They'll have a blowout."

"Don't do that," said Chris. "Don't do that to your-self."

"I hope they're wearing seat belts."

"Stop it. Ouch."

We agreed that it might lift our spirits to clean the rest rooms and really make them shine. After bleaching the toilets, snaking out the drains, mopping the floors, and Windexing the mirrors, we renewed our assault on the chain-saw graffiti using shop towels soaked with starter fluid. The black Magic Marker lines smeared but didn't fade.

"Who does this stuff?" I said.

"Rich businessmen. All this anonymous sex shit's done by businessmen." Chris shut his eyes. "I'm trip-ping, man. I'm crisp."

The driveway bell sounded. Chris flinched and dropped his rag.

"Can you go?" he said.

"I'm going."

"I'll keep scrubbing."

"You keep scrubbing."

"I'll be right here."

"Right where?"

"Here. In the bathroom."

"I don't think I can do this."

Chris said, "I know what you're thinking. Me, too. Those tires."

~ ~ ~

I bought a car, a retired sheriff's cruiser with smears of rust and primer on the doors where the insignias had been sanded off. A partition divided the front seat from the back. The cruiser's big V-8 got lousy mileage, but that didn't matter; I gassed it up for free. On weekends, after closing up the station, Chris and I would drive around for hours just to burn the fuel. Once, for a laugh, we pulled over for a hitchhiker—a girl from school whom I'd heard was sweet on me—and made her sit behind the metal screen as if she were our prisoner.

Except for a brief phone call now and then, Scott had stopped checking up on us at work. We dismantled the Total Satisfaction sign and tossed it in the pit behind the station where we dumped old batteries and tires. We gave up wearing our uniforms except for the caps, which we needed to cool our heads.

Summer was ending. School was in three weeks. During one of our aimless weekend drives, I asked Chris if he planned to stay on and run the place.

"You haven't figured it out yet?"

"What out?"

Chris took a slug from a bottle of chilled peach wine. "Why do you think they don't care how much we steal from them? Why do you think they never check the take or match it against the meters on the pumps?"

"Because they're rich?" I said.

"They act like it. Fact is, they shot their wad a

month ago. The settlement from their Dairy Queen's all gone."

"I thought they owned a Burger King."

"Big dif."

Chris drank the rest of the wine, rolled down his window, and pitched the bottle backward onto the highway. "Here's what I'm saying: those tires behind the station, or maybe those greasy rags around the shop, are going to catch fire exactly two weeks from now. Mysteriously. An hour after closing."

"Right."

"Don't believe me. Stay innocent. It's smarter."

"This job is getting too weird for me," I said. "I've had it. I quit."

"It's a little too late for that."

~ ~ ~

By ignoring the fire until afterward, Chris said, I'd be able to act convincingly shocked by it. He also warned me again not to quit, which might make me look disgruntled to the insurance company and turn me into a suspect. The best thing to do, he told me, was sit tight. The arsonist, a pro from out of town, had already cased the station, he said, while posing as a customer.

"Who?" I said. "That guy in the Ranchero?"

"Black guy. Big arms."

"Is it him?"

"You're prejudiced."

"Who? This is driving me crazy."

"Join the club."

Though I woke every day expecting to be told that the station had burned the night before, nothing happened. I went to work as usual. Chris had begun to deteriorate, though. He hit a deer on Highway 5 one morning and spent the whole day picking fur out of his bumper. The next day he opened a radiator cap and a geyser of coolant sprayed him in the face. That same afternoon I found him in the shop inhaling from a Baggie filled with starter fluid.

Later that week Scott invited us to lunch to celebrate Eva's thirty-seventh birthday. Chris insisted on setting the alarm and walking around back to lock the service door. He also suggested we go in separate cars, but I said that that would be wasteful. We took his van.

Scott welcomed us at a table spread with party food: kiwis and star fruit, jumbo shrimp on skewers, mold-flecked cheeses, wine bottles in buckets.

"Eva will be right out," Scott said. "Drink for you, Justin?"

"Thanks. I'll try the white."

"Try the red. More character."

"Whatever."

Chris gestured at the overflowing table. "This house is all windows—the cops can see right in. Put on a total show for them, why don't you?"

"We eat this way every day," Scott said. "Don't act paranoid."

"I'm out of here."

Chris didn't leave, though. As Scott and I munched shrimp, Eva appeared from behind a potted tree, leaning against an aluminum walker. I'd never seen her standing up before, only sitting down inside her car, and I hadn't noticed the S-curve in her back.

"I was listening to my tapes," she said, but didn't explain.

I wished her a happy birthday. She didn't acknowledge me. Instead, she reached feebly for a hunk of cheese that slipped off the cracker she tried to set it on.

Scott said, "Eva and I treat *every* day as if it was our birthday. Because it is. What's waking up but a form of being born? This whole Anglo-Saxon notion of special occasions, special holidays, doesn't make sense to us."

"That's crap," Chris said. He looked at me. "Ignore them. Two most selfish people I've ever met."

"So, Justin." Eva fixed her pale green eyes on me. "What are your hopes? Your goals in life? Your path?"

"I'd like to talk on television, maybe. Give my views and opinions."

"Interesting. Are you a religious person?"

"Not really. You?"

"We prefer the word 'spiritual,' " Scott said.

The remark seemed to drive Chris over the edge; he spat a mouthful of wine at Scott's clean shirt and swung on him with his right fist. Scott blocked the blow. He grabbed Chris's arm by the wrist and wrenched it back and doubled him over, his chin against his belt buckle. Chris begged for mercy but Scott held on.

"We're the best thing that ever happened to you,"
Scott said. *"Grease monkey."*

"Uncle."

"Fucking *motorhead.*"

That's when I heard the sirens. They started low.
Eva picked up a skewer from the table and poked at her
teeth and gums. Scott ate a cracker. Chris ran tap water
over his sore wrist. As the sirens grew louder, Eva
gripped her walker and executed an awkward, choppy
turn. "I have a tape to listen to," she said. "I'm halfway
to qualifying as a naturopath." Scott held her elbow and
helped her over a rough spot where the kitchen tile
bordered the carpet.

The sirens trailed off. The phone rang. I saw Chris
look at it.

"Don't even think of it," Scott said. *"Mr. Good
Wrench."*

~ ~ ~

Everyone came out to watch the fire, even Mike, whose
store was closed for inventory. I saw him through the
windshield of Chris's van, standing behind the police
line in a jogging suit. Not far away a column of volunteer
firemen aimed hoses at the driveway and the gas pumps,
soaking them down to keep them from exploding. Another set of hoses sprayed the station. Now and then the
fire flared green and purple and sent up hissing plumes
of yellow sparks from all the chemicals stored inside the
building.

"You set it," I said. "It was you."

"No comment, man. I'm sorry about your car, though. Tried to warn you."

My car had already burned up and been extinguished. The charred metal body slumped in the driveway, all four tires melted into lumps. Wisps of black smoke escaped the shattered windows.

"I worked hard for that car."

"You're better off," Chris said. "Scott and my sister were halfway moral people until they test-drove their first Mercedes convertible."

We sat and watched the station burn, not speaking. Chris put a tape in the deck and cranked his seat back and set his dusty ropers on the dash. Fumes had begun to penetrate the van, leaking in through the seals around the windows. They smelled of tires and gasoline and grease and were probably killing my brain cells by the millions, but I couldn't stop breathing them in. They smelled like summer.

"I'm serious," Chris said. "The problem's cars, not people."

I watched my old cruiser smolder.

"It's our machines."

5

Mike spread out a Forest Service topo map on the hood of his new International Scout, bought especially for our trip out west. Unbroken lines denoting elevation overlapped dotted lines representing trails. He shaded in our route with a red pencil as Audrey sat on the tailgate humming cowboy songs and Joel stared up at the sky and softly peed.

"You following this? It's a long hike up," Mike said.

"What if we shorten it some?"

Mike looked at Joel. "You think you can handle nine

miles this afternoon?" Joel's ankles were bruised from an all-day tennis tryout for Adolphus Prep in Minneapolis. He'd come this close to winning a scholarship and been invited to try again next fall. Mike called this a brush-off, but Joel was optimistic.

"How long is nine miles in hours? On average?" Joel said.

"I try not to go by averages," Mike said. "Averages, a wise man told me once, are usually an excuse for something."

Mike got frustrated refolding the map and he gave it to me to fold. He'd been feeling shaky since early September, when Woody Wolff's body had rejected his liver and left him in intensive care, on life support. A second transplant wasn't in the cards, and Mike raged for two days that the doctors had given up. He telephoned former teammates and wept with them, swearing out loud that, if it came to it, he was prepared to sign an organ donor card and drive his car off a cliff. Instead, he got on a night flight to Ann Arbor, but he arrived too late. His old coach had lapsed into a coma. Mike stayed by his side around the clock for days, until Woody's daughter asked him to go home because he was getting in the doctors' way. He wasn't the same person when he got back. God, he told us, was taking the wrong man. He behaved as though this were his fault, perhaps even something he deserved to pay for.

I gave the map back to him, neatly folded, and together we started unloading camping gear: a snakebite kit in an orange rubber capsule, goose-down sleeping bags in nylon stuff sacks, a set of nested aluminum pots and pans. Except for Mike, who'd hunted elk in Idaho, none of us had ever seen the mountains, and the four or five times we'd camped out we'd stayed in campgrounds.

"You didn't answer Joel's question, Mike," said Audrey. "Time-wise, what's nine miles?"

"For me? Three hours."

"That sounds awfully ambitious."

"For you folks, four."

Joel stood still as Mike hung a backpack on him, seating the quilted hip pads on his waist and guiding his arms through the cushioned shoulder straps. Audrey said the pack looked tilted, so Mike fooled around with some buckles and drawstrings. Every time he tightened one side, though, the other side leaned away. Mike's face went red.

"Let me," said Audrey.

Mike raised an arm and blocked her. He tugged on the drawstrings and tied their ends, then patted Joel on the butt and said, "You're done." He picked up Audrey's pack next.

"Looks heavy," she said.

"You brought along half the bathroom cabinet. Of course it's heavy."

"Let's not fight. Just lighten it."

The armpits of Mike's shirt showed sweaty crescents

as he untied and unbuckled the bulging pack and trans-
ferred several items to his own pack. Two blood-plump
mosquitoes were feeding on his forehead and I admired
his ability to ignore them. He could turn off discomfort
at will, it seemed, which meant that when he did com-
plain, he wanted something.

"This trip's a con. You conned me," Audrey said.
"You told me you needed rest. This isn't rest, Mike. I
can't believe the kids are missing school for this."

"I told you I needed to *think*," Mike said.

"Same difference."

"And we call this a family. What a joke. We can't
even walk up a hill together," Mike said. "I hate to
think what would happen if times got hard."

"Times *are* hard," Audrey said. "You make them
hard."

Mike opened his hands and let go of Audrey's
backpack. It struck the ground and stood upright for a
moment, then toppled over sideways, spilling things: a
tin Sierra cup, packets of freeze-dried stew, an envelope
of powdered lemonade. At first we just stood there, staring at the mess, but then Audrey knelt and gathered up
her stuff. She cleaned out the cup with a moistened
fingertip and blew the dirt off the packages of food. By
the end of it she seemed calmer, strangely soothed.
Mike's outbursts had this effect on her sometimes.

"I'm sorry," Mike said. "I've let things get the best
of me."

"The man is almost seventy," said Audrey. "He drank. He smoked. It's his time, Mike."

"So it's *his* fault?"

"I didn't say that."

"Admit it: you never liked him. You thought he was stupid. Crude. Well, I've got news for you: before I met him, I was nothing. Zilch."

"I'm sorry, Mike."

"He's *dying*."

"I said I'm sorry."

After more accusations and more apologies, Mike put the backpack back on Audrey's shoulders. She unsnapped a pocket and fished around for something.

"Did you by any chance remember Vaseline?"

Mike looked baffled.

"My lips. It's dry up here."

"Fine. So quit. The air's too dry, give up."

"A tip from the master."

"What's that supposed to mean?"

Mike threw his arms up and turned his back on us. He hooked his thumbs in his backpack's shoulder straps and walked away down the woodchip-covered trail. I waited for Audrey to call him or to follow, but she stood still and Mike did not look back. As he was disappearing into the trees, Audrey sat down on the tailgate, unlaced a hiking boot, and held it upside down. A stone fell out.

"He *was* crude," she said. "And mean. Mike knows it, too. That's why he feels so guilty."

"Why?" I said.

"He's glad the old bastard's dying. Deep down, he's thrilled."

~ ~ ~

I'd been dreading the trip to Montana since Mike announced it. He was giving me a haircut in the basement, sweeping electric clippers up my neck, and leaving naked swaths of itchy gooseflesh. All my friends got their hair cut by professionals, but Mike claimed he could do a better job.

"Woody had a famous saying," he said. He squirted some 3-in-One oil on the clippers. "Until you're broken, you don't know what you're made of."

"Broken how?" I said. The clippers buzzed and chattered behind my temples.

"Your father could use a trip out west," Mike said. "I think we all could. A chance to push ourselves. I'm starting to feel like a worthless lump of fat. Look at me. Look at this gut. There's no excuse for it."

"Maybe you should start jogging again."

"Or shoot myself."

The threat was upsetting, but it was nothing new; it reminded me of the notes that I'd been finding since Mike had returned from the hospital in Michigan. I'd discovered the first one tucked inside a dictionary after Mike challenged me at the dinner table to define the word "culpable." He sent me to his den to look it up, and when I opened his Webster's, a slip of paper fluttered out.

We were his team, and we deserted him.
There will be a price to pay.
We're culpable.

The next note was under the pillow on my bed. I found it on the morning of my birthday, written across the portrait on a twenty-dollar bill.

They say time is money, but money
can't buy time. I've managed to waste
both things, so I know.

The third, most recent note was on the staircase when I went down to the basement for my haircut.

POSITIVES	NEGATIVES
Michigan varsity	*Made Mom's life hell as a kid*
Married Audrey Brolin, beating out West Pt. cadet	*Tobacco addict*
Paid off business loan six months early; made gym and health bar profitable second yr.	*Lost touch with God & nature & higher self*

Support my family

*Exaggerated minor
injury out of fear of
failure as an athlete,
letting down one man
who ever gave a damn*

The note was still in my pocket when Mike finished my haircut. I'd been thinking about it the whole time. Had he really faked his knee problem, or was he just being tough on himself? Even now, his right leg sometimes sagged after long drives and when he hadn't been sleeping well. Then again, when I thought back to Audrey's story of how the bad knee had cemented their romance—and when I considered Mike's own mother's knack for winning sympathy through misery—playing up pain seemed like something he might have done.

He showed me the back of my head in a hand mirror, but took it away before I could look closely. "Sit tight; I missed a spot. Don't budge." I heard a snipping sound and moved my eyes and saw a red Swiss Army knife, open to its little pair of scissors.

"You'll need one of these when we go out west," Mike said. "You could cut tinder, build a signal fire."

He trimmed around my ears. The scissors were dull.

"Remind me to get you the big one, with the saw," he said.

I didn't ask him why we'd need a signal fire.

~ ~ ~

Nailed to a post where the trail entered the woods was a hikers' registration box containing slips of paper and a pencil stub. I sharpened the stub with my knife and followed the instructions inside the box lid. I wrote down the size of our party, the date, and that we'd be gone for two days. When I dropped the slip in the box, I saw another slip.

> *Don't bother to follow.*
> *I need to be alone.*
> *I shouldn't have dragged you along on*
> *this. I'm sorry. I can get back to*
> *Minnesota by bus.*

I shoved the note in my pocket and kept walking; Joel and Audrey were still five minutes behind me. After a mile or so of level ground the trail started switching back and growing steeper. A trickle of water running down the middle deepened and widened and branched off into deltas, forcing me to jump in certain spots and tiptoe balance-beam style along dry ridges. My boots' waffled soles attracted clumps of mud, creating broad, heavy pads that felt like snowshoes. I trimmed the pads with a stick but they grew back.

Audrey and Joel approached, already puffing. The laces of Joel's boots were loose and dragging.

"I'm parched," Audrey said. "I forgot to carry wa-ter." A dry white crust had formed around her lips.

I handed over my dented tin canteen. "We have to conserve."

Audrey gulped the water and gave the canteen to Joel.

"Conserve," I said.

"Where are the iodine tablets?" Audrey said.

"Mike's pack."

"He thought of everything. Terrific."

The canteen came to me but I barely wet my lips. The sun was high and harsh above the peaks. Audrey brought out a Baggie of salty trail mix but I warned her that eating it would make her thirstier.

"We have to do *something* for energy," she said.

"I think Mike left me a Snickers."

"Starvation rations. He should have just shot us and put us out of our misery."

Out in the woods, so far from towns and people, the Snickers bar tasted unreal to me, synthetic. I outlined my plan as I broke it into thirds. I would go on ahead, walking fast, and Joel and Audrey could follow at their own pace. If, in three hours, I hadn't caught up with Mike, I'd come back and we'd pitch a tent and wait for him.

"So who gets to keep the water?" Audrey said.

I checked the canteen's neck and cap for leaks, then clipped it to a D-ring on Joel's pack. Tears had pearled in the corners of his eyes, and the tip of his nose was already pink from sunburn.

"What if he doesn't come back?" Joel said.

Audrey said, "Of course he's coming back. He's only trying to scare us."

"Why?" Joel said.

"For all I know, it's chemical. He wants us to understand how much we need him. He did it when he played football: walked out of practice until his teammates begged him to come back. It's how he lifts himself up when he feels low."

"I'll see you two in a couple of hours," I said.

"Stay. Don't let him play with you," said Audrey. "This is about attention. Don't give it to him."

I fingered the note in my pocket. Audrey was wrong. This was more serious than attention-getting. I reminded Joel to save water, then turned away. I walked slowly in case they wanted to join me, but when it was clear they weren't going to, I sped up.

~ ~ ~

I lit a cigarette with a waterproof match and looked up the side of the mountain, toward the snow. The zigzagging scar of the trail went up and up, vanishing into a stand of pines with brown exposed roots that shelved out over a cliff. There were hot spots on my shoulders under the pack straps where it felt like the skin was being rubbed away.

My endurance surprised me as I gained altitude. By staring at the ground and counting my steps I found I could easily mount the steepest grades. Each time I looked back to see how far I'd climbed, it was twice as far as I'd expected. My only regret was playing the martyr and leaving my canteen behind. Mistake. Rescuers have a right to be selfish, to put their mission first. Next time I put myself out for someone else I was going to make certain demands up front.

I knew I was weakening when I found myself wanting to pick and eat a ring of mushrooms growing on a log. I opened my trail guide to edible wild plants but couldn't match the mushrooms with any pictures. Horseflies were buzzing around my sweaty scalp. I slapped one with an open palm and combed out the crisp, stubby body with my fingernails. Next a wave of stinging gnats attacked. Their bites raised welts I could feel my heartbeat in.

I needed fluids. I was burning up.

Though Mike had warned me that drinking untreated water could give me parasites, I decided to risk it. I cupped my hands below a dribbling spring and splashed cold water on my face and lips. After the first drink, there seemed no point in stopping; either I'd been infected or I hadn't. I drank until my stomach strained my belt and I wondered how long it would be before the cramps came, if they came at all. I might get lucky. Maybe Mother Nature cut breaks for people when she saw them doing the right thing.

The next priority was to treat my sunburn. Using my Swiss Army knife, I sliced strips of cloth from a T-shirt

in my pack and tied them around my head in a loose
turban. That's when I remembered Audrey's makeup
bag. I took it from my pack, removed the lipstick, and
scooped out a blob of it with the smallest knife blade. I
spread the cool grease across my nose and forehead, sealing out the sun.

I'd come through, alone, with no one's help. I inspected my face in the mirror of Audrey's compact and
liked what I saw: a painted wild man. Appearances no
longer mattered. Just the mission.

I pounded my chest with my fists and whooped my
name. It disappointed me not to hear an echo.

~ ~ ~

I reached a spot on the trail where fires had burned.
Without their needles, the trees seemed thin and spindly, and in the coal and ash green plants were growing,
some of them with yellow starlike flowers. Now and
then I heard a chattering squirrel, but otherwise the
forest seemed deserted. I'd expected the mountains to be
filled with wildlife, but instead they felt like a vacant
stadium or a big house whose owners have moved away.

I stopped and touched my stomach. No discomfort.
Apparently, the water had been pure. I raked another
dead fly out of my hair.

Suddenly, I heard voices up ahead. A man and a
woman came striding down the trail, followed by a pant-
ing yellow Lab with a red bandanna around its neck.
The couple had lean, bowed legs and sun-worn faces.

Various camping tools and cooking utensils dangled from loops on their army surplus rucksacks.

"Down the up staircase," the man said, coming near me. He handed a plastic bottle to his companion, who squeezed the sides and drank the arc of spray. These people knew what they were doing. They were serious.

The woman passed me the water. I drank and drank. I was too far gone to be polite.

"You lose two quarts an hour up here," the man said. He fixed me with a disapproving stare. "Tell me you're not alone up here this evening."

"I'm here with my family. We got separated."

The man faced the woman. "They got separated."

"I'm wondering if you passed someone?" I said. "Tall guy. Unshaven. Orange pack. Green shirt. He has a bad leg, so maybe he was walking funny."

"Don't tell me he's in your party?"

I kept my mouth shut.

"You listen up," the man said, pointing a finger. "These mountains are not a playground. They're not a park. Getting 'separated' has consequences. Lacing your *boots* too tight has consequences."

The woman said, "Loring, regulate. You'll frighten him."

"This is not good," said Loring. "This is bad. Besides your father—and yes, we passed him—how many more of you are there?"

"Only two. How did he seem?" I said. "Upset? Depressed?"

The couple looked at each other with lowered eyes. I got the feeling they'd been alone so long that they no longer needed to use words.

"You're coming with us," the man said. "That's an order. We can send up a ranger once we're down. If your father is having some kind of mental episode, it's better if he deals with an authority figure. Come on, let's go, kid."

"I can't."

"You want to die up here? Is *that* the plan?"

"I don't have a plan."

"I see that. What have you been doing for liquids? Don't tell me."

I sidestepped the couple and broke into a trot. My turban unwound in the breeze and blew away and the heat of my breath began to melt the lipstick covering my face. I realized I must have looked crazy to the couple, and yet they hadn't said a word about it, either out of kindness or from embarrassment. The thought made me want to put more distance between us, and when I heard them calling after me, I pressed my hands to my ears and started running.

~ ~ ~

I began to find things on the ground. Sunglasses. A coil of rope. Some tent stakes. I collected the objects as I walked, but when they got heavy I stashed them under a boulder. A few minutes later I glimpsed Mike's pack lying off the trail on a steep slope, its contents strewn about like crash debris. Either it had burst open during its fall or a wild animal had found it.

It was time to stop and put my thoughts together. I shrugged off my pack and leaned it against a rock, then turned in a slow circle to get my bearings. I was standing at the bottom of a gravel field, below an icy, teakettle-shaped peak. I called out Mike's name but my voice seemed weak and small.

I considered turning back but I didn't feel up to it. I didn't feel up to going forward, either. It hit me then that the hikers had been right: a person could die this way. From indecision. From not being able to do anything but stand there feeling his heart beat and his mouth dry up.

I had to eat. I dug through my pack and came up with a package of freeze-dried Stroganoff. I bit off a chunk that melted to salty broth and looked around for wood to build a fire. I was too high, though—well above the tree line. I started pulling up hunks of dry brown grass, then I tore up my field guide, added it to the pile, and struck a paraffin match. A flame burst up. Even once it was going strong, though, it gave off no real warmth. It seemed to need all its heat just to keep burning.

I called out again. No response. Again. Again.

Finally, an answer. "I'm over here."

"Where are you?"

"Hurry up, I'm freezing. *Hurry.*"

It was dark by then. I followed Mike's voice across

the gravel field, stepping with care but slipping and trip-
ping anyway. Ahead, I saw water shining. Reflected
stars. The moon was an egg, just short of full, and orange. A rodent stood up on a rock in silhouette and
shrilly chuckled, then skittered out of sight.

"I'm coming. Stay still. Are you hurt?"

A wavering groan. Too unsteady and strangled to be
an act.

The footing was swampy. The suction slowed me
down. One leg sunk down to the thigh in muck and
when I pulled it free my boot came off. That's when I
spotted him, lying on a rock slab. His T-shirt was
stained dark around the bottom and one of his legs lay
extended in the pond as if it had been burned and he
was cooling it.

"I cut myself. It's deep. It isn't clotting."

There is the normal brain and the first-aid brain. I
switched on my first-aid brain. The leg in the pond was
surrounded by a haze visible as a distortion of the star-
shine. The water was bleeding Mike, leeching out his
blood. I crouched, got hold of the leg, and lifted it, but
couldn't locate the cut for all the dripping.

"Where is it?"

"Kneecap. Put it down again."

"It needs to be elevated. Christ," I said.

I saw the wound: a pair of ragged flaps around a
shredded lump of oozing meat. The blood welled up and
warmed my numbing fingers as I managed to cradle the
leg with one hand and unbutton my shirt with the

other. I bit down hard on my collar, tore it free, then started bandaging.

"You must be thinking I wasn't serious. I would have cut my wrist if I'd been serious. That's what you always hear about: the wrist. Isn't that what you always hear about?"

The trauma had soured Mike's breath; I turned my face away. "Lie still," I said.

"You followed me."

"I had to."

Mike clutched my arm and pulled himself half upright. "I want to kiss you. You followed me. You came."

The kiss was all beard, all scratch. It scoured my cheek.

"I'm better now. I feel better now," Mike said. "Lighter or something. Clearer."

My stomach gurgled and turned over. "Oh God."

"What is it?"

"Nothing." I gave Mike my shoulder. He held on tight.

"I faked the whole thing. I was fine after the surgery. All the knee needed was a little exercise. Woody knew. I could see it in his face. Your mother knew, too. She just pretended she didn't. She had her reasons, I guess. I had mine, too. Sometimes I wish they'd sawed the whole damn leg off."

It was an interesting speech, enlightening, but I was in no shape to take it in. The parasites had come to life inside me. Millions of them, nibbling their way out.

A breeze blew across the pond and shattered the moon.

~ ~ ~

We started down the mountain in the dark. I made Mike wear long pants to cover the bandage and I broke off a tent pole for him as a cane. And though the limp he'd given himself was real, it seemed like he was hamming this up, too, teasing out the dramatic possibilities. He hobbled, he hopped, he slumped, he stiffened. I told him that if he didn't cut it out I'd take away the cane.

He cut it out.

I was suffering, too. The cramps came on gradually, with mounting force. The first ones struck a minute or two apart; I handled them by clenching my stomach muscles. Then they accelerated and spread out. I couldn't hold back. Hot pliers wrenched my gut. The liquid drained down my leg into my boot and the stench hit me hard and cleared my sinuses. The next gush, full of gas and bubbles, was blisteringly hot, all steam and acid.

"Don't stop," I said. Mike was slowing.

"It hurts."

"Don't whine."

Time flattened out. The woods were quiet, birdless. Every few minutes Mike would start explaining himself. Audrey's love had drained him of his drive, making a pro career seem grim and miserable. But football had spoiled him for a normal life, pumping him full of juice that made his heart pound, even in his sleep. He'd sold his mind and education short by coming on as he-man to sell hunting knives. I asked him to save it; to speak to a professional. I told him my job was to get him down the hill and his job was to look normal when we got there.

The sky was lightening when we saw the glow of Joel and Audrey's campfire. Either they hadn't gone to sleep or they'd just woken up. The couple was with them. Loring sat next to the fire holding a skillet; he flipped a pancake and the others clapped. Their camp smelled of coffee and bacon and burning sap and they seemed to be having a high old time together. Audrey hummed a bar of an old cowboy song and everyone joined in, Joel keeping time with a saucepan and a spoon. The others rocked side to side and waved their cups.

Mike let go of my shoulder and sat down. He rested his cane on his lap and bowed his head.

"You coming?" I said. "I need liquid. I have a parasite."

"I can't."

"New rule. It's simple." Mike raised his eyes to me. "Whatever you can't do, you have to do. You got it? The worse it hurts, the more you smile. Get up. And no sad stories. You got lost. I found you. An everyday adventure in the woods."

Mike took his time, but eventually he stood. I told him to leave the cane behind. He dropped it.

"Good. Now walk. Chin up. No limping. Good."

"You're stronger than I am. I've sold you short," Mike said.

I'd been waiting a long time for him to say this, but somehow it didn't please me the way it should have. I'd hoped we'd be strong together, not just one of us. I hadn't planned on being strong alone.

kingdom come

1

When the doorbell rang and I rose to answer it, putting down a book from the school library on jobs in the communications industry, how was I to know a new religion was waiting on our porch?

They were no more than boys, just a few years older than me. They looked like college athletes dressed for a banquet in suits and ties and name tags. Black vinyl briefcases hung from their right hands and I could smell talcum powder on their skin. One boy was blond, with a smallish, turned-up nose and pebbly cheeks the texture of elbow skin. The other was dark and handsome and wore glasses whose lenses were thickly smudged with fingerprints. A scar from a cleft palate operation knotted his upper lip. He lisped a little.

"My name is Elder Jessup," he said, "and this is my partner, Elder Knowles. We'd like to speak with you, if possible, about God's plan for the American family."

I waited for him to say more. He'd startled me.

"It's Elder Knowles and my privilege to represent the Church of Jesus Christ of Latter-Day Saints."

"The Mormons," Elder Knowles said. "Ever heard of us?"

I had, in fact. I'd seen their ads. Beautifully shot and cast with flawless models, the inspirational television spots, stuck between commercials for cars and wine, had always jarred me a little, but in a good way. Their style was corny but professional, their messages mysterious yet reassuring. They seemed to promise a life of health and peace, of cheerful board games played in front of fireplaces and nourishing suppers shared in cozy kitchens. What's more, I remembered meeting a Mormon boy at Camp Overcome—a bed wetter named Tyson from Salt Lake City who'd covered his ears when the campers told dirty jokes and had the blondest hair I'd ever seen.

I smiled at the elders and let them make their pitch. They couldn't have come at a better time, as far as I was concerned. Woody Wolff had finally passed away that month and things were dire at home. And though later on, when I'd won the elders' trust, they would reveal to me the sneaky trick behind their perfect timing, their sudden appearance struck me as miraculous. They were the sort of help that I'd been praying for, although I didn't call my wishes prayers yet.

"Is the head of the house in?" Elder Jessup asked. For a moment I didn't know whom he was talking about.

"He is," I said.

"Is he available?"

"He should be."

Because it was ten in the morning on a Wednesday, this was an embarrassing admission. Mike had been stopped for drunk driving that weekend while coming home from an ice-fishing trip and he hadn't been to his store for three days. And though I should have been in school myself that morning, I had a valid excuse. Because of a foul-up at the pharmacy (they'd switched my five-milligram tablets for tens) I'd taken too much Ritalin that morning and gone back to bed with a racing heart.

"Tell him we have good news," said Elder Knowles. "Also, a book your family can read and keep."

Just then, from the TV room off the entrance hall, Mike's voice rose in a dreamy, tuneless song that had been bubbling out of him for days: *Nobody knows me. My life is halfway through. Mike Cobb is a pair of footprints. The footprint man . . .*

Elder Knowles bit his lip and turned to face the side-

walk. Our dog sauntered up and licked his fingertips.
Elder Jessup set down his black briefcase on the thresh-
old.

"I think we'd better come inside," he said.

~ ~ ~

It could happen anywhere, at any time—Mike making
crazy music of his thoughts. The sporting goods store, a
Saturday afternoon. Mike and I are restocking the thermal underwear. I misplace the price list from the whole-
saler and Mike pipes up with a droning, distant jingle
that sounds like an ad from the radio, but isn't: *Time's
running out. Don't shout. Don't run about. Everybody
knows time's running out.* Or maybe we're in the high
school gym at the district speech meet and I've just
concluded an impromptu talk on "Polluted Rivers, Polluted Dreams." As the judges and coaches shake my
hand, a voice warbles up from the middle of the audience: *My son is proud. He thinks he's made his stand.
So did Michael Cobb, the footprint man.* And though
everyone pretends that they don't hear this and goes
right on congratulating me, I hear the song loud and
clear. It's all I hear.

The nights at home were even harder on me. Audrey
had left Maple Glen and had found new job at the hospital, working the late shift again, and after she left the
house I'd lie awake trying to drown out the singing I
knew was coming by listening to *Night Hearts* on the
radio. The program's host, Joe Sloane, a former baseball

player and certified social worker, counseled anonymous callers nationwide, advising Jim D. to throw away his diet pills and start a regular exercise program, encouraging Catherine L. to leave her boyfriend and finish her law degree. *Night Hearts'* signal came in sharp and clear from its Omaha home station, and listening to it in the dark while Mike yodeled softly and spookily in his bedroom helped me to view our family's hurts and troubles as part of some vast American misery that it was no disgrace to be a part of.

In the daytime my big concern was visitors. If Mike was at home and a car drove in our driveway, I'd leap into action, shutting all the doors between whichever room he happened to be in and the entrance hall. I'd turn up the TV or blast the stereo while Audrey, zonked out in her bedroom wearing earplugs, slept through the whole crisis. And whatever it took to get rid of people, I'd do it: sign for packages, order Girl Scout cookies, sponsor some fifth grader's diabetes walkathon. No one got past me, no one heard Mike's singing. The Mormon missionaries were the first.

~ ~ ~

When Elder Jessup and Elder Knowles first saw him, Mike was propped on his side on the sofa, reading the blueprints for the gym and health bar he was opening behind the store. His eyes were red and had no eyelashes. He tended to pluck them when he felt anxious, and lately I'd been finding them everywhere—lying in the bathroom sink, floating in glasses of milk. Without any lashes, his eyes grew sore and runny, filling with dust and forcing him to blink a lot.

"Morning," he said, not bothering to sit up.

The elders extended their hands. Mike raised himself partway and shook them limply, letting go before it was polite to.

"We're from the LDS church," said Elder Jessup. His scar kept his upper lip from fully extending when he tried to smile.

"I've seen you around town," Mike said. "I figured you'd have to hit this house eventually." He set his blueprints on the floor and sat up the rest of the way. "Are you boys thirsty?"

"Thank you. Yes. Plain water would be fine."

Mike looked at me. "Get these boys a glass of water."

"We have some orange juice," I said.

Elder Jessup gave his strained half-smile. "Plain water. And a moment of your time."

Already, just a few minutes into the visit, our house felt lighter, less gloomy, better ventilated; I wanted the elders to stay all morning, if possible. I fixed a pitcher of ice water with lemon slices, the way I'd seen Audrey do for summer parties. The elders held out their glasses as I poured, making throaty sounds of gratitude, then took simultaneous sips and grinned.

"It can't taste *that* good, it's from the tap," Mike said.

"It's the lemon," said Elder Knowles. "I've never had that."

"You're overdoing it, boys. Sit down," Mike said.

After I pulled up armchairs for the elders, Elder Jessup squared his briefcase on his lap and fingered the brass latches near its handle.

"What do you know about man's fate?" he said. His tone was businesslike.

"You tell me," Mike said.

Elder Jessup touched a latch and his briefcase sprung open with surprising suddenness. Inside it were elastic pockets holding an assortment of colorful pamphlets. He chose a red one and put it on the coffee table, snapping it down like a winning card.

"The basics are all in here," he said. "God's plan for mankind, from preexistence on. Mormons believe that everything that happens to us is the result of choice, of conscious choice. You see, we believe that souls come down to earth already knowing about their lives to come."

Mike turned over the pamphlet and scanned the back. "Meaning I don't have to read this twice," he said:

"How's that?" Elder Knowles said. He looked truly confused. "Have you had missionaries here before?"

"He read it in preexistence," I said. "He's kidding you."

The elders didn't laugh. Their eyes grew clouded. Elder Knowles turned his glass of water in front of his face as if inspecting it for particles. I wondered if he'd spotted a stray eyelash.

"You've caught me at a busy time," Mike said. He picked up his documents and shuffled them. His filthy white T-shirt was smeared with mustard stains. "Tell me something, though. I'm curious. How often, when you knock on someone's door and they're polite enough to let you in, do you actually get a new member? What's your batting average?"

Elder Jessup shut his case and stood. Elder Knowles stood, too, with a slight lag. He was the follower here, the apprentice.

"Did my question offend you?" Mike said. "I didn't mean it to."

"We don't keep statistics," Elder Jessup said. "Ideally, what happens is what's happening here: first there's resistance, then curiosity, and then—when the person's had a chance to think—a phone call inviting us back. That's what we're hoping for."

"In the meantime, you'll pray for me," Mike said.

"Yes, we will."

"Good luck with it. Don't strain yourself."

"Good-bye, sir."

I showed the elders out to the front porch, where Elder Knowles reached deep into his case and brought out a dark blue book: the Book of Mormon. I thanked him for it and promised him I'd read it, although I suspected I wouldn't. I was mad at the elders for giving up so easily after promising so much.

"Our number's inside the cover," Elder Jessup said. "How old are you?"

"Seventeen soon."

"Any siblings?"

"One little brother. Fourteen."

"Take care of him. My partner and I are leaving you in charge here, so call us when the time comes. We'll be waiting. Remember, you chose your life in preexistence, so you already know inside what you have to do."

"Explain that to him further," said Elder Knowles.

"It's in the book. He can read it for himself. I don't want to spoil it for him."

"Thanks," I said.

The elders said good-bye to me and left. In the driveway they fastened clips around their pants legs and mounted two old-fashioned bicycles with baskets. They had to stand up on their pedals and push down hard to get some traction on the snow and ice. Behind me, as I was turning to enter the house, I heard a song beginning. I couldn't go in. I opened the Book of Mormon and started reading, standing in the cold.

~ ~ ~

Before the missionaries came, the only religious book I'd seen at home was a dusty, untouchable antique: the Cobb Family Bible. We kept it sealed in plastic, stored in a chest with diplomas and insurance policies. As thick as a dictionary and written in German, the Bible was covered in brittle, cracked, green leather. The only real contact I'd ever had with it came when I was in second grade and told a lie about seeing a timberwolf lurking on the playground. Mike asked me to set my right hand on the Bible and tell the truth, but I didn't, and nothing happened. The only other item in the house that seemed to have anything to do with God was the framed copy of the *Desiderata* Audrey had hung on the wall above Joel's bed after he'd lost an important tennis match and was considering quitting the whole sport.

Maybe because it seemed so unfamiliar, from its crisp gold-edged pages to its long concordance full of ancient-sounding names, I approached the Book of Mormon with real reverence. After poring over the first few chapters, though, I knew I'd never finish it. The language was stiff and old-fashioned and repetitive, worse than the *Desiderata* even, and I found no mention at all of preexistence, let alone any convincing explanation of how a person could live a life he'd already previewed in detail and still tell lies he knew that he'd be caught in or ask out girls he knew would cut him cold.

The pamphlet the elders left behind was better. I read it one night while listening to *Night Hearts*, which made its message seem more vital somehow. The pamphlet said families come together on earth in order to help one another achieve salvation. Each individual has a role to play, for no one can gain perfection on his own. We choose these roles before birth and then forget them, but after death we remember them perfectly and see how, in fact, they worked out for the best.

I was rereading the pamphlet when Audrey came in on her way to work.

"Your brother has pinkeye," she said. "I put some drops out. Make sure he uses them first thing in the morning."

"Sure will," I said with my newfound sense of usefulness.

"What's that thing?" Audrey nodded at the pamphlet.

"The Mormons left it."

"The Mormons? When were *they* here?"

"The other morning. You were still in bed. Mike gave them a hard time and made them leave, though."

Audrey's mouth shrunk.

"He kidded them, that's all. It's nothing to worry about. Just a little kidding."

After I heard Audrey leave the house, I turned off *Night Hearts* and did some quiet, hard thinking. The idea that our family had volunteered to live together, knowing our fates were in one another's hands, convinced me of my duty. It was time.

Mike was propped up in bed with a wineglass, holding a pen above a blank new legal pad.

"Come to see the footprint man," he said. The phrase referred to a show on ancient man, *Footprints in the Sands of Time*, that we'd been watching the night of Woody Wolff's death.

"Do you do this when Audrey's around, or just when I am?"

Mike blinked his naked, lashless eyes. He rubbed his

fist in one. I picked up the bedside phone and handed it to him.

"We're calling the Mormon elders," I said. "I'll dial."

Mike held the phone. He wasn't stopping me. I dialed, then heard ringing and an answer.

"It's me," Mike said. They talked for almost two hours.

~ ~ ~

Elder Jessup set up a movie projector like the ones we'd used years ago at school. It weighed a ton and was made of dull gray metal. He clipped on the reels and threaded the film through while Elder Knowles stood ready to dim the lights.

"Most of our movies are on video now, but this one's not for some reason," Elder Jessup said. "It's a shame. It's my favorite. *Extremely* powerful."

The elders went on fussing with the projector while the rest of us sat patiently in the dark, facing a square of stark white light on the living room wall. Mike and Audrey held hands on the sofa. Joel and I sat at their feet on the rug. Tonight was our first lesson, our new beginning. Audrey had date bars baking for afterward.

The movie began with a scene of freeway traffic. Horns honked. Exhaust rose. The sky was smoggy, foul. A narrator's voice said, "Man is in a hurry. But why? To what purpose? Does he even know?"

"This next part's incredible," Elder Knowles said quietly. Elder Jessup raised a finger to hush him.

The camera zoomed in on a red-faced well-dressed man stuck in a luxury car behind a semi. His jaw was clenched. He was muttering under his breath. Suddenly, he grimaced and clutched his chest. His head tipped forward and rested on the wheel. The very next instant, we were at a funeral. Flowers. A crowd. A pretty young woman dressed in black flanked by two blond little girls wearing hats.

The voice said: "Separation. Death. The end."

Elder Knowles snapped his fingers. "Happens just like that."

The voice said, "Nothingness. Blackness. Is that what *you* believe? Well, we don't. For us, the family is eternal, and earthly death is merely the beginning of the amazing story we want to tell you."

The movie grew complicated after that, dense with experts, quotations, and history lessons, and even the elders' attention seemed to drift. I watched Mike through the corner of my eye. He crossed and uncrossed his legs and scratched his arms as Audrey stroked his neck and swirled his hair around. "What is it?" I heard her whisper at one point, during a scene where the resurrected father hugged his wife and girls with ghostly arms. Mike didn't answer her.

As the movie was ending the projector broke. There was an awful smell of burning plastic and the picture turned brown at the edges and started bubbling. Elder Jessup jumped up and pulled the plug.

"Almost wrecked our only print," he said.

Elder Knowles rushed in to cover him. "So what did you think, Mrs. Cobb? Did you enjoy it?"

"I liked the scenes of the pioneers the best. The sacrifices those women made. Incredible."

"*Mr.* Cobb?"

Mike didn't answer immediately. He had the about-to-sing look on his face. Tiny muscles struggled near his mouth. His eyes were dreamy, absent.

I flared a look at him. "It was great," I said.

Mike seemed to recover slightly. "Very emotional. Very professional job. Realistic heart attack."

Elder Knowles looked thrilled. "That actor, you might like to know, is a convert. He's actually a bishop in Los Angeles. There's lots of Mormons in entertainment these days. There's a rumor around that we might get Elton John soon."

"The famous singer," Mike said. " 'Rocket Man.' "

"One of his all-time best," said Elder Knowles. He began to hum the melody. Elder Jessup sang some of the words. Then Mike joined in.

But it was a false alarm. Just normal singing. It ended after half a verse and Audrey went to the kitchen for the date bars.

~ ~ ~

Although we were only halfway through our lessons and still four weeks away from being baptized, we started attending Sunday services at the nearest Mormon church. Thirty miles away in north St. Paul, the chapel was built of pale yellow brick and looked like a clinic or elementary school. The only color was an American flag in a bed of budding daffodils. The flagpole was even higher than the steeple, which seemed odd to me. Also, the steeple was plain—it lacked a cross. I asked Elder Jessup how come.

"Let's think it through. Say Jesus Christ had been murdered by a firing squad. Would people put sculptures of rifles on their churches? Or say he'd been hung. With a noose."

I pictured these scenes.

"Anything else?" Elder Jessup said. "Don't be the least bit embarrassed. It's what I'm here for."

"Preexistence still confuses me sort of. Let's say I have children someday."

"Of course you will."

"Well, my children already exist as spirits, right? So does that mean they're watching everything I do trying to decide if they still want me and how they're going to help me out in life?"

Elder Jessup nodded. "That's basically accurate. Why? Does it scare you?"

"It makes me dizzy."

"That's natural. You're taking in lots of new information these days at a pretty incredible pace. I'm proud of you."

The next Sunday was a fast Sunday. Except for Joel, who'd eaten an English muffin when Audrey became concerned about his blood sugar, we arrived at the chapel with empty stomachs. Mike seemed grumpy and tired, but I felt fine; pleasantly light-headed and alert. Elder Jessup seemed cheerful, too, but Elder Knowles, a much huskier kid, looked dazed. He had his digital watch on upside down and there were oozing shaving cuts on his chin.

The meetings and services lasted half the day. Audrey went to Relief Society, the organization for Mormon women, while Mike joined the elders at a priesthood meeting. Joel and I went to a younger priesthood meeting. All faithful Mormon males were priests, I'd learned, and possessed such powers as healing and tongues, which Elder Jessup explained to me once as the ability to translate languages, both foreign and ancient, without studying them.

The topic in priesthood that morning was survival. The church believed in preparing for emergencies and all Mormon families were urged to stockpile two years' worth of food and water, I learned. Various methods of storage were discussed and soy pellets were praised for their longevity. I left the meeting depressed. The goal of outliving the general population after a nuclear war or major catastrophe seemed selfish to me. And lonely. Very lonely.

At the sacrament service following the meeting a squad of teenage boys in suits and ties passed around silver trays of torn-up bread and tiny paper cups of water. It was the elders' first food of the day, but the rest of us had to pass. We weren't full Mormons yet.

Afterward, when we were finally free to eat, we drove the elders to a Perkins restaurant. The elders tucked their ties inside their shirts and dove into their sausage links and hotcakes, surprising me with their lazy table manners. Mike ate an omelet bursting with orange cheese and Audrey and I had Belgian waffles piled high with berries and banana slices, while Joel ordered oatmeal from the Lite-Line menu.

"So?" said Elder Jessup, leaning back once we'd cleaned our plates. "Think you can do it?"

"I feel good," said Audrey.

"Describe that feeling."

"The church is like a community," she said. "It's not just us on our own now. Just the four of us. We have all these new friends who want the best for us."

"Joel?" Elder Jessup said.

"I'm scared. The war. In priesthood they said there's going to be a war maybe."

The elders looked at each other with merry eyes. "Don't you go worrying," Elder Jessup said. "That war won't be for a while, and you'll live through it."

"We all will," Elder Knowles said. "Guaranteed."

It was my turn to comment. I didn't know what to say. I felt like our family had gotten itself into something that we might have trouble getting out of. If only I could remember my preexistence. If only I could remember what I'd seen when I'd surveyed our future before my birth.

"You keep thinking, Justin," Elder Jessup said. He turned to Mike. "So tell us: is it a go?"

"Whatever they want. They seem happy."

"What do *you* want? You're the father. The decision maker."

The waitress came with our check then. She seemed unsure about whom to give it to, so she tucked it under the pepper shaker in the middle of the table. Mike slipped it out. He reached behind himself, got out his wallet, drew out a credit card, and held it high, trying to catch the waitress's attention. Everybody started chatting again, as if we'd forgotten a question had been asked. When it was time to go and we stood up together, I saw Elder Jessup open a small brown date book and scribble "Cobb baptism" across one square.

~ ~ ~

Audrey moved a step stool into the liquor closet and started handing things down to me: pint and quart bottles of whiskey, gin, and vodka, packets of powdered margarita mix, jars of cocktail onions, tins of cherries. I packed everything in a cardboard box lined with plastic so it wouldn't leak, then taped the box shut and got another one. The last item was a stack of paper napkins printed with truth-or-dare-style party questions. "Have you ever pinched a waitress? Where?" "How long was your worst-ever hangover, in days?"

"I feel like I ought to donate all this junk," Audrey said as she stepped down from the stool. "Who to, though? The VFW? The Elks?"

Next we collected tobacco products. Raiding drawers and closets all over the house, we threw away pipe cleaners, ashtrays, lighters, matches. Mike talked about keeping a couple old briar pipes—one of them had been his grandfather's, he said—but Audrey advocated a clean sweep. We crushed packs of cigarettes, tossed out cans of snuff, and even got rid of the filthy mason jars Mike kept in his workshop as spittoons.

"Maybe we're going overboard," he said as Audrey twist-tied another garbage bag. "It feels like we're sacrificing family history."

"We are," Audrey said. "That's the point. Be ruthless, baby."

Tea and coffee things went next, including a new Mr. Coffee machine that Audrey had bought the same day the elders showed up. On top of it we piled magazines—*Esquire*s and *Vogue*s and *Harper's Bazaar*s. We saved our *National Geographic*s and Mike's *Field and Stream*s but discarded some old *Life*s. The difference between the publications seemed clear to us.

But we still weren't finished. We kept finding things. Decks of cards. Poker chips. A Ouija board. I knew that the project had gotten out of hand when I saw Audrey hovering near the shelf containing the series of Time-Life

Ancient Mysteries books that Joel had secretly ordered off TV once by memorizing the number on Mike's Visa card:

"What are these about exactly?" she asked me.

"They're fine," I said. "They're the only books he reads. One's about Stonehenge."

"Joel, can you come here?" she yelled.

She thought for a moment and then called out, "Forget it." Then, to me:

"I'm losing it. Need food."

The porch was overflowing with boxes and bags by the end of the day, but rather than hauling them out to the street for the garbage truck, Mike insisted on driving them to the dump. I volunteered to go with him but he said no. I suspected he wanted to salvage a few things.

~ ~ ~

I woke up early the morning of our baptism and waited in the kitchen for the elders. Audrey was still at work and Mike was sleeping. Joel was in the bathroom, learning to tie a tie. I boiled water for Postum, a coffee substitute that Mike complained tasted like moldy toast but drank by the mugful nevertheless, then opened my Book of Mormon for a quick, last skim.

Audrey came in yawning from her night shift.

"Bad one. Full moon. Lots of accidents," she said. She spooned some Postum into a blue cup. "You ready?"

"I am. I'm all dressed."

"That tie looks nice on you. Is that one of Mike's? It's so dashing."

"It's mine," I said. "Elder Knowles helped me pick it out."

"That lifts my spirits. Maybe we won't lose touch with everything, after all."

While Audrey was upstairs changing into a dress, the elders drove up in a borrowed car and came to the door with a bouquet of flowers. I put them in water, then read the clipped-on note: "Your Heavenly Father welcomes you to his garden."

"We're going to drive you ourselves," said Elder Jessup. "I hope that's okay with your folks. It's safer."

"How?"

"The devil loves to play tricks at the last minute. He might cause a wreck or something. We've seen it happen."

I heard a toilet flush upstairs and wire hangers scraping on a clothes bar. Joel appeared in the kitchen with his tie tied wrong, its thin part hanging lower than its fat part. Elder Knowles said, "I'll show you a trick," and started adjusting it.

"The thing I still wonder," I said to Elder Jessup, "is how you knew. How you knew we needed you. Is that preexistence, too?"

"God led us here."

"Go ahead and tell him," Elder Knowles said. "He'll be out on a mission of his own soon."

Elder Jessup fiddled with his cuffs. "My partner and I are detectives, in a way. We scout around for clues. For leads. We hear things."

"You saw him somewhere. You caught him singing," I said.

"No," Elder Jessup said. "It's nothing like that."

I sensed him growing nervous, backing off. I faced Elder Knowles, who'd just finished arranging Joel's tie.

"This town has an LDS pharmacist," he said. "Sometimes we eat dinner at his house. Don't worry, he's not a spy, just very helpful. He gets concerned about certain customers, the ones who are maybe taking too much medicine."

"The store where we get our prescriptions?" I said. "The *Rexall*?" I was shocked; this seemed illegal. Unfair.

"Tim, that was stupid," Elder Jessup said. "That was idiotic. What a moron. Somebody's going to kick your Mormon butt for that."

We were late getting going, though only by a few minutes. Elder Jessup drove with special care, checking his mirrors in a steady rotation and staying five miles per hour below the speed limit. Audrey, Joel, and I huddled in the backseat and Mike rode up front, wedged in between the elders. I found it hard to look at him. His new short haircut and clean white collar, the dabs of shaving cream behind his ears and smell of witch hazel coming off his neck, reminded me of a man on trial, a suspect being escorted to a courtroom.

To block out this thought and some others that were bothering me, I rehearsed the baptism in my mind, going over the ritual step by step just as Elder Jessup had described it for us. We'd enter the chapel. We'd put on soft white robes. There would be an audience. A crowd. We'd pray together as a church and family, and then, one by one, we'd be led to the baptismal font. We'd go down barefoot into the clear pool, rest our bodies against the elders' arms, and let ourselves be slowly lowered, backward. We'd have to trust them, they'd warned us, or we'd flinch. We'd have to go limp, like dolls, or we might splash.

Despite our nerves, things went off without a hitch. The water was cool and clear and deep, and afterward, when I dried my hair, I could smell swimming pool chemicals on the towel. We gathered in a room with a buffet table and snacked on corn chips and cheese dip prepared by our new Mormon brothers and sisters, who offered their hands in welcome and gave us hugs. Mike kept his arm around Audrey, their faces glowing, and Joel was surrounded by a flock of girls in frilly blouses and long, old-fashioned skirts. Elder Jessup settled his hands on my shoulders and said, "When you're on your own mission, remember this. This is the payoff: bringing in new souls. I swear, there's no better feeling in the world." He looked in my eyes and I looked into his, thinking back to our talks on preexistence and wondering why, if I'd known him before my birth, he seemed like such a stranger suddenly.

2

Mike started taking his Mormonism seriously. At church he made friends with a group of men his age who heated their homes with wood, owned diesel generators, and stockpiled Krugerrands in safe-deposit boxes. Though some of these men had higher-level jobs at major corporations in St. Paul, they didn't let their families watch TV, and they traded books with titles like *Prepare!* and *Riding Out the Crash*. They attended gun shows and swap meets throughout the state, and Mike would come home from these outings all fired up about our family's potential for self-sufficiency.

"Living in town," he said to me one night, "is like being on life support in a hospital. Sooner or later they're going to pull the plug."

"Why?"

"Because they can. To show their power."

"What would it get them?"

"A terrible satisfaction."

In anticipation of the time when nothing modern could be depended on, Mike began pulling plugs of his own. He moved our TV set out to the garage and fitted our thermostat with a governor that kept the house at a nippy sixty degrees. He kept the cassette deck and stereo receiver but threw out all but two of our tapes: the Mormon Tabernacle Choir's rendition of *The Man of La Mancha* and *A Nat King Cole Christmas*.

Audrey, who'd grown pious in her own way, tried to relieve our sense of deprivation by focusing Joel and me on mystical matters such as the power of prayer. Her enthusiasm was touching, but slightly frantic. Now that we had no TV to pass the evenings, we'd sit with her at the kitchen table listening to stories she'd heard at church concerning sudden cancer remissions and miraculous recoveries of long-lost valuables.

Her favorite story, which she told us twice, was of a young woman who learned that she was pregnant, had an abortion, and then regretted it. She spent a whole weekend praying with the bishop, and a few months later gave birth to healthy twin girls. That Audrey, a nurse, could believe this story worried me.

"You're saying the Heavenly Father restored her pregnancy?"

"The person who told me this story doesn't lie," she said.

"Maybe the girl didn't really have an abortion."

"The rational mind can't handle it. I know."

The more Mike got down to basics around the house, the deeper Audrey's mysticism grew. The week he in-stalled a basement backup generator, she brought home a book which purported to demonstrate, by assigning nu-merical values to the Greek and Hebrew alphabets, the divine perfection of the Bible. " 'Jehovah' adds up to twelve," she informed me. "So does 'Jesus Christ'. An accident?" Armed with a pencil and a spiral notebook in which to record her cryptic calculations, she studied the book every morning after breakfast and by noon she'd be in a tizzy of speculation.

"I added our names up. My name comes to nine. Yours is seven. Mike's is also seven. Nine plus seven plus seven is twenty-three. Two plus three equals five. And guess what five is?"

I shook my head.

"The word 'family' comes to five."

"You left out a number for Joel."

"He's seven."

"*I'm* seven."

Audrey's face fell. "You're right. He's six." She scribbled something. "Give me a little time to readjust this."

I began avoiding Audrey in order to escape such con-
versations. For the first time since I was eight or nine
years old, I started spending time with Joel.

He'd grown into an interesting kid. Slim and strong
after years of dieting, made confident by his successes at
junior tennis, Joel was physically fearless. Nothing
scared him. Along the river were cliffs that people dove
from, and one afternoon Joel got a running start and
jumped from the highest one as I watched and shuddered. Eighty feet down a canoe was gliding past. The
paddler looked up. Joel plummeted toward him and the
paddler screamed. Joel sliced the water just inches from
the stern.

He didn't resurface. A minute or two later he snuck
up behind me and tapped me on the shoulder.

"I thought you were dead," I said. "That really
stunk."

"I like it when people think I'm dead."

"That's sick."

"It makes me feel all warm."

Joel had grown mentally fearless, too. Despite Mike's
standing orders about our clothing—that Audrey was
only to buy it from Sears and Penney's and never pay
extra for national brand names—Joel had amassed quite
a wardrobe for himself by trading clothes with friends.
One day, after locking his bedroom door, he gave me a
fashion show.

"This pair's for tennis. These are running shoes. I like Adidas because the leather's soft. The polo shirts with the penguins are Monsanto, the alligators are Izod. Feel how thick."

I stroked the fabric. "Don't wear these in the house."

"Don't worry, I just like to look at them. To own them. Check these jeans out: Sergio Valente."

He tried them on. It almost made me cry. The too-small jeans were threadbare in the seat.

"They're designer," Joel said. "I like designer things."

"Why?"

"I don't know. They feel special. Nicer lines."

Joel modeled the running shoes. They were huge on him. Though he was only three years younger than I was, I'd noticed that he and his classmates lived different lives than I had at their age. They styled their hair with gel. They wore real shorts instead of cut-off corduroys. And schoolwork that I would have gotten C's for earned them A's. They knew how to use computers.

Joel returned his treasures to their box, slid the box to the back of his closet, and draped a blanket over it.

"Come on. Let's go watch TV in the garage," he said. "I hooked up an extension cord."

"What's on?"

"I don't care. Commercials. The commercials are better produced than half the shows."

As we passed through the kitchen on our way outside,

Audrey said, "Hold on. This ought to interest you." She was hunkered down at the table with her writing pad.

"I found out our family's true number. I did the math. The numbers of our names make twenty-nine, and two plus nine is eleven."

"What does that mean?"

"Well, eleven—one plus one, that is—is two. So our number is two."

"Is two significant?"

Audrey consulted the index of her book. Joel was already out the door. "Go on," she said. "This book's more complicated than I thought."

~ ~ ~

On Wednesday nights, like Mormons across the country, we held Family Home Evening in the living room. Mike opened the church-written workbook on his lap while Audrey scooped strawberry ice cream into bowls. Since our conversion we'd turned into sugar fiends. All the Mormons I knew were sugar fiends.

That night's topic was "Glories of the Temple." We'd never been inside a Mormon temple. Before new converts were allowed this privilege, they had to put in a year of good behavior.

Mike quizzed us from the workbook: "Name and list the Utah temples. Justin?"

"Salt Lake City. Ogden. Logan . . . Manti?"

"Good," Audrey said. "And one more."

"St. George?"

Mike turned a page. "It's your turn, Joel. Sit up."

Joel stretched his arms and spread his fingers and yawned.

"Explain the meaning of the sealing ceremony."

"Can't remember. To keep people from dying?"

"You can do better than that."

"I trashed my racket. I need a new Prince. A graphite."

"Pardon me?"

"Listen, I'm pretty beat. Big match tomorrow. I think it has something to do with never dying."

After Joel left, Mike made another suggestion for stripping down our lives. "That dryer in the basement just gobbles energy. Line-dried clothing smells fresher anyhow."

"I like my washer," Audrey said.

"I'm talking about the dryer. Just the dryer."

"We could have both: a dryer *and* a line."

Mike shook his head. "That's overlap. Overlap's what we're trying to avoid here."

The statement had a grim, definitive ring. The discussion halted and Audrey fetched more ice cream. I imagined her in the kitchen as she scooped, standing among her endangered gadgets and wondering what would go next. The toaster? The microwave? Week by week our house was emptying out, becoming less convenient and up-to-date. It was getting hard for me to tell what year it was.

When Family Home Evening resumed, Mike said, "I'm sorry. It's all these other men. They wind me up. I'm going to try to spend less time with them. The washer and dryer can stay. They're basic necessities."

"You're sure?" Audrey said. "I can try to do without."

"You'd make that sacrifice?" Mike said. "For me?"

"I'd like to think I'd be doing it for God."

~ ~ ~

I felt myself slowly falling out of the culture. Even at church, among other Mormon teens, I was at a disadvantage. We'd be in the sacrament room behind the chapel, tearing up slices of bread before the service, and someone would bring up that week's Happy Days and quote their favorite gag. I wouldn't know what they were talking about. I'd blank. And at youth dances, when a popular new song came on, everyone would rush onto the floor as if a switch had been flipped, while I'd hang back. At school, it seemed that all the jokes and wisecracks were based on catchphrases from TV commercials that I hadn't seen.

It was worse for Joel. Mike caught onto his trick with the extension cord and locked the TV in his basement workshop, where Joel and I sometimes heard it through the floorboards tuned to the national news. Mike justified his news-watching by telling us how important it was to monitor the economy. Now and then Mike would report on some statistic—a rise in inflation, a hike in interest rates—and warn us that America was on the brink.

Home became a scary place. One day, to get away, Joel and I swam to the sandbar in the river where kids from town liked to gather on hot days. Steve Hanson, a kid who'd graduated years ago but still hung out with students, was playing a radio.

"Turn it up," Joel said. "I like that song. I never get to hear it anymore."

The girl Steve was with was tanning on her stomach, paging through a beauty magazine. Joel read over her shoulder. The girl looked back at him. "There's a whole stack in my beach bag. Be my guest."

Joel and I consumed the stack, hungry for color, for ads, for celebrities. Joel made me give him a sex-appeal quiz intended for young women: "Have you ever dressed entirely in red?" "Do you prefer cars with cloth or leather interiors?" Joel scored strangely high on the test. We read columns on dating and wedding etiquette and how to order wine. We lingered over the photos of the models, forgetting ourselves so completely that sun blisters developed on our backs.

The girl volunteered to spread lotion on us. "Guys who are into beauty have guts," she said.

"We're not really into beauty," Joel said. "We're bored."

"They're Mormons," Steve Hanson said. "No media. Personally, I call that child abuse. Kids have a right to be part of the big show."

Joel and I swam back to shore and started home. He ground his jaws and sulked and kicked small rocks. He snapped twigs and branches off the trees we passed.

"I can't believe it—we're missing the whole punk thing. Everything's changing. Shirts are changing. *Styles.*"

"What does that have to do with you and me?"

"Justin, can I ask you something?"

"Sure."

"Do you even *care* about the outside world? Isn't there anything you *want* out there?"

"I'd have to think."

"If you have to think, forget it."

When we got home we went to dry our towels and found an empty square of lint where the dryer had stood. In the yard we found Audrey stringing up a line. She squeezed out the towels and hung them up with clothespins.

"Two is the number for Jew," she said. "I solved it."

"Where are my white shorts? They clean?" Joel asked.

"I'm doing the laundry by hand. It slows things down, hon."

"It's like we're not even *Americans,*" Joel said.

~ ~ ~

Joel rebelled openly a few days later. He started wearing his designer clothes.

No one noticed at first. Mike was absorbed in a project in the basement, building shelves for our stock of protein pellets. He looked happy, healthy, strong. His abstention from coffee and cigarettes and liquor had pinked up his complexion. His hair seemed thicker. Missing the punk thing seemed to me like a reasonable price to pay for his well-being.

I had a project, too. I had a talk to write. Every week the bishop picked three laymen to stand and speak to the congregation, and this week it was my turn. "How about an upbeat talk on thrift?" he said. "Mormons, you see, are people of the beehive. The beehive's our symbol. Now, what are beehives for?"

"Honey?"

"They're little factories. Nothing wasted. They're symbols of efficiency. Of purpose."

I'd made little progress on my talk; honeybees did not inspire me. They scrambled over one another's bodies while carrying out dull, repetitive missions on behalf of a queen who barely noticed them.

Audrey, too, was preoccupied. Her interest in numerology had waned and been replaced by a fascination with angels. Mormon angels were not like other angels. They dressed in normal clothes and didn't have wings. Their bodies were not translucent but solid, physical. In fact, they were indistinguishable from humans. According to Audrey, they wandered the earth like hitchhikers, seeking out faithful Mormons in distress.

"Sister Hutchinson's car broke down in Utah. It overheated," Audrey said. "There wasn't a service station for fifty miles. Then a man with a pail came walking down the road. He didn't say a word, just filled her radiator, then turned and disappeared the way he'd come."

As Audrey finished the story, Joel came in. He had on the jeans, the Sergio Valentes. "I'm going diving. Justin, want to come?"

I followed him out. "Those pants don't even fit."

"Tight's the trend."

"They look painful."

"Sort of. It's worth it."

Joel's dives that day were riskier than ever. He showed off to a group of girls by somersaulting backward off the cliff. He practiced spins and flips and cannonballs. Just when we were ready to go home, Steve Hanson came by with his radio and tape player and dared Joel to climb an overhanging pine tree and dive from one of its branches.

"What will you give me if I do?" Joel said.

"What do you want?"

"Your boombox."

Steve agreed and Joel scrambled up the tree trunk. Pine needles and chunks of bark rained down. I yelled for Joel to jump from halfway up, but he had his eye on the top.

"Too high," I called.

"Go for it," Steve Hanson yelled. "I'll throw in my set of Ted Nugent bootleg tapes."

That made the difference. Joel shouted, pushed off,

and dove. He never cleared the tree, though. He'd mis-
calculated. He crashed down level by level through the
branches, falling straight, then sideways, then straight
again. Twigs cracked and snapped. Joel's body did a cart-
wheel.

Steve Hanson laughed. The fall was taking forever.
Joel landed all wrong, with one arm out. I heard the
bone pop. A stripe of hairless, abraded scalp showed
above one of his ears. He'd lost some fingernails.

Steve Hanson's idea of emergency assistance was to
stand there and warn me not to touch Joel's neck. I
ignored him, knelt down, and propped Joel's head up.

"I get hyper, too, sometimes," he said.

We loaded him into the beer-can-strewn backseat of
Steve Hanson's Barracuda. I rolled up the Valentes and
tucked them under Joel's head for a pillow. "You owe
me, Steve," Joel moaned. "I want those Nugent tapes."

"Fucking born-agains."

"Sticks and stones," Joel said.

"Fucking Holy Rollers."

"Eat me, Steve."

~ ~ ~

I sat by Joel's sickbed, writing my beehive speech. I
envied the Percocet pain pills he'd been prescribed. They
mellowed his eyes. His broken arm, in a cast that smelled
of glue, lay across his lap, as yet unwritten on. He'd said
that he didn't want people signing it because he thought
pure white casts looked more distinguished.

Steve's boombox sat on Joel's nightstand, playing Ted Nugent, but the stunt Joel had pulled to earn it had been unnecessary. Mike had fallen out with his survival pals over his refusal to pitch in for an underground shelter they were building in the northern Minnesota iron range. He'd returned the TV to the living room, sold his generator, bought Audrey new Maytags, and sprung for a minivan to shuttle Joel back and forth from tournaments and tryouts. The crash Mike expected hadn't come to pass and I could tell he was tired of waiting around for it.

The only reminder of our self-sufficiency push was Audrey's laundry line, which she still used, agreeing with Mike that line-dried clothes smelled fresher. I watched through the window above Joel's sickbed as she hung up his Valente's with a clothespin next to his pink and yellow Izod polo shirts.

"You won," I told Joel. "You stuck it out. Good job."

"Is everyone else at church faking this like we did? Pretending the world's going to end? It's not, you know."

"No, you're probably right," I said.

"You want one?" Joel held out a pain pill in his palm. "Just take it. God could care less. He isn't watching."

"You still believe in him?"

"I always have. That's how I know we're going to be okay."

3

After six months of regular church attendance, of fasts and fund drives and hymns and scripture classes, Mike told me he needed a breather, a little holiday, and I agreed that I could use one, too. His plan was for us to drive to Canada—just the two of us, no Joel and Audrey—and fly two hundred miles in a floatplane out to the middle of Lake Nipigon, where we'd be dropped on an uninhabited island equipped with a two-bunk cabin and a motorboat. We'd fish for three days, alone, with no distractions, and cook our meals on a propane stove.

We'd talk. Though Mike let me know that the trip would be expensive, and that he'd paid a hefty surcharge for a Labor Day weekend reservation, he said he'd consider the money well spent if we could deepen our bond as father and son.

I didn't know such a bond still linked us, and I wouldn't have known how to deepen it if it had.

We left late at night, Mike's favorite time to drive. Ignoring Mormon dietary rules, he stoked himself with black coffee and chewing tobacco. He said it was important to stay alert. Every few miles he rolled his window down and spat a mouthful of juice into the darkness. I played the AM radio. The news came on at the top of every hour, heralded by a burst of pounding music, and most of the stories had to do with politics, which Mike claimed to have an inside understanding of because he'd been attending Republican fund-raisers. In his view the country had been going downhill ever since Nixon had been hounded from office by the Kennedy-loving eastern elite.

"I need this trip," Mike said. "I'm overdue. I don't think it's any secret what I've been going through."

I didn't know what he meant, and didn't ask him. Mike's life, from what I knew, was proceeding well. His business had finally taken off that summer, boosted by the health bar and the gym. The money had allowed Audrey to quit her job and paid for Joel to attend a St. Paul boarding school whose tennis team was regionally ranked.

"Becoming a saint was not my goal," Mike said. "I did this for you, for the family. We needed structure."

"I guess we did."

"It's gotten out of hand, though. I'm finally in a position to enjoy life, financially speaking, and now . . . I timed things wrong."

Mike spat tobacco and faced out the window, not sharing what he was thinking. This didn't bother me. What bothered me was his new desire to tell me things—to use our trip as a chance for big discussions that I wasn't sure we needed to have.

We stopped for gas at the border. I cleaned the windshield. Mike came out of the station after paying and stood by the hood and unwrapped an Almond Joy bar. He offered me the first bite. I took a small one. We gazed at the stars, which were low and clear, and chewed. The smell of a nearby pulp mill soured the air.

"Remember this moment," Mike said.

I promised I would.

"It might not come again."

I nodded solemnly.

"I've been in a lot of pain. I guess I hide it. Maybe you think I'm asking for pity here."

That's just what I did think, but I knew not to say so. Mike's pain was important to him—he wore it proudly—but something convinced him no one else could see it. He believed for some reason that he suffered in secret, when anyone could have told him he looked miserable.

"I miss my old coach," he said. "I know you hated him."

I wasn't going to touch this.

"Some people hated him. Woody could be a terror, I admit it. Personally, I think I needed a terror."

"Why was that?"

"I couldn't get off square one. I needed a good swift kick to get me moving. Still, I can see why some people hated him."

At the border post a uniformed official stood in a floodlit glass booth and asked Mike questions about the nature of our visit to Canada. Mike lied for some reason: "An illness in the family." The guard played a flashlight over Mike's driver's license and handed it back with a nod and waved us on. Mosquitoes danced in our headlights. The car was quiet. I tried the radio but nothing came through. I tried it again farther on but nothing came through.

~ ~ ~

The next morning, a floatplane bobbed at the end of a long dock. An Indian with a sleek black ponytail pumped fuel into its side. "What do you know?" he asked me. I shrugged my shoulders. It seemed to be all the answer he was expecting.

Mike and the pilot pushed dollies down the dock loaded with fresh supplies for the cabin. The Indian stood in the hold and helped them stow things: cartons of canned fruit salad and baked beans, packages of hot dogs, jars of coffee, boxes of powdered milk and mashed potato mix. A case of bottled ale went by and a propane cylinder. The Indian stacked the supplies with care, distributing their weight around the plane.

"Last call for luxury items," Mike said to me. "Anything from the dock shack? Cigarettes?"

Mike had never let on to knowing I smoked sometimes. He sounded almost approving, which surprised me.

"I'm fine," I said. I already had my stash: three packs of Old Golds, some cough syrup, some pot, and a Scrabble board in case of rain.

Before I could offer to help him, Mike picked up all three rod cases, our tackle box, and both our duffel bags, leaving nothing for me to carry. He grunted and made low, complaining sounds. We followed the pilot into the plane and sat down behind the cockpit on wooden seats that folded out of the wall. I buckled my seat belt.

"If we crash over water, that belt won't help," Mike told me. "In fact, it might drag you down with it."

I kept it on.

The pilot took off across the flat blue lake. He was a kid in his twenties, blond and handsome, and flying seemed to come naturally to him. He ate M&M's from a bag inside his jacket, tossing them popcorn style into his mouth and washing them down with a can of 7 Up. On his lap was a map he didn't bother to look at. He appeared to be navigating visually, scanning the sky like a bus driver in traffic.

"The walleyes and pike have been hot and heavy," he said. "The lake trout so-so. I'd concentrate on wall-eyes."

Mike and the pilot talked fishing for a while and Mike made it sound like he was less experienced than he really was. He grilled the pilot for tips on bait and fishing spots while I looked out a small window at the lake. It curved to the horizon, filled with islands.

"My son and I don't get much time together," Mike said. "We're looking forward to this."

The pilot nodded.

"It's hard raising kids these days. You're just one influence. And not the most important one, at that."

"I don't have a family," the pilot said.

"You will."

"I enjoy being single."

"We all do. Doesn't matter."

Mike rose from his seat and crossed the cabin and got his duffel bag. He dragged it back to his seat and loosened the drawstring and shoved his arm down inside it to the elbow. The canvas bulged where Mike's hand was digging around. He drew out a bottle of Black Velvet whiskey, cut the seal with his thumbnail, and unscrewed the cap.

"You want a drink?"

The pilot held out his can of pop and Mike dribbled

whiskey inside, then looked at me. "You want a shot? We're on a fishing trip."

I made a face as the whiskey coursed down my throat, pretending I wasn't used to alcohol. I'd had a few drinks since becoming a Mormon, too.

The plane landed hard. It bounced and skipped and shuddered. We taxied around to a planks-and-barrels dock with tire halves nailed to its sides and started unloading. When we were done the pilot shook our hands and climbed back inside the plane and taxied out. Mike held up the bottle in a kind of toast as the plane gathered speed and lifted off. It circled the island, dipped its wings, and vanished. Mike took another drink, and so did I. I got out my pack of Old Golds and offered him one.

"Thanks. I'd rather chew. You go ahead."

I lit a match one-handed.

"Neat trick," Mike said. I was hoping that he'd notice.

"Here we are," I said.

"Nothing to do but fish and talk."

"It's nice."

"It *is* nice," Mike said. He dipped Red Man from his chew pouch. I was waiting for us to start talking. I was braced for it.

~ ~ ~

We went out fishing after we unpacked. The boat had a small slow leak we couldn't find. Rusty water sloshed around our feet. In it floated uncrinkling balls of cling wrap from the Velveeta sandwiches we'd eaten. While Mike read a map, I organized the tackle box, untangling treble hooks and sorting sinkers. We'd been running into the wind for forty minutes, crossing bays and flying up narrow channels, but only now was Mike checking our location.

"The legendary Trout Inlet," Mike announced. He folded the map and slid it under his butt so it wouldn't blow away.

"You're sure?"

"Trust me. For once just trust me, Justin."

"Fine."

I let down the anchor——a cement-filled coffee can. The rope raced off the winch and spun the handle. The water was deep, the deepest I'd ever fished in.

"Man's age-old dilemma: worm or leech?" Mike said.

"Leech, I think."

"I was afraid of that," Mike said.

He raised the bait bucket's perforated lid. The leeches came out of the water long and snaky but curled into tight, leathery balls on our hooks. We fished them just off the bottom, attached to jigs, but nothing happened. A strikeless hour passed. Growing bored, we gave our leeches names. I named mine Leif for some reason. Mike named his Luscious. Eventually, we gave them voices. Leif was a male, a bully, and said things like: "Kiss my ass, you wimpy little walleye." Luscious was a seductive female leech. "Hey there, killer," she'd purr, "you want to dance?" Mike's Luscious voice was funnier than my Leif voice.

"Let's change around," I said after a time. "I'll be Luscious now."

"Forget it, fella. I'm starting to feel lucky. One lucky lady."

I opened a bottle of ale from the cooler and drank while I bailed out water from the boat. Suddenly, Mike's pole jerked down and bent. He brought up a walleye after a brief fight and whacked its head on the motor mount to kill it. Amazingly, his leech survived the battle. He pretended to kiss it before he cast it back out. He caught another fish immediately.

"*Now* can we switch names?" I said. My jealousy of Mike's success surprised me. I wanted him to share his lucky charm.

"Sorry, tiger. Got a date," said Luscious.

I drained my ale and opened another one. Mike didn't seem to notice how much I was drinking—catching walleyes had put him in a spell. The breeze blew our boat in circles around the anchor line. Finally, I said, "I'm chilly. Let's go back."

Luscious said, "Leif is a quitter. What a pussy."

"We still have two days to fish," I said. "I'm hungry."

"Pussy," said Luscious. "It isn't even dark yet."

I reeled my line in, unhooked my limp, dead leech, and flung it over the side. I hated fishing. I threaded a worm on my hook. I hated leeches. When Mike made

another comment in his Luscious voice, I said, "Use your
real voice. This is stupid. I thought the idea of this trip
was that we'd talk."

"But darling, this *is* my real voice," Luscious said.

~ ~ ~

The cabin was sided in curling asphalt shingles and I
could tell that only men had stayed in it. Enormous dead
moths with outspread wings clung to the rusty window
screens. The sofa was covered in cracked brown Nauga-
hyde, its wooden arms heavily notched with cigarette
burns. In the kitchen no two cups or glasses matched,
and in the cluttered silverware drawer I found more
bottle openers than forks.

For dinner we had canned green beans and panfried
Spork, a Canadian version of Spam. Mike flipped the
pink, spongy meat with a spatula while I boiled the
beans.

"You said you weren't feeling well yesterday," I said,
trying to start our long-awaited discussion. I was just
drunk enough to want to have it now. "What's been the
problem? Woody? Is it just Woody?"

"Pass the pepper, precious," Luscious said.

I handed Mike the shaker. "I mean it. Seriously. I'm
asking how you've been feeling. I want to know."

Mike wiggled his hips and turned a slice of Spork. He
sipped from his plastic tumbler of Black Velvet. "Set the
table, honey. Be a dear. Luscious is almost ready to dish
up."

Mike served the Spork and beans on paper plates that quickly soaked through with grease. We didn't speak. We alternated bites of salty meat with long cold gulps of ale. Our stomachs rumbled. Mike had the smug, self-satisfied expression of a fisherman who'd caught his limit, and after we'd eaten dessert and thrown our plates away, I made one last stab at mature conversation.

"I really like drinking. It worries me," I said. "Did you drink much at my age?"

Mike frowned and shrugged.

"Sometimes I wonder if I'm going to make it. Is that how you felt after football? Unprepared? Like everyone else has a secret they aren't telling you, or maybe you're just too dense to understand it?"

Mike took one of my Old Golds off the table. He lit it and blew out a smoke ring. He crossed his legs.

"I know what you mean about hurting inside," I said.

"Darling," said Luscious, tapping off her ash, "you have no idea."

~ ~ ~

It was raining when I woke up. The cabin was freezing. I looked down from my bunk and Mike was at the stove, scrambling eggs and frying up more Spork. Five minutes later he called me to the table and I noticed his voice had not returned to normal. He wasn't Luscious anymore, thank goodness, but some other creature: weary, moody, put-upon. His strange high spirits of yesterday were gone.

"I drank all the coffee," he said. "I'll make some more."

"I can make tea," I said.

"There isn't any."

"Let me make the coffee."

"I don't mind. I'll do it."

After breakfast we put on rain gear and went out. The rain blew straight into our eyes in stinging pellets. Mike started the motor after several tries and steered us out into the lake. The rain was freezing. When Mike opened the bait bucket, the leeches lay slack and dead. He emptied the bucket over the side, said, "Fuck it," and drove us back through the downpour to the dock.

We changed our clothes, and I set up the Scrabble board. Mike had never been a fan of board games, considering them a waste of time, like jigsaw puzzles, but there was nothing else to do. Our big talk was not going to happen—that seemed clear to me. We set out a bowl of potato chips and pretzels and opened two bottles of ale. While Mike chose his letters I visited the outhouse and rolled a joint with toilet paper. I held my hits for as long as possible, then dropped the roach down the hole.

I went first. My opening word was *dervish*. My best words in Scrabble were words I'd never spoken, words that I was surprised I even knew.

Mike examined his rack and rubbed his lips. He set down his letters deliberately. *Dungeon.*

"Nice," I said. I was finally enjoying myself. I spelled out *hose*, reconsidered, and put down *hove*. I counted my points out loud, then tripled them because I'd landed on a bonus square.

Mike seemed unimpressed. He put down *gloom.*

"That's weird," I said. "You ever notice that? A Scrabble board's like a Ouija board sometimes."

"Explain," Mike said.

"It's raining. Your word was *gloom*. It just seems odd." I knew I was stoned and should probably shut up, although my point was sound.

"Just odd to you."

I spelled *exalted* and Mike spelled *loathing*. It was his last big word for several turns. While I kept drawing scarce, high-scoring letters—Z's, V's, and Q's and plenty of vowels to use them with—Mike drew nothing but common consonants. In round after round, the best that he could do was to add an *s* to an existing noun or form a puny *its* or *if* or *let*. Confidently, he'd reach for new letters, moving his hand around inside the bag as if he could distinguish the tiles by touch, but his fortunes didn't change. It struck me that I might be smarter than him. The thought depressed me, and I pushed it down.

I spelled out *queries*. "Sorry. Lucky letters."

Mike stared at his rack for a while, then spelled *violate.*

"A few more like that one and you'll catch up," I said.

Mike left the table and went into the kitchen and came back holding the bottle of Black Velvet. He stood and looked at the board. His face was red. He tipped the bottle up against his lips.

"Let's finish the game," I said. "It's getting interesting."

Mike shook his head. "This isn't what I pictured."

"Come on. You've got momentum."

"This is sad."

I laid down my letters: *sparkle*. I hoped to win still. Mike never gave me a chance to win at things.

"Two weeks ago I wanted to die," he said. "I even called the doctor for some pills. My head wasn't right. I felt paralyzed, defeated. I shouldn't have joined this church. My business bores me. And I married far too young—I know that now. I married for sex and I should have married for friendship."

Mike's confession didn't move me. It seemed like an excuse to quit the Scrabble game. He talked about wanting to die quite often since the Montana trip, usually when he wanted to worm out of something.

"Tough luck," I said in a voice that wasn't quite mine. "Spell a word. Quit whining."

Mike set the bottle down. "This trip's a failure. I thought we'd finally get close up here. Push through all this bullshit that's between us."

"Sit down and play."

"I should have known."

"Sit down and play," said Leif.

~ ~ ~

It was clear the next morning. We woke up late, hung over. Mike wound new line on his reel while I made pancakes. We doused them in syrup and slathered on the butter. The board from our abandoned Scrabble game was sitting on the table, its words intact, and I found myself idly reading them while I ate. I couldn't believe that for a moment yesterday I'd found the words significant.

We hit the lake. Above us, blue sky was piled up in layers all the way out into space. The sun was fierce. With our leeches dead and our night crawlers inert, we decided to troll with artificial lures. Mine was a silver Rapala minnow. Mike used a gold Meps spinner with a tail. We didn't name them this time. It just caused trouble. We fished with a grim methodical intensity, trolling back and forth across the channels as though we were coastguardsmen dragging for a body.

I caught the first walleye, a small one.

"Good," Mike said.

He caught the next fish. A pike.

"Nice job," I said

Courtesy and politeness ruled. We took great pains not to bruise each other's feelings. When Mike lost the biggest walleye of the day by mistakenly letting his line go slack while fighting it, I praised his skill in hooking it in the first place. When I overweighted my line with sinkers and snagged a log and snapped my rod tip off, Mike blamed the rod's manufacturer, not me. At one point, when I'd caught more fish than Mike and sensed him growing grumpy and discouraged, I switched to a lure that I knew fish didn't like and let Mike even the count.

It wasn't a fabulous day, but we got through it. I learned that there's nothing shameful about a standoff. It seemed to help things that we'd run out of booze—a three-day supply consumed in less than two.

By midafternoon we'd caught our limit of walleyes. We cleaned the fish on the dock, flinging their guts and heads into the lake. Schools of minnows swarmed around the waste and a mink slunk down to the shore and dipped a paw in. We stored the cleaned fish in the propane-powered chest freezer. Afterward, Mike suggested a game of cards, but I begged off. "That's probably smart," he said. We lay on our bunks and browsed old *Outdoor Life*s that someone had left behind in the cabin.

"Listen to this one," Mike said from underneath me. " 'A Wolverine Stole My Elk.' It's true, supposedly. This guy was in Wyoming on a pack trip, hunting above the tree line . . ."

We took turns reading articles aloud. It wasn't the same as talking. It was better. The tales of swarming hornets and charging grizzlies were utterly preposterous for the most part, and we read them in comic, exaggerated voices, adding music to create suspense. For the story of one young woman's lonely trek across the Alaskan tundra in December, Mike used his Luscious voice. I laughed out loud. As Leif, I related the story of a duck dog so tenacious he swam across Chesapeake Bay pursuing a crippled goose.

Then something happened: we switched characters. Halfway into a tale of hungry timber wolves, Mike became Leif. He sounded better as Leif. And I sounded better as Luscious, I discovered. She came naturally to me, her jadedness, her bite.

We were still reading when we heard a plane. It buzzed the cabin. We went outside to look. It wasn't supposed to arrive until tomorrow, but there it was, descending toward the lake. It landed and turned and approached the dock. The pilot waved out his window. We waved back.

"There must be bad weather coming," Mike said.

There was. The pilot apologized for it as we packed. Afraid that the front would keep him grounded for days, he'd flown in early. He offered Mike a partial refund.

"We'll make it six hundred instead of eight," he said. "I know it's an act of God, but I feel bad for you."

"Couldn't be helped," Mike said. "You used good judgment."

We boarded the plane and took off over the island. That evening, during the long drive home from Canada, we talked as if we were deeply disappointed in having our trip cut short. "A shame," we said. We complained about the fish we'd been denied, the night of fresh-air sleeping that we'd missed, the day of relaxing boating that never was, the hard-fought Scrabble game we might have finished. We agreed that the trip had just been getting good the moment it ended. "I liked that Spork," Mike said.

I told him I liked Spork, too. We laughed about it.

We laughed because we were delighted by our good luck. We'd gotten off that damned island just in time.

4

A couple of months before my mission, when I would leave home to spread a religion I hadn't chosen but couldn't quite abandon, if only because I had nothing to replace it with, I joined a tour of Mormon holy sites. Two chartered buses idled outside the church, surrounded by dozens of teenagers in shorts. Adults with clipboards were giving out seating assignments. Elder Tinsdale, our leader, spoke my name and I stepped forward, carrying a suitcase.

"Stow your stuff and climb on," he said. "Bus two."

"I'd like to ride in back, if possible."

"The seating arrangements are fixed," said Elder Tinsdale. "They're the result of careful prayer. I'm sorry."

I climbed the steps of the air-conditioned bus and moved down the aisle, looking for my name tag. Boys were on one side, girls on the other. The chaperons sat up front, behind the driver. He was the only non-Mormon on the bus—a black man in a white shirt with silver epaulets. In his hand was a plastic no-spill coffee cup and in his shirt pocket I saw a pack of Camels. I wondered how far from the bus he'd have to go when he wanted to smoke one.

My seat was an aisle seat halfway down the bus. I was grateful for it: an aisle seat made it easy to reach the bathroom. Lately, I'd been peeing more than usual, at least twice an hour. I blamed my medication. That spring, when word had reached the school psychiatrist that I'd been disrupting teachers' lectures and flubbing easy quizzes, he'd upped my dosage.

I stood up to let in my seatmate, Orrin Cord. He seemed preoccupied and didn't speak to me, just turned his face to the tinted window and laced his fingers together on his lap. Orrin was our youth group's leading skeptic, perpetually in crisis about his faith. His four older brothers had all been missionaries, in countries from Japan to Guatemala, and the stories they'd brought back of foreign cultures—of revolutions put down by brutal governments, of American factories that paid their workers twenty cents an hour to sew tennis shoes, of peasant families who sold their daughters as prostitutes—had bred in Orrin a bitter sophistication. It was an open secret that he drank tea, and he sometimes wore a beret to sacrament meetings. He'd warned me that he knew more about church history than anyone else on the tour, including the chaperons, and he swore he'd speak out if he caught them teaching lies.

The trip hadn't started but already I had to go. The bathroom was narrow, like an upright coffin. A deodorant pine tree dangled above the sink. I aimed, released, shook off, and zipped back up, aware that I had a long three days ahead of me. Part of me wished I could quit the Ritalin, but I feared the withdrawal symptoms I'd heard about: headache, irritability, mood swings, lethargy. The only time I'd missed my daily dose I'd slept for twelve hours and awakened in a rage, shaking so hard I could barely brush my teeth.

The girl who had taken the seat across the aisle from mine smiled when I sat down. I smiled back. Opal Singer was Mormon aristocracy. According to Orrin, whose hobby was genealogy, she was a direct descendant of Brigham Young and his second-youngest wife. The blood of prophets ran in Opal's veins. For her, our tour of Mormon sacred sites would be a kind of homecoming, a pilgrimage, while for me it would be an introduction.

"Excited?" I asked her.

"I am. I couldn't sleep."

"What place do you want to see most?"

"I can't decide. What about you?"

"Missouri. The Garden of Eden."

"You're sure it's in Missouri, not in Kansas?"

We both looked at Orrin for help.

"Missouri," he said. "The Garden of Eden is defi-
nitely in Missouri."

~ ~ ~

In the first few months after my family's conversion, all
I'd seen were restrictions, impositions: no R-rated movies, no "hard" rock, endless services, monthly fasts. I
imagined that my life would turn dry and boring and
that I'd drop out eventually. What I hadn't counted on,
however, was the novelty of a religion whose sacred
places—the farm in upstate New York where God and
Jesus had appeared to Joseph Smith, the trail of exile
across Nebraska's plains, the promised land of the Utah
desert—were located in America, close by, where a person could actually see them for himself.

Ever since winter, when the trip had been announced, I'd been looking forward to this Memorial Day
weekend. Our goal was to tour the Midwest shrines,
beginning with Nauvoo, Illinois, an early settlement, and
ending at Independence, Missouri, where Joseph Smith
had prophesied that Jesus would come back to earth and
summon all faithful Mormons to build a glorious temple.

The bus crossed from Minnesota into Iowa and I for
one had no sense of gathering history. At noon I swallowed another pill, washing it down with flat black-

cherry soda. I imagined the pills dissolving in my esopha-
gus, tiny white bombs of sunburst energy. The belief
among people who didn't take it was that the medication
made you drowsy, but in fact it pepped you so relent-
lessly that you could lose yourself for hours in simple
activities such as folding clothes. In fact, I'd been kicked
off the speech team that spring because I could no longer
wait my turn to talk.

"What's wrong? Is something wrong? You feeling
sick?" Apparently, Opal had seen me take the pills.

"Yes." It was always easier to say yes.

"Maybe you need a laying on of hands. You could ask
Elder Tinsdale to bless you next time the bus stops."

I gave her a nod that said I would consider this. In
truth, such hands-on healings didn't work for me. Six
months ago, at Christmastime, I'd come down with a
terrible earache and asked for help. Two elders sat me in
a folding chair, settled their palms on my skull, and
started muttering. After requesting Heavenly Father's
aid, they went on to predict my future. They foresaw a
life of shining promise: important work, wide influence,
a loving wife who would bear me many children.

My earache subsided over the next few hours, but
when I woke up the next morning my head was throbbing. Afraid that the relapse might further harm my
family's weakening faith, I tried to ignore the pain. It
didn't work. After lunch Audrey gave in and phoned a
specialist. Mike looked disappointed, let down. Part of

what had attracted him to Mormonism was the prospect of no more medical bills.

In central Iowa the landscape flattened and Opal drifted off to sleep. A silver stream of drool ran down her chin. Her left arm hung over the aisle, charm bracelet jingling. I'd never known a girl with so much jewelry. Her abundance of tinny lockets, fake gold chains, clip-on earrings, and cutglass rings gave her an ancient, almost Persian, appearance, as if some sultan had weighed her down with gifts.

Orrin elbowed me. "Got the Holy Ghost yet?" His joke referred to Elder Tinsdale's promise that we would feel a warm stirring in our stomachs as we approached the tour's first stop.

"Not yet." I stood up from my seat. I had to pee again.

"Where you going?" asked Orrin. He knew full well. I'd made the mistake of confiding in him once about my condition.

"Shut up," I said.

Orrin looked at his watch. "One minute—I'm timing you. Anything over a minute, I'll break the door down."

I flushed with embarrassment as I walked away. The time limit was an antimasturbation trick promoted in booklets distributed by our bishop. Other recommendations included sleeping with your hands outside the blankets and wearing a jockstrap inside your underwear. Apparently, the church believed that convenience was a big part of masturbation and that the slightest delay in getting going would cause a young man to give up.

Unfortunately, Orrin's warning got me thinking, and once I was inside the bathroom with the door locked I wanted to linger there. The image of Opal's wet chin was getting the best of me. To control myself, I employed another technique—one that Bishop Salaman had taught me during our monthly moral fitness talks. "When you feel like you're going to touch yourself," he'd said, "imagine your fantasy woman has a wound. A deep, bleeding cut. You'll snap right out of it."

My medication made the image vivid. The oozing wound in Opal's side—a slash of luscious red beneath her rib cage—succeeded only in heightening my excite-ment.

"You went overtime," Orrin said when I returned. He'd put on his brown beret and mirrored sunglasses. A notepad lay on his lap, its top page headed: "Distortion and Misinformation Checklist."

"If it was me next to Opal," Orrin said, "I'd go overtime, too. It's no coincidence."

"What isn't?"

"That they sat you two so close."

"They?"

"The powers that be. The bishopric. They must be afraid you're going to leave the church. Most converts do. So they sat her there as bait."

Orrin enlarged on this theory as we rode. The

church, he believed—and he cited several examples—
perpetuated itself through sex and romance. The lure of
marrying pretty Mormon women was, finally, what kept
Mormon men in line. My own observations supported
Orrin's idea. Mormon girls, unlike the others I went to
school with, were precociously poised and seductive,
strangely lush. They pitched their voices low and used
mascara. They rarely wore sneakers, preferring shoes
with heels, and were always smoothing cold cream on
their hands.

"The church is against premarital sex—it *says*—but
in fact it promotes it. It has to, to survive. It's been that
way since the beginning, since pioneer days. And believe
me, the girls know their duty. They *do* their duty."

"Opal, too?"

"The moment she saw you next to her, she knew she
had an assignment. She blushed bright red."

"You're lying. You're making fun of me again."

"It's bred in a Mormon girl's bones. She has this
instinct. She sees a straying sheep, she herds it back. But
fine, don't believe me."

"I don't."

"Smart attitude. Don't take statements on faith—
hold out for proof." Orrin gazed back out the window
at the highway. "You feeling the Spirit yet?"

"No."

"Me neither," he said. "I'll let you in on a secret:
there's no such thing."

~ ~ ~

"Before the Saints trekked west to Utah, driven out by hate and persecution, they built this city, the largest in the state. They raised a militia. They built a towering temple. The Prophet, Joseph Smith, campaigned for president. Nauvoo, Illinois, was a nation within a nation, thriving and vibrant, the envy of its neighbors."

Elder Tinsdale finished speaking and asked for questions. Orrin raised his hand.

"What about plural marriage? You left that out. That's the *real* reason the Mormons were driven west."

Elder Tinsdale turned to Sister Helms, the sternest and oldest of our chaperons. "Polygamy," she said, "is not church doctrine."

"It used to be," Orrin said.

"What's past is past. The church moves on. It changes."

"I thought the idea of this trip was learning *history.*"

The group formed a line and we followed the chaperons into the church-run visitors' center. We passed a painting of a farmer at prayer and another of Jesus Christ in Central America, where Mormons believed he'd appeared to the natives following his death and resurrection. In a diorama of Joseph Smith at home, life-size mannequins sat in antique chairs around a fireplace. Elder Tinsdale flipped a switch that lowered the lights and caused movies of human faces to shine on the mannequins' featureless heads. The plastic figures came eerily to life, their "voices" filtering out from hidden speakers.

Polygamy wasn't spoken of again, and Orrin moved along with shuffling feet. "What a whitewash," he kept whispering. My eyes were fixed on Opal, in front of us. Her skin was the glossy brown of caramel apples, plumped by the thinnest layer of baby fat. Her lashes were so long that they looked false. She asked no questions and seemed annoyed when others did. I envied the simple faith she seemed to radiate, her willingness to be guided and instructed. It impressed me almost as much as Orrin's wit.

Lunch was a buffet picnic on the lawn. The chaperons sat together under a tree, drinking grape Kool-Aid and gnawing chicken drumsticks. They were all women except for Elder Tinsdale. Ever since his divorce, six months ago—a split that the church considered honorable because Sister Tinsdale had joined the Scientologists—he'd been surrounded by helpful older women who cleaned his house and shopped for groceries for him. Now they leaned forward slightly and watched him eat. Whenever he spoke they nodded, sighed, or laughed, and when his glass was empty they refilled it.

"I talked to Opal," Orrin said, snatching the uneaten drumstick off my plate.

"What happened?"

"She thinks you're a fox. She loves your hair. She thinks you could maybe wear it shorter, though."

"When do you think she'll make her move?"

"Don't know. I just wish *I* was a convert," Orrin said. "Layer by layer, you get to go inside. Uncover the mysteries. Find the buried treasure. Me, I was born inside. It's all so stale now."

After lunch we toured Nauvoo on foot. The Mississippi gave the town a fishy smell and drew my attention to the western horizon. In the house where Joseph Smith had lived, we stood behind velvet ropes and viewed a kitchen where mannequin women were canning beans and corn. I stood back to accommodate the shorter kids and found myself next to Opal. Our elbows knocked.

"I hear you're related to Brigham Young," I said.

"Who isn't?" Opal joked. It made me like her more. "At the turn of the century, in St. George, Utah, there was a man with over a thousand grandkids."

"I'll bet he was tired."

"Tired of what? You *pervert!*"

Next we admired the Prophet's study. Opal turned her bracelet on her wrist. She examined the back of one hand, as if for flaws. "My skin's getting wrinkly," she said. "I'm seventeen. A hundred years ago, I'd be married by now. I wouldn't have to worry about my looks."

"I like your looks."

"Thank you. That helps. I like your looks, too."

Elder Tinsdale sidled in between us and Opal edged away. He rested his broad, hairy hand on my shoulder. His talent for "getting down on kids' level" was famed throughout the ward, though all it consisted of was lots of touching.

"Spectacular trip," he said. "What a way to learn."

"What are we seeing tomorrow?"

"Carthage Jail. That's where the mob shot Joseph Smith, the bastards."

I looked at him.

"Excuse me."

"I swear, too."

"I take the Prophet's death personally. I shouldn't. It all worked out exactly according to plan."

A silence fell. Elder Tinsdale's stomach growled. I was starting to wish I had eaten lunch.

"Opal's a special young woman," said Elder Tinsdale. "Heavenly Father gave her singular gifts."

"I know," I said softly.

"How's your family doing?"

"Better. Much better. My brother's a tennis star. My father got a big offer for his business. We're moving to a big house beside a golf course."

"Sounds like their prayers are being answered. I'm glad. Listen now: you enjoy this trip, okay?"

"Yes. I promise." I glanced at Opal's shoulders.

Elder Tinsdale squeezed my arm. "Spectacular."

~ ~ ~

We slept that night on the cold linoleum floor of a church gymnasium. I woke after midnight with an urgent bladder and quietly peeled off my sleeping bag. I tiptoed between the rows of snoring Mormons, feeling pleasantly guarded and surrounded. Before the conversion I'd belonged to nothing, nothing but my family and my school, but now I was part of a movement, a community. I had friends all over the country, all over the world.

Coming out of the bathroom, I heard a sound. I turned to see Opal in shorts and T-shirt, barefoot. There was a crust in the corners of her mouth and one of her cheeks was red and grooved from lying against the zipper of her sleeping bag.

"I can't fall asleep away from home," she said. "I miss my ferrets."

"Do ferrets make nice pets?"

"Until they grow up and get fat. They start to stink then. Let's go outside—I'm smothering in here."

From the church's back lawn we could see the Mississippi, its surface slick and luminous and vast. The stars were so near they appeared to have volume. A blinking satellite arced across the sky. Opal shivered and took my hand and squeezed it.

"It's up there, I know it," she said. "In all its glory."

I took her to mean the Celestial Kingdom, the highest realm in the three-tiered Mormon heaven. The lower two realms, the Terrestrial and Telestial, were nice enough places, but not truly exalted. Only in the Celestial Kingdom could a faithful Mormon husband summon his wife by calling the secret name divulged to him in the temple wedding ceremony. The couple, once reunited in the afterlife, could then go on to reproduce eternally, populating new planets with their offspring and ruling over these worlds as God rules ours.

"I feel sorry for kids who don't have our beliefs. They look at the sky and all they see is . . . sky." Opal moved my hand onto her knee. "Is it selfish to want other people to have what I have?"

"No. I think it's the opposite of selfish."

"Scoot closer. I'm cold."

I put my arm around her.

"I'm a happy person," Opal announced. "I know that's uncool to admit these days, especially if you're young. Tough luck—I'm happy. I know where I'm going. I know where I'll end up. It shows in my eyes, people say. In my expression. It used to embarrass me, looking so contented, but now I don't care. I've decided to let my light shine."

At this, Opal rested her head on my shoulder. My nose filled with the smell of Prell shampoo. She shifted around and blew air against my earlobe, a series of delicate, regulated puffs.

"That tickle?"

I nodded.

"Did you take drugs?" she said. "Before you converted, I mean."

"I took a lot of drugs."

"What were they like?"

"It depends."

"On what?"

"The drug."

Opal yawned and opened my hand. She traced an index finger along the branched lines in my palm. She licked my neck. Her strokes started short and gradually grew longer, until she was licking me from ear to collar-bone. I felt my artery pulsing against her tongue tip. I felt my chest heat up inside my shirt. Opal slid a hand between the buttons and did something technical to one of my nipples.

"Unbuckle your belt," she said. "I want to touch you there."

I hesitated, and Opal said, "You need me. It's fine that you need me. Unbuckle."

I did as she said. Cool air blew through my zipper, followed by the warm grip of Opal's fist. My skin was numb and rubbery at first, but soon I began to respond. My shoulders fell. Opal worked her cheeks to juice her mouth up, then lowered her head. She pushed her hair aside. The last thing I saw before I shut my eyes was Opal's hand slipping under her own waistband.

Her efficiency charmed me. The act was tidy, polished. It left me feeling shiny, spiffed up.

Afterward, Opal said, "No more drugs—you promise? I tasted them in my mouth. They taste like chemicals."

I kissed her hair, her forehead. "That felt perfect. I want to do more with you. When can we do more?"

Suddenly, Opal seemed shy. She hid her face from

me. She plucked a handful of grass and let it fall. "Maybe never. I don't know. It's tricky."

"Why?" I said. "We can switch around next time."

"I'd like that. I'm sorry. I just don't know," she said.

"The drug thing?"

Opal shook her head and sighed.

"Why?"

"Because other people need me, too."

~ ~ ~

The stairs at Carthage Jail were narrow, so Elder Tinsdale divided us into groups before we went inside. He lowered one hand like a railway-crossing arm between my chest and Opal's back, and she went on ahead. She didn't look back. She'd been friendly to me that morning but not quite warm, and I wondered if she was testing me, somehow, or if I seemed different to her in the light. As requested, I'd thrown out my Ritalin at breakfast and now I was in a state of nervous self-monitoring, waiting to see if my symptoms would return: the toe-tapping, the yakking, the antsiness.

Opal's group, which included Orrin, filed out of the jail as mine filed in. Orrin was shaking his head. He looked disgusted. "Smith was a Mason," I heard him telling Opal. "When they shot him, he gave the Masonic cry for help. Why does the church have to keep things such a *secret*?"

"I'm sure they have their reasons," Opal said.

Upstairs, in the jail cell, Elder Tinsdale dramatized the Prophet's martyrdom. "The mob burst in *here*," he said. "Joseph Smith was *here*. They chased him to this window over *here*." He invited us to gather at the window and gaze at an old stone well some distance below, where the assassins had propped the Prophet's body. "Allow me to give a personal testimony. Standing here, on this spot of blood and horror, I know the gospel is true. I feel its power. I ask you to quiet your minds and share this knowledge."

Someone sneezed, and then the group fell silent.

"That warmth in the pit of your stomachs—do you feel it?"

"Yes," a girl said.

"Do you feel it, Justin? *Justin?*"

I looked up, startled. "Not yet," I answered truthfully.

"Give it time. Be still and concentrate."

I feared that my foot might start tapping, but it didn't. Amazingly, I managed to clear my mind, and for me this was a miracle in itself. Slowly, I grew aware of a low tingling that might have been the Holy Ghost, withdrawal, or a feeling left over from my night with Opal. I chose for it to be the Holy Ghost.

"What's happening?" Elder Tinsdale said.

"I feel it."

"You don't sound very convinced."

"I am. I feel it."

My testimony, despite its hesitancy, made me an instant hero. I'd scored big. On the way downstairs the group congratulated me. Girls hugged me and boys slapped my back. "Good work," one said. I felt lifted up, admired, wanted. I'd attracted a fan club, a cheering section When someone thrust a stick of gum at me and I bit down on it, the taste transported me. It was the taste of knowing that I belonged.

The bus drivers revved their engines and opened their doors. Elder Tinsdale called us to attention. "You'll notice we've changed the seating, so check for name tags. Kids who didn't have windows should have windows now. What's more, this should give you a chance to make new friends."

As I made my way down the aisle my spirits fell. I didn't see my name tag anywhere. A kid named Tim Kriss had taken Orrin's old seat, and Orrin was in mine, across from Opal. She hadn't moved. When I passed her, she looked down and turned a page in her Book of Mormon. I felt a spike of anger. My forehead tensed. The headache that I'd been waiting for materialized.

Finally, I found my place—in the very last row, a three-seater by the bathroom. I sat down. Beside me was Sister Helms, the chaperon.

"We thought you might be more comfortable back here. We noticed you had to go a lot," she said.

"That was my medication. I'm off it now."

"Medication for what?" said Sister Helms.

The headache intensified, spreading down my neck.

My breathing sped up, but it seemed to yield less oxygen. I was falling apart. I couldn't concentrate.

"You're grinding your teeth," Sister Helms said.
"Settle down."

"I am settled down. I'm completely calm."

Sister Helms nodded and moved over a seat.

~ ~ ~

We parked in the Garden of Eden's parking lot, next to
the outdoor toilets and the garbage cans. We'd stopped at
a Burger King that afternoon and everyone had trash to
throw away. Kids stretched and yawned and took deep
breaths, then walked in circles, working out their leg
cramps. It was evening, and cool, with a breeze that
riffled my hair and sent me back to the bus for a jacket.
I spied the bus driver's Camels on the dashboard and
snatched the whole pack, as well as his matches. What I
really needed was some aspirin, but Mormons viewed
pills with suspicion, no matter what kind, and even if I
found the courage to ask for some I doubted that anyone
would admit to having any.

The group formed a circle in the parking lot to listen
to Elder Tinsdale's lecture. Orrin and Opal seemed to be
avoiding me. They stood at Elder Tinsdale's side, shoulders identically hunched against the chill, and gazed in-
tently at his moving lips. Orrin's face had lost its
pinched expression. He'd pushed his sunglasses up into
his hair and there was a bright smudge of mustard on his
chin. Opal licked a finger and wiped it off for him.

I felt a twitch of betrayal. My hands made fists. I couldn't believe how quickly she'd moved on, how easily she'd shifted her devotion. To forget her, I turned my attention to Elder Tinsdale, but I found what he was saying hard to swallow. I had ideas about the Garden of Eden, particularly concerning its location. I pictured it in the Middle East somewhere, covered in sand, an un-marked, windswept ruin. I pictured dry riverbeds, mountainous horizons—not an ordinary Missouri valley covered in brush and grass and knotty hardwoods. Still, Elder Tinsdale assured us that it was true: God had breathed life into Adam on this spot, and it was here that Jesus Christ himself would someday return and gather the elect—a hundred and forty-four thousand faithful saints who would follow him, carrying tools, to Independence, and break the ground for his everlasting temple.

Elder Tinsdale concluded his talk with yet another personal testimony. Next to me, Tim Kriss had started shaking. Sister Helms reached over and patted his hand. Even more palpably than in the jail cell, deep waves of feeling were surging through the group—though not, this time, through me. A boy cried, "Father!" A girl began to bawl. Our basketball team's star center hugged himself and gently rocked from side to side, eyes shut. Even Orrin seemed moderately uplifted; he tilted his face back to catch the setting sun while Opal, serene as ever, stood by him, smiling.

Elder Tinsdale brought order to the scene by instructing us to wander as we saw fit along the footpaths that led from the parking lot into the surrounding woods and fields. "Find somewhere peaceful to sit and pray and meditate. In forty-five minutes the buses will honk their horns."

My plan was to go off alone to smoke a cigarette, but when I saw Opal and Orrin leave the group and sneak off together through a stand of sumac I decided to follow them. They held hands as they walked. Their steps were light and synchronized. I hung back, downwind, and lit a Camel, toying with the idea of tossing the match into the dry brush along the path. To burn down the Garden of Eden would be a feat, and I was surprised it hadn't been tried already. Orrin and Opal were out of sight by then. I had an idea about what they planned to do together, but I wasn't sure that I wanted or needed to see it.

I dropped the match on the ground and stamped it out, crediting myself with a good deed simply for having avoided an evil one. My thoughts had grown scattered, and when I closed my eyes and tried to pray I forgot what I was asking for halfway through. "Heavenly Father, preserve my family. Heal my antsiness. Guide my future mission." I opened my eyes and started down the path again, following Orrin and Opal in spite of myself.

I heard them before I saw them. Someone was sobbing—great snuffling, rattling sobs. Opal's voice said, "Okay, okay, I'm stopping." I stepped around the bush and looked below me. Orrin was sitting on his spread-out jacket with his Levi's pushed down around his knees. Opal was beside him, kneeling, her open shirt revealing a shiny pink bra. Orrin kept slapping his hands against his cheeks, the way men do when applying after-shave. His eyes were wet red messes. He muttered the antisex incantation over and over.

"She's cut, she's hurt, she's bleeding . . ."

The scene made me angry and a little sick, but I couldn't stop looking. Opal grabbed Orrin's wrists, but he resisted. "Off me. Let me be. Get off," he said. Opal relented and started buttoning her shirt.

"She's bleeding, she has a wound . . ."

"Shut up with that."

Orrin worked his pants up over his legs and fiddled with his belt. He'd held the line against something, he'd beaten temptation, but instead of respecting him for it I felt contempt. He was everything he pretended not to be: programmed, afraid, intimidated, weak. His skepticism, which I'd admired, was fake, which made me suspect his goodness was also fake. And though Opal's idea of saint-liness disturbed me, at least she had the courage to see it through. Orrin's faith in God embarrassed him, while Opal's, which seemed more real to me, confused her.

I respected confusion. Confusion I understood.

I crouched in the weeds and waited for them to go. Opal stood up and stepped into her sandals while Orrin sat on his jacket and hung his head. I could see his white underpants through his open zipper. My headache, which had receded for a moment, returned with new strength. I noticed my knees were trembling.

Orrin raised his face. "Come back. Don't go. Maybe I did the wrong thing."

"Of course you didn't. You *never* do the wrong thing."

"I'll pray for you."

Opal gave Orrin the finger and walked away. I waited, then followed her. I rehearsed my innocent face. I took a side path that cut across the path Opal was on. I got ahead of her. I tried to look pleased and surprised when she approached me.

"Hi. I was meditating."

"Good for you," said Opal. She tried to step past me, but I kept up with her.

"Incredible place. Inspiring. I felt the spirit again." My words ran together.

Opal walked faster. "Go away. Stop bugging me."

"I miss you. I want to talk. Let's talk. Wait up. Isn't this place incredible? What's wrong?"

Opal halted and spun around and faced me. The wings of her nostrils were pink and flared and wet. "I mean it, back off. I'm tired of clingy guys. I'm tired of being everybody's mother."

I couldn't stand still. I nodded. I jiggled one foot. "Right," I said. "Right. Okay. I see. Okay."

"You're vibrating," Opal said. "You're scaring me."

"I'm fine."

"Get a blessing, okay? You need a blessing."

"I tried once. It didn't work."

"So try again."

~ ~ ~

On the trip's final day we drove to Independence and stood around a grassy hilltop lot where Mormons believed the great temple would someday stand. Everyone seemed cramped and underslept. A virus had broken out inside the bus, recirculating through the ducts and ventilators, and every other person had caught the flu.

Even Elder Tinsdale had fallen ill. As he lectured us about the temple he shifted a cough drop around inside his mouth, and some of his words were hard to understand.

"The summons to build might come soon. Tomorrow, perhaps. Some of you kids might even join the effort. Imagine the thrill of wielding spade and chisel with Jesus as your foreman. What a feeling."

I gazed around at the dirt and weeds, at the restaurant and parking garage across the street, at the cars and trucks and traffic lights, but I couldn't picture the spires and buttresses Elder Tinsdale was describing.

As usual, Orrin gave me the straight dope. "The church doesn't even *own* the Temple Lot. Another religion does. Pretty ironic, don't you think?" he said.

"I'm tired of thinking. I'm trying faith."

"In what? A bunch of fairy tales?"

"In some of them."

On the long ride home the seating system collapsed. People sat down wherever they wanted to and tended to their colds with wads of Kleenex. Elder Tinsdale, exhausted, fell asleep, and didn't wake to eat the boxed Big Mac that Sister Helms set kindly on his lap. At sundown the driver dimmed the overhead lights and someone put on *The Osmonds' Greatest Hits*. I walked to the back where Opal was sitting alone, the Book of Mormon open on her knee. She slid over to make room.

"I caught the bug," she said as I sat down.

I shrugged.

"It's fine if you're mad at me," she said.

"I'm just run-down."

"That's the bug."

"It's not the bug." I said.

The Osmonds tape played as we crossed a long steel bridge back into Illinois. It felt odd to be leaving the Holy Land so suddenly, not knowing when, if ever, I'd be back. I let my eyes close as Opal told me stories about the part of her family that lived in Utah. "I've been thinking about my grandpa. He had four wives. He lived in the desert—big tall man, with a beard. I visited him with my mom when I was nine. His fourth wife, June, was nursing a baby—my uncle. I watched my own uncle breast-feed. That must seem weird to you."

"What?" I said. "I'm sorry. I'm not all here tonight."

"Those pills you take."

I shook my head. "I quit them."

"Why?"

"I don't know. They were in the way of something."

The tape switched sides. The bus was dark and cold. Opal put away her Book of Mormon and I fetched a blanket from the overhead rack. We kicked off our shoes and huddled closer together and spread the thin blue blanket across our laps. Beneath it our hands moved, quietly, like spirits.

5

Of all the places the General Authorities could have chosen to send me on a mission—South Africa, South America, South Carolina—they picked New York City. I couldn't believe the letter. We'd moved to a house on the golf course that summer and Mike and Audrey were playing with the pro when a Federal Express van drove up with the envelope. I could see them out on the fairway as I opened it, and after I'd read it over a couple of times, I yelled to them to come over in their cart. My fingers were tingling. My mouth was dry from shock.

I passed the letter to Audrey in the cart. She pushed her sunglasses up onto her forehead, under her white billed cap. Mike put his arm around her and leaned in. Golf, the new house, and the club's packed social schedule had brought them closer than I'd ever seen them.

Audrey's tan seemed to fade as she read. She angled the letter toward Mike. His eyes went round. "Ding, ding, ding," he said. "You hit the jackpot."

Audrey's face hardened. "Well. I guess this changes things. No more second thoughts. Excited? Must be."

To spare her feelings, I tried not to grin. She'd been working on me to stay in Minnesota, attend the U of M, back off from church life. She and Mike spent their Sunday on the course now, attending services only when it rained. Joel, whose prep school had sent him to Chicago for a total-immersion summer tennis retreat, didn't go at all. He'd found a new faith. On the strength of a book promoted by his coach, he called himself a Buddhist now. He claimed its teachings and practices helped his serve.

"I still have some thinking to do," I said to Audrey.

"Come on, Mike. I'd like to finish the whole eighteen."

To double-check the letter's accuracy, I had Bishop Salaman contact Salt Lake City. I sat in his office in a suit and tie as a chain of receptionists passed him up the line to someone who could speak definitively. I was thrilled about my assignment, but anxious, too. In New York, as opposed to Russia or Brazil, say, I'd come as a pest, I feared, an interruption. People were busy there. Their clocks ran fast.

When Bishop Salaman reached a higher-up, he flashed me an okay sign with one hand. "Interesting," he said when he was finished.

"Tell me everything. I'm going crazy."

"After the interviews they held with you, they agreed you have a special power. You know how to break down barriers with words. New York is the perfect place for you, they feel, because residents tend to be tough, impatient, skeptical. We haven't had much success there recently."

"It's final?"

"Of course it's final. The church has spoken. Enjoy yourself these last few weeks. Be proud. You're taking a blessing to people who sorely need it."

As word leaked out about my destination, people at church started giving me advice. Elder Munsen, who'd served his mission in Bolivia, wrote down a prayer for me and laminated it so I could carry it inside my wallet. The prayer dated back to the days of Brigham Young, he said, and was meant to be recited in emergencies, when a missionary faced danger or hostility. It called on Heavenly Father to strike mute anyone who opposed his earthly plan.

The girls had advice for me, too: stay strong, stay chaste, and write. I suspected Bishop Salaman was coaching them. One by one, at dances and softball games, they took me aside and breathily assured me that when I returned to the ward two years from now they would be waiting for me, all grown up, eager to date, go out, get serious. They reminded me that, according to church tradition, returning missionaries had six months to do nothing but rest, and socialize, after which they were expected to get engaged.

"If you're interested, I'll be waiting," Marla Larson said, "but not if you do something stupid with some New York girl. I know they're very experienced out east, but I can give you something those girls can't." She brushed my ear with her lips. "A family."

Jane Hatch's proposition was more tempting. She promised to correspond with me about her deepest, most secret thoughts and fantasies; to open up her soul with no holds barred. "I've already done my first letter. It's pretty filthy. I didn't know what I had in me until I wrote it."

"Like what?" I said.

"That's for me to know," Jane said, "and you to find out." She kissed me on my nose. Her breath smelled of butterscotch ice cream and mint sprinkles.

The other young men who were headed out on missions grew resentful when they heard my news. Sven Lind, who was off to Hungary that month after nine grueling weeks at the church's language institute, accused me of pulling strings with higher-ups. Rob Farrell, who was Costa Rica-bound, hinted that missionaries in New York were favorite targets for pickpockets and muggers. When I told him I wasn't afraid of criminals because I'd be making my rounds with a partner, Rob warned me that New York muggers worked in packs. "And that badge on your shirt pocket saying Latter-Day Saints tells them that you're basically defenseless. You don't have a knife, a gun, or anything."

I mentioned the prayer Elder Munsen had given me. "I have God," I said.

"That's good. That's funny. Make sure you know how to say that prayer in Spanish."

Elder Gorman, an old man in a wheelchair who'd spent his mission in postwar Germany bringing former Nazis to Jesus Christ, gave me the most unusual advice. "You'll see it all in that town," he said. "The best, the worst, and everything in between. Maybe you'll stick it out or maybe not. Maybe you'll find a new life. It happens. Often."

"You came back, though."

"From Düsseldorf? Who wouldn't? There was nothing there for a young man. My friend Elder Bragg, who went to Rome, however . . ."

"I'll try to be careful. I'll do my best," I said.

Elder Jessup raised a knobby hand and waved me in next to his chair so he could whisper. "Ignore what the girls say. Go wild, kid. *Let rip!*"

~ ~ ~

At night, after Mike and Audrey went to bed, I'd lay out the clothes I'd purchased for my mission: dark suits, dark ties, white shirts, black socks, black shoes. I tried them on in my bedroom, standing in front of a full-length mirror that made me look like a cross between Abe Lincoln and a Chicago mobster. To complete the picture, I'd tuck my Book of Mormon under my arm and rehearse a line of greeting: "Hello, ma'am, I'm Elder Cobb. I'm here to help you." If it didn't sound convincing, I'd lower my voice.

Through the ceiling I could hear Audrey crying in bed. I'd thought that the fact I was staying in the U.S. might comfort her, but the opposite had happened. Whenever New York was mentioned on TV or came up in conversation, fresh tears would surge up and she'd have to leave the room. One night I asked her what the trouble was. "Say you were going to Belgium," she said, "or Chile. I wouldn't be able to picture you. You'd vanish. In New York, though, I'll have to imagine your every move. Justin at the fountain in Central Park. Justin in a taxi on Fifth Avenue."

"You can always come visit me. It's a two-hour flight."

Audrey blotted her leaking eyes. "Don't kid yourself. The minute that plane lands, you'll break into a run. I know you, Justin."

"I'm going to spread the gospel."

"Don't kid yourself. This isn't Korea you're going to. It's Manhattan. They don't need a gospel. You won't, either."

~ ~ ~

There was a lot to take care of before I left. Audrey helped me shop for luggage. Mike bought me a watch. I had a physical. At a bookstore I bought invitations for my send-off party and snuck a peek at a guide to New York nightlife.

I also needed a general dental checkup. I chose Perry Lyman, though I didn't have to. Our family had another dentist by then, Dr. Synge, a transplant from Chicago who practiced downtown in the old county creamery, just one of the many historical buildings that had been taken over by new businesses as Shandstrom Falls became more prosperous. People who'd driven Fords drove foreign cars now and soaked in hot tubs on decks behind their houses. The kids wore nothing *but* designer clothing.

I chose Perry Lyman for my checkup because there was something that only he could do for me. He'd fallen into another slump, I'd heard. His farmhouse was window-high with uncut grass. He'd sold his helicopter and quit the Guard.

I drove alone to the new clinic he'd opened in a run-down strip mall. The sign on the door listed no other partners. The parking stripes in the lot were dull and cracked.

He greeted me in a shabby waiting room that lacked a receptionist's desk. He had on a wrinkled short-sleeved smock that revealed the sort of fatty muscle of a body-builder who's quit the gym.

"The young man of God," he said.

"Just drop it, Perry."

The examining room was bare, no posters; only a clock that looked salvaged from a grade school, with rounded, childish numbers and a white face. He'd kept his old chair, but its leather was lined and brittle. I decided to wait until after the exam to tell Perry Lyman what I wanted from him.

"New York City," he said.

"Got lucky."

"Did you? I'd call it the ultimate double bind. Young, white, and unattached in Gotham, but a Mormon missionary. Ouch."

I looked up at him, past the yellowed dental lamp. "Are you going to examine me or not? And what's with the beard? What happened to G.I. Joe?"

Perry Lyman eyed me, flat and cold. Again and again, it had come down to the two of us, and now we were circling each other for the last time. Some strangers become more important to you than family, maybe because you're not expected to love them. You can leave them whenever you want to. They can, too. Every moment together is a choice.

Perry Lyman turned on the water in the spit sink. On one of his knuckles I noticed the raised scar that dated back to my wisdom teeth extraction.

"I gave up fighting the facts," he said. "I accepted myself, in all my human disorder. Before you bury yourself in this religion thing, I suggest you consider doing the same."

"Admit I'm a mess?"

"A certain kind of mess. The King Kong of oral obsessives. Open wide."

I sealed my lips. I refused to let him in.

"I have patients coming. Open up."

"Your parking lot is filled with dust," I said. "There hasn't been a patient here for days."

"Hope, my boy. I live in hope. Like you."

Perry Lyman picked up a scraper from his tray and I opened my mouth as wide as it would go, straining my cheek muscles. He hesitated. He wasn't sure he wanted to go back in there, and I didn't blame him. My mouth was deep and dark.

He fumbled around a little, then lost his nerve. He set down the scraper, put aside the tray, and took a pack of cigarettes from his trousers. He shuffled out two of them, and lit them both. He offered me one and I took it; my last, I told myself. My last with someone else watching.

"Peace?" he said.

I needed one last service from him. "Peace."

"I remember when you were on nitrous once and babbling. You're quite the babbler," Perry Lyman said. "Most patients chatter about their private lives. Spill dark secrets. But you were pure ambition. I was surprised; I don't think of you that way. I wouldn't have guessed that underneath it all what you want most is to host your own TV show."

I folded my hand on my chest. "I really said that? It's something I used to toy with in my head."

"New York's the perfect place for you, in that case. Make the contacts. Knock on certain doors. Get the right haircut, take voice lessons. Might work."

I looked at my watch. The morning was going by. Unless I paid for my airplane ticket by noon, I'd lose my economy fare.

"Let's get down to it," Perry Lyman said. "I know why you're here today. It's obvious."

I squirmed.

"You want your thumb back."

"Yes," I said.

"Fear of authority. Failure. Strangers. Loneliness. Need that pacifier. Need that tit."

I rose from the chair. "Forget it. Big mistake."

"The mistake in your case was stopping," Perry Lyman said. "This won't even take an hour. Close your eyes."

"But I'll lose my cheap plane fare."

"We can't have everything."

~ ~ ~

After delicate negotiations, Mike's parents agreed to attend my going-away party. Their opening position had been no Mormons, since Grandma believed that the church was a cult intent on taking over the government. For once, Mike stood firm against her and won approval for twenty LDS guests. Grandpa's issue was the serving of alcohol. Mike crumbled on this one, and I wasn't surprised. For months he and Audrey had been regulars at the clubhouse happy hour.

On the day of the party Audrey blew up balloons as Grandma supervised from a lawn chair, perusing the latest issue of *True Crime* through a pair of wraparound dark glasses. She'd gone downhill since I'd seen her last, and there was a plan afoot to move her into a Minneapolis elder-care facility. Her hearing was shot, distorting her speech, she'd developed a substantial bald spot, and though she still smoked as much as ever, she used supplemental oxygen at night. Grandpa was the same, though maybe a bit fatter and quieter. The Horizoneer had a For Sale sign on its windshield.

Picnic tables and pop-up canopies arrived from the rental shop on a flatbed truck. Mike and I unloaded them as Joel drove a mower, borrowed from the greenskeeper, in circles around the yard. We'd set up a badminton net and a croquet set, though I didn't imagine the Mormon guests would use them.

The guests began arriving early, laden with cardboard barrels of mint chip ice cream, coolers full of decaffeinated cola, and not one but three tall, decorated cakes featuring plastic statuettes of the Empire State Building. I assumed that one woman had made all three cakes, but I found out otherwise. On big occasions Mormons thought alike, it seemed.

I showered, then went to my bedroom to dress. I put on my grandparents' going-away presents: a lightweight navy-blue suit and a black belt containing a hidden money pouch lined with several fifty-dollar bills. I was counting the cash when the door opened.

It was Opal. She spread her arms. We hugged. Stripped of her usual load of jewelry and wearing a clingy rayon dress that highlighted the buckles of her bra straps, she looked like a fresh-picked flower. And she smelled like one.

We chatted for a few minutes and then I said: "You don't have to promise to wait for me. It's fine. Two years is a long time. I understand."

Opal smoothed her dress over her lips. "I have some news," she said. "I'm following you. I got into college at NYU. Surprise!"

I sat down on my bed. Opal's big news was not entirely welcome. She slid her cool hands around me and locked them tight between my shoulder blades. "You happy?"

"Sure."

Mike appeared in the doorway, just in time. "You'd better come down. Your mother is in tears. My parents are locked in the camper, on strike. Also, that speech coach friend of yours hooked up a sound system. He's playing disco tapes."

"Be right there," I said.

Mike backed away. "Let's make this look good today. Big smiles. Strong handshakes. After that, you're on your own. Out of sight, out of mind." Mike left the bedroom.

"What did he mean by that?" Opal said.

"They don't think I'll last. They think I'll quit my mission."

"Not with me checking up on you, you won't."

I looked at the wall. I clenched my teeth. I was going to have to ditch this girl.

~ ~ ~

Special occasions designed to make memories—birthdays, graduations, holiday feasts—had always done the opposite for me. The slightest pressure to savor the moment blanked me out. That's what happened at the party. Fuzzy blessings, anonymous kisses, and the faint taste of cake were all I could remember.

Except for Joel's speech. It stuck with me, every word. He stood on a picnic table and waved a salad spoon to get the crowd's attention.

"My brother has always been good at trying new things and now he's trying this thing. Hope he likes it. Every time he turns over a new leaf, the one underneath it has problems, too. As for converting people to the church, I'm sure he'll do fine, if he puts his mind to it. His mind jumps around a lot, though. Whose doesn't, I guess. My only advice for him is: be less sarcastic. Notice people's feelings better. Listen.

"To be honest, I'm pretty concerned to see him go. I don't know how to put this. He's used up a lot of excuses in his life and he doesn't have many left. Does that make sense? Anyway, I propose a toast to him."

Joel raised his paper cup. The crowd raised theirs. "Take good care of yourself out there, okay? Make sure to try new things. Be kind. We love you."

Audrey moved close and put her arm around me. I could smell that she'd been drinking non-Mormon punch.

"I'm not sure I know what your brother meant," she said, "but that was beautiful." She squeezed me, hard.

I knew very well what he'd meant. I squeezed her back. The guests fell into a line to shake my hand.

~ ~ ~

After a stretch of rough air above Wisconsin the plane leveled off and cruised smoothly through the night. I fell asleep with one cheek against the window. Air from the vent nozzle gusted across my face. I woke up when a light flashed on: my seatmate's reading light. I looked at her through half-closed, spying eyes. My age. Pretty. Slim. Red hair. Black boots. Something told me she wasn't from Minnesota, that she lived in the East and had been here on a visit. On her lap was a copy of the *New York Times*, open to the arts section. The headline was about a play on evil French aristocrats.

I watched her read. I wondered if she'd seen my badge yet; in case she hadn't I furtively unclipped it and put it in the ashtray in the seat arm. She folded down her dinner tray and accepted a foil-wrapped meal from the flight attendant.

I stretched and sat up. I wanted the girl to look at me.

"Did I wake you up?" she said. "I'm really sorry. I can move if this light is in your eyes. Here, it'll just take a second. I'll move over."

It was only just then, when I started to ask her to stay (no, your light doesn't bother me, I'd tell her, and by the way my name is Justin Cobb, I'm flying to New York to spread the gospel, although, to be honest, I'm thinking of going AWOL, which everyone is half expecting anyhow; and in fact when my mother said good-bye tonight she told me in a whisper that I was free now, that God could probably get along without me, so why not just go *live*? Lord knows you've earned it), that I noticed what was in my mouth.